That Mysterious Woman

A SHAKER OF MARGARITAS ANTHOLOGY

TWENTY-SEVEN NEW SHORT STORIES

EDITED BY L. S. FISHER

D1417223

www.MozarkPress.com

Published by Mozark Press, www.Mozarkpress.com
© 2014 Linda Fisher
PO Box 1746, Sedalia, MO 65302

Cover design and book layout by H. Ream.

ISBN: 978-0-9903270-0-4

DEDICATION

This anthology is dedicated to those mysterious women who enrich our lives and tease our imaginations.

OTHER TITLES
SHAKER OF MARGARITAS SERIES

HOT FLASH MOMMAS
(A Show-Me Book Award Winner)

COUGARS ON THE PROWL
(Missouri Writers' Guild Anthology of the Year Award)

A BAD HAIR DAY

CONTENTS

ACKNOWLEDGEMENTS

We are grateful to every author who submitted a story to *That Mysterious Woman* regardless of whether the story was selected for this edition.

Deepest appreciation is extended to all who proofread and assisted the editor in any way. Mozark Press would like to especially acknowledge Harold Ream for the countless hours he spent on the website and providing technical support throughout the publication process.

INTRODUCTION

Everybody loves a mystery! Our fourth *Shaker of Margaritas* anthology, *That Mysterious Woman*, includes twenty-seven mysteries.

The collection began with a callout for mysteries featuring a female protagonist. We asked for cozies, soft-boiled mysteries, suspenseful tales, capers, or whodunits with a strong emphasis on character, plot, and good old-fashioned storytelling. And our authors delivered! We received a record number of submissions and had the difficult task of paring down the stack to the best of the best.

The authors in this *Shaker* edition used their imaginations to produce stories of a mysterious woman involved in a wide array of circumstances. Stories cover murder, retribution, paranormal activity, thievery, strange disappearances, deception, and other surprising situations.

An anthology includes authors with different writing styles, which makes watching the story unfold more unpredictable. Isn't that one of the reasons we read mysteries?

For an enjoyable evening, prop up your feet, relax with an icy margarita, and enjoy the mysteries within these pages featuring *That Mysterious Woman*.

L. S. Fisher

SINS OF THE DAUGHTER

DONNA VOLKENANNT

For as long as I can remember, I've wanted to be a police detective, just like my old man. Being a single parent and a cop wasn't easy for Dad. In fact, it ruined his life. Before Mom's death, Dad's job was his religion. He won medals and commendations for valor. He volunteered for overtime, worked midnights, weekends, holidays. After his shift, he'd stop at a bar, usually until the wee hours of the morning. My folks fought about it all the time.

I was only eight when Mom died. I remember hearing screams and seeing her lying in a pool of blood at the bottom of the stairs. Everything else is blank.

Police speculated a perp, attempting to get even with my father, sneaked in through the unlocked patio door and was encountered by Mom, who was either shoved, or lost her balance, and fell down the stairs.

After Mom died, Dad was inconsolable. He transferred to the day shift and turned down most overtime to be home with me at night. Friends and neighbors pitched in. Jackie O'Malley, mother of Lily, my childhood bestie, provided free babysitting after school and during summer vacations. With Dad working less, there never seemed to be enough money for extras. Later, I learned about Dad's gambling problem. He spent Mom's life insurance payout in no time. We would've lost our home, if Lily's father, Kevin, hadn't bailed us out—although he bragged about his generosity to everyone who would listen.

It's funny how life can change in the blink of an eye. The first time was when Mom died. Then two years ago, Dad was sentenced to seven years for extortion. But I know he's innocent. And I'm going to find the truth.

Having a father labeled a crooked cop isn't an easy road. And if you're a rookie cop yourself, you can kiss your law enforcement career goodbye.

After resigning from the police force, I dedicated myself to get Dad's verdict overturned. Hired an expensive attorney. Spent countless hours doing investigative work, which ended my engagement to Mark, who complained I was ignoring him. When money for legal fees ran out, so did the high-priced lawyer. My shrink has tried to equip me with coping skills to deal with my grief and abandonment issues. During one session, she predicted I'd have a breakthrough. A smell or sight or sound might stimulate repressed memories. Hope she's right. If I ever figure out who killed Mom and framed Dad, I'll get my revenge.

Where are my manners? Here it is the second page of my story and I haven't introduced myself.

I'm Sophie Weslowski, daughter of Stanley, who prefers to be called Stash. He's built like a fireplug: short and squat, gray on top, and he explodes under pressure. His icy blue eyes can drill a hole through you if he thinks you're lying, which is how he made me feel when I started dating. Mom's name was Mary Kathleen Gallagher Weslowski, Katie for short. She was a long-legged Irish-American beauty with silky black hair and emerald eyes. I'm tall with raven hair like Mom and have Dad's cool blue eyes, along with his hot temper.

Now, I'm a licensed private investigator about to get evicted from my storefront office in a low-rent district of my hometown. Then there's this month's electricity bill, which explains why I've turned off the air conditioner and am using an oscillating fan while the temperature and humidity hover around the ninety-degree mark. Welcome to August in the Show Me State!

I need a miracle. Fast!

Maybe if I close my eyes, a knight in shining armor will charge through the door. Or maybe I'll dream myself a new life. The whirl of the fan and ticking of the wall clock tug my eyelids; after the turkey and tomato sandwich I had for lunch, a nap sounds perfect.

I'm dreaming about lounging on a sandy beach, when my office door squeaks open. So do my eyes.

My nostrils fill with the heady scent of cologne. Bergamot. Patchouli. Woodsy. Oddly familiar.

Even half-awake, I recognize the silver-haired man, who says, "Must be nice to take a nap in the middle of the day."

Without an invitation, he plops down in my faux leather chair, and in a raspy voice he says, "Sophie Weslowski. You've grown into a beauty. Just like your mom."

Sitting across from me is the backstabbing phony Kevin O'Malley, who's not a knight in any kind of armor. Best man at my parents' wedding. Husband of Jackie. Father of my former best friend, Lily. O'Malley is a corrupt businessman, the ruthless president of the pipefitters' union—and the richest man in town.

Shuddering, I say, "Well, look what the cat drug in."

Flicking an invisible piece of lint from his white linen suit, he asks, "How long's it been?"

Arms folded across my chest, I say, "Since Dad's trial. No. Wait. You never bothered to show up. Didn't return his calls either, not even before Jackie got sick."

At the mention of his late wife, he winces. "Keep Jackie out of this. And Stash knew I was there in spirit. What can I say? I'm a busy man."

"If you're so busy, why are you here? Don't you have a politician to bribe or a business owner to shakedown?"

"Always wisecracking, just like Stash." He loosens his tie and unbuttons his shirt collar. "Why's it so hot in here?"

"Air conditioner's broken." I lie as I slide a hand inside my desk drawer and thumb on my tape recorder—just to be safe. O'Malley's notorious for recording his conversations then altering them to suit his purpose.

Wheezing, he uses a monogrammed handkerchief to cover his mouth. After catching his breath, he says, "I need your help."

Leaning forward, I ask, "Why should I help you?"

His pupils widen as he fights off a coughing fit. In a moment of pity, I stroll to the file cabinet.

"Can I get you a drink?"

"Sure. Whatever you've got."

I dig out two plastic cups and a bottle of Tullamore Dew. It was Mom's favorite whiskey, imported from County Offaly, Ireland, where her folks were born. I fill the glasses then set one on the desk in front of him. "Guess it's fitting I share this with you, although I don't understand why you sent me a case for my birthday. Let me guess. It fell off the back of a truck?"

"Don't look a gift horse in the mouth. I was a lousy godfather. Missed your birthdays when you were little. I'm trying to make amends." He picks up the silver-framed wedding photo of my folks. "Katie was one in a million. Stash didn't deserve her."

Flattered and insulted at the same time, I swallow hard and ball my fists.

"*Slainte!* To Katie." He raises his glass in the traditional Irish toast then takes a sip.

I do the same before opening my notebook. "So, why are you here?"

"I need a good detective." He spreads his palms. "And I heard you could use the work."

"Just so we're clear. I don't accept charity and don't work cheap. It's a hundred bucks for a fifteen-minute consultation." I drain my glass and wait for his response.

"It's not charity. You're the only one I trust."

He peels off a wad of Ben Franklins. "Here's a thousand for a retainer." He takes a deep breath then continues. "I need to find out what's going on with Lily."

When he mentions Lily's name, I flinch. When we were young, we shared our dreams and deepest secrets. In grade school, she wanted to be a nun. In high school, we vowed to be maids of honor in each other's weddings. Then Lily left for college and took a u-turn to crazy town. While I attended community college before entering the police academy, Lily got kicked out of two expensive private universities for drug abuse and drunk driving. Her dad bought her way out of trouble more times than I can count.

"How is she? Last I heard she was teaching Yoga in California."

"You know Lily. A free spirit. But her heart's in the right place. Came home to—" He chews his bottom lip. "Take care of Jackie."

Patting O'Malley's leathery hand, I say, "I was so sorry to hear about Jackie's death. She was always kind to me."

He wipes his eyes then blows his nose. "Thanks for the Mass card. Jackie thought the world of you. Wished you and Lily would've stayed friends."

"So what's the problem?"

Leaning on my desk, he whispers, "I've hurt people. Ruined lives. Need to make amends."

Surprised by O'Malley's display of remorse, I say, "You don't need a detective. You need a priest. Haven't you heard confession's good for the soul?"

"Already done that."

"So, what can I do?" I ask.

"Something's up with Lily. She won't open up to me. But she trusts you."

"I haven't talked to her in years."

"Doesn't matter." He rubs his temples. "Before Jackie died, I heard Lily say you're the only true friend who never turned your back on her. Said she could trust you with her life."

Chills dance across my arms. Our friendship ended the last time I helped Lily. But I'm curious and desperate for cash. "What can I do to help?"

His words tumble out. "Find out her secret. She's going to inherit everything, but I want to make sure she's not using drugs again and that no one's taking advantage of her." He folds his hands. "I'm praying she'll get married. My biggest regret is I won't live to see my grandchildren."

When he mentions the word grandchildren, I avert my eyes. "I'll see what I can find out."

Tears stream down his wrinkled face. "Sorry for crying like a girl." Wiping his eyes, he asks, "Where's the toilet?"

"Down the hall. First door on the left."

Alone in my office, memories flood back of the warm summer evening after my first year of college when Lily showed up at my house.

Hysterical, she told me she was pregnant by a guy she got high with on spring break. Didn't even know his name.

She grabbed my hands and sobbed, "I need to have an— "

Mentally finishing her sentence, I asked, "Are you sure?"

"I know. I know," she wailed. "It's a mortal sin, but I don't have a choice."

"You always have a choice, Lily. Being an unmarried mother isn't the end of the world. Your folks will love you and your baby. And if you decide not to keep it, there's always adoption."

"I can't disappoint Dad again. Last time I got arrested he almost stroked out."

Knowing I couldn't abandon my best friend in her darkest moment, I asked, "How can I help?"

"Give me a ride across the river. There's a doctor. Real expensive and hush-hush. I've got the money, but I'm scared to go alone."

That night I drove Lily to Illinois. On the ride home, she blamed me for not talking her out of her decision. After that, she blocked my calls and refused to talk to me. That's when I realized she was just like her dad—a user and false friend.

I'm lost in my painful memories when O'Malley taps my desk, returning me to the present.

"Sorry I took so long. Everything takes longer when you get old. Hey? Something wrong? You look upset."

"Must've zoned out."

O'Malley points to the stack of cash on my desk. "That's just a deposit. When you find out what's up with Lily there'll be a lot more."

On his way out the door, he says, "Your old man did a lot of rotten things, but he wasn't a dirty cop. He'd never take a bribe, especially from scumbag drug dealers. He was set up."

As his footsteps echo down the hall, I plot my strategy. For the next few weeks, I tail my former best friend. Lily's days begin at dawn with a three-mile run, followed by morning Mass then a bike ride to the diner where she works. Twice a week she teaches Yoga at the senior center before driving her dad to his medical appointments. Once a week she volunteers at a women's shelter. Sunday morning she attends Mass, followed by a visit to the cemetery where Jackie is buried.

Lily's Mother-Teresa-on-steroids act convinces me she's hiding something. Determined to uncover her secret, I drop by the diner to catch her off guard.

As soon as she spots me, she rushes up and gives me a bear hug.

Her words flow non-stop. "Sophie! I've been praying I'd run in to you. I started to call several times but lost my nerve. I can't tell you how sorry I am. Can you ever forgive me? It was all my fault. You were just being a good friend. And I was devastated to hear about your dad. I don't believe a word of it."

Just like the old days. We're besties again. Except I still don't trust her.

Joy spreads from her lips to her eyes. "I'll be off work in a few minutes. Can you stay? Please?"

Over a tuna salad sandwich and a glass of iced tea, I feel guilty saying, "I was out of town when I heard about your mom." That's a lie. I didn't go to Jackie's funeral because I was afraid of being turned away.

I casually ask, "So, what've you been up to?"

After she fills me in with her life after college, I open up about my abbreviated law enforcement career and cancelled engagement. Telling her about my PI business, I compare client confidentiality with a priest hearing confession, hoping she'll open up.

She takes the bait and shares her secret then asks me to swear not to tell a soul.

Relieved to finally know what she's hiding, I ask, "Why haven't you told your dad?"

"He expects me to get married and have kids. I promised Mom I'd take care of him until—"

Lily wipes her eyes. "Dad has lung cancer. Stage four."

I start to tell her I've seen him and he looks like hell, but catch myself.

Driving home, I call O'Malley and ask him to drop by my house. My jaw drops when I answer the door. Over the past few weeks, he has lost at least thirty pounds and walks with a cane.

I lead him to the kitchen table and pour him a shot of Tullamore. "Lily's fine," I say. "Apparently you're not."

"Docs give me six weeks. Tops." Shrugging, he takes a drink. "What do they know? Nothing but quacks out to get rich." Elbows on the table, his breathing is labored. "What'd you find out?"

I flip open my notebook and report my findings. When I tell him how often Lily visits Jackie's gravesite without him, tears stream down his sunken cheeks.

After he composes himself, I say, "This afternoon I stopped by the diner. We talked for hours. She opened up to me, just like old times. There's no shady character influencing her."

His shoulders shake; relief spreads across his face.

I lean forward, "She confided in me that she regrets how she disappointed you in the past. She promised Jackie to be a better daughter and take care of you."

Squeezing my hand, he says. "Losing Jackie was so hard on her. I can't imagine how you felt after losing your mom so young. Katie was a beautiful woman."

His hand trembles when he takes another sip. "Anything else?"

Shaking my head, I lie. "That's all."

I commit a sin of omission when I don't tell him Lily has no plans to get married after he's gone because she's going to enter the convent and become a nun. And I definitely can't tell him about the grandchild he almost had.

He reaches inside his jacket, peels off a stack of hundred-dollar bills. The final payment amounts to ten times what I expected.

"I told you I don't accept charity. This is way too much."

"Consider it a gift to make up for all the grief I've caused. And there's something else." He slides a package wrapped in one of his cologne-laced handkerchiefs across the table.

I unfold the handkerchief and hold up a videotape. "What's this?"

"A confession from the rat that framed your dad. I might have one foot in the grave, but I still got some juice."

He holds up his index finger. "One final request. Don't turn it over until after I'm dead."

As soon as he leaves, I slip the videotape into the recorder. I recognize the back room of the bar Dad used to hang out with his partner, Leon Cashman, who appears drunk or drugged or both, confessing to O'Malley about how he set Dad up to take the fall for extortion. He's terrified, slobbering that it's only a matter of time before a drug dealer gets him.

I turn off the recorder and hide the tape behind a family photo album in the living room cabinet.

Whoever said revenge is a dish best served cold was wrong. It's actually best served on a warm night, while dressed in a hoodie, carrying a gun with a silencer.

The day after O'Malley's funeral I'm parked in a remote spot down the street from Cashman's favorite bar watching raindrops meander down my windshield. When Cashman staggers outside, I ease out of the car. Dodging puddles, I stroll toward him, trying to muster the nerve to put him out of his misery, when a dark SUV whizzes by then screeches to a stop. A mountain-sized thug dressed like a ninja jumps out, fills Cashman with lead, then hops back into the SUV as it speeds away.

Filled with relief that Cashman's dead and I'm not the killer, I drive home. Once I turn over the videotape to the authorities, my dad will be a free man.

In the living room, a wave of nostalgia washes over me. I remove the videotape and open the family album. Memories gel as I flip the pages.

Church shot: I'm wearing my white First Holy Communion dress and veil. Dad's in his tan sports coat. Mom's wearing a periwinkle dress and a gardenia corsage.

Angelic Shot: Lily and me in our white dresses, our hands are folded around our rosary beads.

Group shot: Mom and Dad and me with Lily and her parents at the restaurant after the church ceremony. Mom's waving the camera away.

In a flash of clarity, I remember her voice. I'm in my bed when she yells, "Hurry! He's home."

Flashback: I rush through my parents' bedroom door. Mom's slipping on her nightgown, telling me I've had a bad dream, to go back to bed.

Back in the present, I study another group photo. Kevin O'Malley lovingly gazes at Mom, who looks like she has a secret.

I unfold O'Malley's handkerchief and lift it to my nose and remember the shadow of a man buttoning his shirt before slipping out the patio door. As he hurries past me, the strong scent of his cologne lingers: Bergamot. Patchouli. Woodsy. Expensive.

Another memory floods back.

Flashback: I'm peeking out my bedroom door watching Dad run up the stairs. He's yelling, "Who is it? I'll kill him." Mom shouts, "Stash! Stop! You're hurting me." A deadly scream. Dad's sobbing. Shocked and scared, I run back to my bedroom and close my eyes, hoping it's not real.

My stomach twists as I turn the final page.

Favorite shot: The final photo of Mom and me. It's her birthday. We're smiling. She's holding my gift. A gardenia plant, her favorite flower.

With a steady hand, I strike a match then light the gardenia-scented candle on the coffee table. While the flame grows tall, I pull the videotape apart, ripping the thin film from the plastic case.

The thought of Dad spending six more years in prison for extortion, a crime he didn't commit, makes me sick. But that's a small price to pay for the worse crime he did commit—murdering Mom.

My fingers warm as the evidence melts against the flame.

I close my eyes and pray for forgiveness.

AN AURA OF DEATH

CAROLYN MULFORD

Jessamyn Volari ran her fingers over the dates on the waist-high tombstone. Sure enough, 1873. She'd found the right Thomas Snowalter. She stepped back and lifted her new camera, delighted to see that the salesman had been right when he guaranteed a glare-proof screen.

Intrigued by an odd play of light on a nearby slope, she zoomed to 20x and focused on a burial service some forty yards away. In spite of the blue sky, a distinct gray cloud hovered above a green canopy. Puzzled, she lowered the camera and strained her excellent eyes. No mysterious baby rain cloud.

She relaxed as she remembered that telescopic lenses make distant objects appear close to each other. She photographed the canopy and cloud to document the camera's failings.

A man said, "You a *Missourian* photographer, miss?"

Assuming he'd mistaken her for a journalism student on assignment because of her gold Mizzou Tigers T-shirt and black running shorts, she stretched to her full five foot three. "No. I'm an electrical engineer."

He towered over her, a middle-aged man with close-cropped brown hair and an inch-wide broccoli-green aura—a sign of purposeful curiosity—arching over his head. In spite of the heat, he wore a summer sports jacket. And a shoulder holster.

Jessica guessed he was an undercover cop. "I'm a volunteer headstone hunter. I photograph local gravestones for genealogists. All perfectly legal."

"I'm Sgt. Earl Korman, Columbia Police. Mind if I have a look?"

She held up the camera and hit Review.

He frowned. "Why did you photograph the canopy?"

Jessamyn knew better than to explain. She'd learned by age four not to tell anyone but Gram that people wore colors around their heads. Even at work, where she almost fit in, she never revealed that she saw individuals' auras as well as rooms' gradations of light. "I saw a big white bird there."

He arched an eyebrow. "Out of courtesy to the victim's family, please don't take any more photos."

"I didn't know anyone had been murdered. I was out of town on business all week."

"I didn't say *murder* victim." The officer's aura dulled, hinting that he lied. "He died in a hit-and-run. Have a good day." He strode away to stand in the slender shade of an obelisk, pulled a small camera out of his jacket pocket, and focused on the departing mourners.

Curiosity aroused, Jessamyn moved out of his line of sight and zoomed in to photograph the mourners. She saw shades of grief's charcoal gray and flashes of anger's red.

What color would a murderer's aura be? But auras changed. The girl who'd made third grade the most miserable time in Jessamyn's life had fluctuated from blood red to bright orange and crow black to ash gray. Shuddering at the memory, Jessamyn hurried to the parking lot and her Honda Civic.

Ten minutes later she parked in the shade of a Bradford pear and walked up the stairs to her apartment. She smiled with pleasure at having it to herself. Much as she loved Tommy, she welcomed the respite from his Saturday afternoon regimen of TV sports. Today he watched his beloved Cardinals at the stadium.

Going straight through her sparsely furnished living room to the den, she downloaded the photos onto her iMac and opened the shots one by one. The clarity of the carving on the tombstone delighted her. The clunky no-name camera had unique capabilities.

She expanded the cloud photo. Above the canopy floated an irregular silver-gray elliptical form interspersed with purplish red streaks—depression, anger, and something else. Fascinated, Jessamyn zoomed in. Splotches of black—hate—darkened the gray.

"What on earth is it?" She played with the image, zooming in, pulling back, changing the screen resolution. Nothing enlightened her. She printed it out. No sign of the cloud. Frustrated, she got up to pace and think. Finding herself in front of the refrigerator, she took a bottle of pomegranate nectar from Tommy's special stash. If she told him about the cloud, he'd think she'd drunk something a lot stronger.

"Not an aura," she muttered. "Much too big." About the size and shape of Tommy snoozing on the beige leather couch. An aura for all the people under the canopy? Doubtful. She'd never seen a collective aura.

Back at the computer, she opened her photo of the departing mourners. No cloud. She zoomed in on a white-haired woman with a gray aura outlined with blue. Jessamyn had seen that aura around Gram's head when Gramps died.

She went to the *Missourian's* Web page, and typed "hit and run" into Search. Opening an article headed "Pedestrian Dies in Hit and Run," she stared at a picture of the round-faced young man who'd sold her the camera last Saturday. She skimmed the article. Hardware store employees had found the body of Ronald Cort, twenty-four, in the parking lot Monday night after closing. Sgt. Korman must suspect the driver knew the victim well enough to attend his funeral.

The scene at Mo-Foto flashed through her mind. When she told the salesman she needed a camera capable of capturing variations of light in a hotel ballroom, a typical worksite, he'd shown her his best digital single-lens reflexes. None met her standards. Finally he went into a back room and returned with a prototype, an ugly, heavy, black square camera his boss had brought back from a trade show. She tested it in the store. The results more than made up for the camera body's bad design and high price.

The salesman—the late Ronald Cort—couldn't locate a warranty or instructions and asked her to come back Monday to talk to the owner. Jessamyn persuaded the salesman to let her buy the camera to use on her upcoming business trip.

He'd been nice, poor man. She didn't remember his aura, so it probably had been the grass green common to people who like their work. As a child, she'd exhausted herself in crowds trying to figure out what the different colors meant. As a teenager, she'd suffered headaches from sensory and emotional overload. As an adult, she'd disciplined herself to ignore all but the brightest colors.

She felt ashamed that some of her regret at Ronald Cort's passing came from not being able to ask him to explain the cloud. She was an engineer. She'd figure it out herself.

Thrusting the camera into her shoulder bag, she strode to the car, drove to the cemetery, and parked. With no canopy to guide her, she strolled up the slope until she spied a wisp of gray. Seeing no one around, she hurried toward it.

The cloud—a despairing thunderstorm gray—hovered over the fresh grave. The hairs stood up on Jessamyn's arms. What was it? The dead man's aura magnified hundreds of times? His troubled spirit? His soul in limbo?

She stood frozen, seeking a scientific explanation. Finding none, she raised the camera and zoomed in on the center of the long, slender form. The lens revealed small black and red blotches—hate and anger. Feeling she was intruding on the dead, she murmured, "I'm sorry. Rest in peace."

The cloud's colors vibrated.

Jessamyn whirled, raced to her car, and headed for home.

A blur whipped past her. Two cars lengths ahead, the blur became the cloud, now a lighter gray with a long streak of lemon yellow, a common color during stress. Jessamyn's fear waned and her curiosity rose as she concluded whatever it was could think.

The cloud kept pace ahead of her. When she stopped at the light, it hovered until the light turned green. Coming up to another light, it shifted to the right. She signaled for a left turn, and the cloud flung itself at her windshield. Stunned, she braked and signaled to turn right.

Approaching another intersection, the cloud edged to the left. She followed. She anticipated the next turn—toward the hardware store where Ronald Cort had died.

The cloud turned into the store's large parking lot. It led her down a row of cars, lingered above an SUV, and then zoomed out, stopped short, flew upward, and dove to the ground.

A car drove over the cloud.

The cloud repeated its maneuvers.

"I get it," Jessamyn said. "The car hit you on purpose."

The cloud drifted to the lot's exit, and Jessamyn followed. She soon guessed where it was leading her—Mo-Foto. She parked as the cloud floated through the store's glass door. She debated whether to go in. If the cloud led her to the hit-and-run driver, what could she do about it? No one would believe her. Would she be in danger if the killer saw her? She forced herself to stay calm. She'd be safe. No one here knew her or why she'd come. She went in.

An older man with a faint orange aura indicating annoyance stood at the do-it-yourself photo-editing machine.

Under a gray-green aura, a teenage blonde at the register held up a red camera and its box. "I'll put the camera in the case for you and discard the box and packaging."

"Please put it in the box," a woman said. "It's a gift. I may have to bring it back."

The cloud had disappeared.

A thin blond middle-aged man in a short-sleeved white shirt and black tie charged into the store and hurried to take over at the register. His aura—steel gray with swirls of red and a river of black—extended almost two inches from his head.

Jessamyn shrank back behind a display of dusty picture frames. She gave herself a mental slap. That black tie hinted he'd just come from a murdered employee's funeral. He wasn't going to radiate a tranquil green.

The teenager finished the transaction and hurried toward the back door.

The man smiled as he handed prints to the next person in line.

Jessamyn expected his aura to alter as he smiled, but it didn't. She gasped as the cloud appeared inches above the man. Could he be the murderer? Her urge to know overcame her instinct to flee. She moved toward the counter and bumped into a new arrival, a skinny man with an open sore on his cheek.

Both jumped back, and a bulging camouflage backpack slid off his left shoulder.

"Sorry," Jessamyn said, and he darted away to study a display of hot-pink, lime-green, and mellow-orange cameras, the sort favored by adolescent girls.

Jessamyn recognized a meth addict using her own observation tactics. To justify her presence, she picked up a sixteen-gigabyte memory card and got in line.

When her turn came, the cloud enveloped the man in the black tie, almost blocking her view of him. Startled, she dropped the memory card on the counter.

He picked it up. "Cash or credit, miss?"

She reminded herself he didn't see the cloud. "Credit." She fished for her card and handed it to him.

The cloud zoomed to the door.

Jessamyn recognized a warning, but running would only give her away. She searched for something forgettable to say: "Are you the owner?"

"Yes. I'm Gary Whilton." He glanced down at her card, and red flames rippled in dense black around his head.

A murderer's aura, Jessie thought, and he had recognized her name. He could know it only because she'd bought the prototype. How stupid she'd been to give him her credit card.

"Are you a Columbia resident, Mrs. Volari?"

Fear had dried her mouth. "Yes." She didn't correct the "Mrs." He mustn't learn she lived alone. She signed the credit screen and forced herself to walk away at a normal pace. After a few steps, she glanced back and saw the meth head place a pricey Nikon SLR on the counter.

Gary Whilton shifted his gaze from the camera to her, and black smoke erupted among the flames.

Somehow Jessamyn made it to her car. She'd driven halfway home when she realized the cloud had abandoned her.

Now what? The police suspected murder. She could tell them who did it. No, she couldn't. Who would believe a cloud identified the killer? If she said she'd seen disturbing colors in Gary Whilton's aura, the police would leave him free and send her to a psych ward. She had to find another way. Perhaps an anonymous tip to Crime Stoppers.

What tip? What did she know? She knew the shop owner had recognized her name but not her face. That could only mean he knew her name from the record of her payment for the camera. So the murder involved the ugly prototype that captured images not visible to most people's eyes. No manufacturer would give technology so valuable to a small Midwest camera shop. Conclusion: the killer had stolen the prototype to sell to a competing brand, not to a customer.

She parked in front of her apartment and hurried inside. The answering machine on the lamp table by the couch blinked. She punched Play.

"Hi, Mrs. Volari. This is Mo-Foto. We just received an urgent recall notice on that camera you purchased last Saturday. A faulty electronic connection can spark fires. I'll pick it up and bring you a new Nikon SLR to use until it's fixed. See you shortly."

Jessamyn collapsed on the couch. She'd been right. He'd killed Ronald Cort because of the camera. Whilton would kill her, too, if he realized she was suspicious. She sprang up to run to her car. Hand on the doorknob, she hesitated. She couldn't leave her job, her fiancé, her home. Why not give Whilton the camera and forget about it? Because he wouldn't forget about her. She wouldn't be safe until he was in jail. No time to email a tip to Crime Stoppers now. She had to come up with a reason to call the police.

"Think, Jessamyn." She dropped her bag on the end table by the couch. "He wants this valuable camera back, but that's not a reason to murder the clerk. So why?" She remembered the checkout girl asking the customer to leave the camera's packaging and the addict showing Whilton an expensive Nikon, probably the camera he was bringing her. What if the salesman discovered that Whilton repackaged and sold stolen cameras?

The cloud floated through her door with gold flashing in steel gray. Jessamyn knew she'd guessed right. "You were going to turn him in."

For a second, gold dominated.

She had the truth but not the proof. And no time for subtlety. She had to persuade the police to arrest Whilton. She dialed 911. A woman answered.

"My name is Jessamyn Volari. I know the killer who drove that hit-and-run car, and he's coming after me. Please send officers to my apartment, 120 Lumpkin Road, Apartment 2 C, immediately."

Keys clicked. "Who are you afraid of, Jessamyn?"

"Gary Whilton. He owns Mo-Foto, and he's selling stolen cameras there."

"Hold a moment, please." She came back a minute later. "Sgt. Korman is on his way. ETA ten minutes. Why would the Mo-Foto owner run over his employee?"

"I bought an expensive camera from Ronald Cort last Saturday. This afternoon when I bought a memory card, Whilton saw my name and—reacted strangely. When I got home, he'd left a phone message with a ridiculous story about a recall. He said he's coming to pick up my camera."

Someone knocked on the door.

Jessamyn tiptoed over and peered through the peephole. Whilton. She scurried away back to the phone and whispered, "He's here."

"Does your apartment have a back door?"

"No. I'm on the second floor."

"When he knocks again, say you just got out of the shower. Tell him to come back in fifteen minutes."

Jessamyn breathed deeply, waiting for the second knock. When it came, she called, "Who is it?"

"Gary Whilton from Mo-Foto."

"I just got out of the shower." Did her voice shake? "Could you come back in fifteen minutes, please?"

He didn't answer for a moment. "Make it five. I have to pick up my kids."

"Okay, five," Jessamyn said. She put the receiver down and ran to the den to pick up the receiver there. "Could you hear?"

"Yes. Stay calm. Lock yourself in a room."

"None of them has a lock that works." She searched her desk for a weapon, rejecting ballpoint pens, a stapler, a marble paperweight. She settled on sharp scissors small enough to fit in the pocket of her shorts.

The knock came again.

A shiver ran down Jessamyn's spine. "He's knocking," she told the 911 operator. "Where's Sgt. Korman?"

"Almost there. Stall."

Jessamyn put down the receiver and, knees trembling, tiptoed to peer through the peephole. The cloud, all black and red, swarmed around Whilton's head like angry bees. He waved his left hand as though swatting gnats.

Jessamyn realized the cloud couldn't help her or harm Whilton. Only proof of Whilton's guilt could assure her safety. How could she reveal his secret without exposing her own? "Just a moment."

A plan beginning to form, she crept to the phone by the couch and whispered, "How long until Sgt. Korman gets here?"

"Two or three minutes."

Jessamyn glanced at her pocket to be sure the scissors didn't show. "I'm going to let Whilton in. Please, please stay on the line and listen." She punched the speaker button, hung up the receiver, and gathered her courage to open the door. "Come in, Mr. Whilton."

A thin line of green outlined his aura's red and black. He enjoyed the challenge of fooling, and possibly hurting, her.

Smiling, he held out the Nikon. "Sorry about the recall."

Ignoring the camera, she closed the door and edged nearer the phone. "I've decided to keep the camera. I used it to take photos at work last week. It works great."

Flames flared in his aura. "Sorry, but the recall is mandatory. Five people have been injured in fires."

Knees buckling, she perched on the couch three feet from the phone. "I'm an electrical engineer, Mr. Whilton. I can handle the problem."

He stepped closer. "Even engineers make mistakes."

Jessamyn gripped the scissors in her pocket. "You're the one who made a mistake. For $100,000 and the camera, I can forget you killed Ronald Cort."

Red and black intertwined, but his face didn't change. "Why would I kill Ron?"

"To keep him from telling the police that you fence expensive cameras."

Red rage overpowered black hate. "You're crazy!"

"No, I'm a reasonable person." She paused to listen for footsteps. Nothing. Stall. "I'll give you time to raise the money. You can pay me half now and half in six months."

He threw the Nikon on the couch and leapt at her, pushing her onto her back. "Your mistake! Your *fatal* mistake!" His hands closed on her throat.

Jessamyn yanked the scissors from her pocket and jabbed at his ear.

He screamed and jerked back.

Frantically she churned her knees to knock him off her.

"Police!" Sgt. Korman burst through the door. "Hands on your head, Whilton."

Gasping for air, Jessamyn lay back on the couch.

The cloud, flashing gold, hovered in front of her an instant and metamorphosed into a brilliant blue. It dissolved from each end until it disappeared.

Jessamyn exulted a moment for Ronald Cort and for herself. An unexpected wave of loneliness swept over her. She could not share the true story of her ordeal with anyone.

Whilton moaned and wiped away blood running from his ear. "That bitch asked me to come over here and then she attacked me."

Sgt. Korman motioned to a uniformed female officer to handcuff Whilton's wrists. "We got her entire call on tape. Good work, Ms. Volari." He looked at her for the first time. "You're the one who photographed the burial."

Jessamyn sat up and tried to speak, but words wouldn't come through her aching throat. She reached for the pad and pen by the phone and wrote, "I looked up the death online. I saw the victim was the man who sold me my camera."

Sgt. Korman bent to look at her throat. "Just bruised, I think, but Officer Landry will take you to the Emergency Room for a checkup before you give your statement." He pointed to the Nikon. "We'll need the camera for evidence."

Jessamyn raised her pencil to correct his mistake and hesitated. He'd seen only the back of the prototype. She wanted that remarkable camera nestled in her handbag more than she'd ever wanted anything, even if only for a few more days. Both cameras had been stolen; neither was in the store's records. But her fingerprints weren't on the Nikon.

Jessamyn grasped the Nikon with both hands and gave it to the detective. For now at least, she could keep her secret and the remarkable prototype.

TROPHY WIFE

FRANK WATSON

I sit demurely at the edge of the black leather couch beside James, my husband of almost three months. His arm is around my waist, orchestrating the interview. The reporter sitting across from me in the living room is only in his twenties. My age.

He is not the type I used to go for. He is not at all like James. Though one learns from experience.

The reporter is cute. Shy. Naïve. He has no understanding at all of how my leg really got shattered—what this interview is really all about. Or how much time I may have left. If my life could be different, this young man could be a threat to James. But James is still in control.

"You were hurt pretty badly?" the reporter asks in an earnest voice.

He works for the county's weekly newspaper. His cheap Bic pen shadows the slim notebook. I sit in such a way that he can see my good leg. I wear a pink, flowered sundress that James has bought me at McKenna's, what passes for a high-end clothing store in this little Ozark town, though it is a big city compared to where I grew up. Hell, compared to the hog farm where I was raised, any place is a metropolis. The reporter tries to be a gentleman and keep his eyes from my leg and the swell of my breasts.

"The accident shattered my leg," I say, following my script. "I was in the hospital for weeks."

"I'm sorry," he says, and sounds like he means it. He has an out-of-town accent, maybe from St. Louis or Kansas City. How did he wind up so far from home? I figure he may be just out of college on his first newspaper job. I wish I could tell him the real story. I hope he asks more questions about the accident. Though what could I say if he does?

James jumps in, squeezing my shoulder so hard it hurts.

"We weren't sure she would walk again," he says. "But my Marie is full of surprises."

"Physical therapy can be very painful."

"But it hasn't stopped her from achieving her dream," James continues. "She just got her nursing degree. I'm so proud of her!"

"That's what you told my editor, why he sent me out to talk with you all," the reporter says. "It's a good story."

Who's playing games now? James? Showing off his pretty young wife, getting her picture in the paper, showing everybody in the county that the local boy returned from the military a rich man? Me? Having my picture in the paper for the first time since I started my scrapbook with photos taken when I won the Miss Spring Festival contest? Or this reporter, who has already learned how to use the right words to get quotes to shape his stories, just another article for *his* scrapbook, regardless of the real story?

On the other hand, this reporter is awfully young to be cynical. And he has a nice smile.

"Thank you," I say, and return the smile.

When James plucked me from the farm, it seemed at first like my dreams had come true. He made gifts of expensive clothes, a mansion to live in, and a Cadillac in which he chauffeured me around town. It wasn't until too late that I learned the price I would have to pay.

James gave me no choice when he said he could arrange to get my picture in the newspaper again, to make up for his latest outburst. When I found out what he had in mind, I decided I would cooperate as little as possible. But I like this young man and change my mind. I will give him a good story.

"Marie just got her nurse's uniform," James says. "You want a picture?"

"Of course." The reporter reaches for the camera bag at his feet. "My editor told me—definitely—get some good photos of your wife. To go with the story."

James pats me on the back.

"Go change into your uniform," he says, giving me a push.

James has me on display. Why not give a good look? I lean forward, to provide a better view down the top of my dress. The young man pretends to examine his camera. He watches me, but does not have *that* look. I used to be flattered when men looked at me that way. Now, I feel like they are all so dumb that they can't see past the cleavage. Maybe this one is different.

In my dressing room, adjoining the bedroom, as I shed my dress, I can hear the two of them talking quietly through the door I left open a crack. They aren't aware I am listening. Just as James is not aware that I understand more than he thinks I do.

"Interesting to see you again," I hear the reporter say. "It's too bad about your...previous...wife."

Bridget. *One* of his previous wives. The woman who looked so much like me. Though James has not yet fully realized that I am not another Bridget.

"She had a lot more problems than I realized," James says, in his sympathy-seeking voice. "I never realized she was that depressed. When she left me, I had no idea she would kill herself."

"And to think she was also being stalked."

"She was a beautiful woman. Almost as pretty as Marie. What do you think of her?"

"I don't know how you get all the luck." James laughs, pleased with the compliment. But the reporter shows more grit than I would have thought. "Police learn anything about the alleged stalker?"

"I gave Bridget the gun to protect herself. It was too bad she used it on herself."

The gun. The funeral home director serving as coroner decided it was a suicide, and returned the gun to James who then gave it to me. James didn't know that, unlike Bridget, I know how to use it. Back on the farm I was in charge of shooting the varmints that tried to kill the piglets. Or maybe he did realize it, which is why he did not also give me a clip for the weapon. One never knows exactly what James is planning.

I pull the starched uniform out of the drawer, along with the black fishnet stockings. It is one of James' favorite outfits. But he will not want me to wear the complete outfit today. He will want to show off the scars. Hose and panties cover the gun in the drawer. To one side, in a Victoria's Secret box—James often likes to surprise me with little gifts—are the bullets I purchased on one of the few shopping trips when James was not with me. He was visiting one of his girlfriends and was more than happy to let me entertain myself. However, he apparently suspected something wrong when he returned, because he hit me harder than usual, and now when he visits his other women or drives to St. Louis or Kansas City he makes sure that I am locked up—alone—in the house.

"I understand the police considered you a suspect, before they found out about her depression," the reporter continues. "That must have made it even more difficult for you."

"The police were just doing their jobs. I respect that. In fact, I am now very good friends with the investigating officer."

"They tell me they never found her stalker."

"I think it was Bridget's ex-boyfriend."

"They say he left town."

"That's all behind us, now. I prefer to think about the present." He calls out, "Marie!"

"Be there in a sec," I reply.

Then, to the reporter, James continues, "I appreciate your cooperation in keeping the way Bridget died out of her obituary. She had...I have...a lot of friends, and it would have been embarrassing to...her...if the details were made public."

"You know how it is. People like to read about other people's misfortunes. Blood and shootings, even suicides, sell newspapers. After you talked to my editor, however, he killed the story. He said there was no need to give you any more pain than you already experienced."

"He's a good guy," James says. "Plays a helluva golf game." He yells out again, "Marie! Our friend has a busy schedule! Don't keep him waiting!"

I place stockings and panties back over the gun, but not before I open the pink box and fit a clip in place.

Both men smile when I walk back into the room, with my low-cut shirt and short skirt. James wants me to put on a show, so I might as well do it right. James has a look of ownership, pride, and lust. The reporter has a look of confusion, pleasure, and surprise. I suspect that he doesn't usually see this much boob or leg when he visits the hospital ER for stories.

"Turn around, show him how good you look, in spite of your accident," James says, motioning to me, as if I were a show dog. I follow his orders, as the reporter plays with his camera. Now I'm doing it for the reporter. "Honey, show him your scars."

I pull up my skirt, revealing not just the scars, but also most of my thigh, up to where the thong panties would be if I had been wearing them. In spite of the scar, I still have good legs.

"Impressive, isn't she?" James says.

Our eyes meet. The reporter seems almost apologetic. I find myself liking this young man more all the time. If things were different, he and

I might even want to get together. Have a drink or two. See how things would work out. He couldn't afford to buy me pretty dresses or show me off at the country club. Maybe he would treat me with kindness, respect, dignity. What I never got from my dad back on the farm. What I thought I would get from James, when I mistook expensive presents for love, not knowing that James was like my dad—only worse.

James sets me back down on the couch, arranges me so that my legs can be easily seen. He smoothes my skirt far above the knees, opens the top of my shirt a little more. "Be sure to get a picture of her legs." The reporter complies, then moves in closer for a head and shoulders shot, which is not quite as revealing, but might be more appropriate for this story. James loosens another button on my shirt, arranges me into a slightly different position, and orders, "Take more photos." The reporter uncomfortably snaps another few shots. "When will the story be printed?"

"Probably tomorrow," the reporter says. He looks at his watch, and says, "In fact, I'm on deadline. Need to get back to the office, get the film processed, and the story written. Sorry to run. Hope you understand."

"Sure," James says. "You can go now." Then, walking the reporter to the door, without even turning his head, my husband also dismisses me. "Go to your room, honey. I'll join you in the bedroom. But leave your uniform on for now."

I find it more and more difficult to follow his orders, to allow myself to be controlled, and abused by him. I am not Bridget or his other wives and girlfriends. Even so, I again obey. I walk to the dresser for the fishnet stockings. I know that now he will want to see me in them. As I grab the stockings, my fingers touch the cold metal of the gun. I pick it up.

As he closes the front door, James calls out to me, "This'll be a great story! You were terrific."

"He seems like a really nice guy."

The words just slip out.

"So you're hot for the young pup, are you?" His voice grows tense, even angry. I should have known this would be part of the script. "Well, then, I'll just have to teach you a lesson."

The gun feels good in my hand.

"Give me another minute. I'm getting my stockings on."

"You've had enough time!" I hear him taking off his belt, slap it a few times across his palm. "I'm ready for you. And when I'm ready, you're ready. I *own* you. I took you off that pig farm and made you what you are now. I made you pretty. I made you into a woman that all men want. But I'm the one that has you." He slaps his belt a few more times. "And I'll have you until *I* decide I don't want you anymore."

I look at the gun. I am suddenly certain that it will be a good story. A flattering story about a brave young woman who overcame her awful circumstances. The young reporter will choose a photo that fits the fantasy James packaged for him. I will be pretty.

I place the gun back in the dresser, cover it with the panties, but leave the drawer open just a bit, to retrieve the gun easier when the time is right.

My picture will be published in a day or two. I will make it the first page in my new scrapbook.

Then I will give that young reporter a *real* story, which will not be about a crime but about a brave young woman who overcame her awful circumstances.

Because James will no longer be in control.

REMEMBER ME?

GEORGIA RUTH

"My face is tingling."

"My darling Shelley, you've been through this five times already. You know what to expect. In six months, you'll be a different woman. Call my office if you have problems." My old classmate Dr. Anthony Papaleo had collaborated with me to preserve my youthful appearance with a pinch here, a nip there, and everywhere a tuck.

Following this session of plastic surgery in Atlanta, I stayed in a local hotel suite as I had after the other operations. This time, recuperation was agonizingly slow and painful. My mirror told me something had gone wrong. The doctor's office told me I would have to wait until the swelling receded before they could make an assessment. After a month of whining, I dropped by Anthony's office. The physician assistant repeated that adjustments could not be made for at least six months because my face had to heal. She would not admit it was disfigured. I retreated to my winter home in Boca Raton to heal in seclusion.

Two months later, I drove up for another unscheduled visit when I couldn't get an appointment. I didn't know Dr. Papaleo was at a convention in Las Vegas. His nurse suggested a change in medication and begged me to be reasonable. She confided that Dr. Papaleo was going through a critical personal dilemma, and he might lose "everything." Nobody cared that I couldn't go home to New York. Continual phone calls to his office and home resulted in a threatening letter from his attorney. A year passed. The last time I called his office, I was told he was on an extended European vacation.

I heard nothing from Dr. Anthony Papaleo. I never got to tell him my nose now sloped sideways. My lips were still puffy except for the side that suddenly swooped, and my speech was garbled. My eyes looked like pee holes in the snow. I hid behind a long mane of blonde hair. I tried to comfort myself with the southern cooking that had always made me feel better when I failed an exam or lost a boyfriend. Every crisis in my life was battled with macaroni and cheese followed by chocolate, anything chocolate. When I was a teenager, I had easily lost the extra comfort roll. Now they were piling up.

Almost two years after the operation, I was able to make an appointment with Dr. Papaleo but the first available day was not until September. My thirtieth high school class reunion was in August. I didn't want to go because I was unrecognizable even to myself. The swelling in my face was less, but now I was swollen all over. As I confronted my doubts with a two layer chocolate cake, I went through my senior annual. I saw my best friend's promise to be close forever, but we lost touch when I met a hot engineering student in college. That marriage fizzled out as his career skyrocketed.

The second marriage didn't fare much better. I missed the twenty-year reunion because I was engaged in a divorce with a husband attracted to a physical fitness coach. I had been working so hard to manage Manhattan properties, I was not even aware I had competition for my bed.

I decided it was time to get my priorities straight and forget my divorces and expanding waistline. I was the same person who graduated in 1982, just a little older and chunky. Everybody else would be changed, too. I made my reservations.

"Shelley Winter," I said to the baggage claim agent. He looked at the photo on my license again and squinted at me, returning it with a shrug. I wheeled my carry-on through security and down the concourse to wait for my plane to board. The walk exhausted me.

Charlotte, North Carolina, had also changed in the last thirty years. High-rise residential towers and open spaces replaced clusters of homes and neo-classical buildings. Uptown seemed to be all glass and steel. I arrived at the Omni Hotel in mid afternoon, with time to rest and prepare for the casual event scheduled for Friday night. The luau was modeled after the event I planned years ago to celebrate our state basketball championship. The desk clerk directed me to the Oakwood reunion registration area. Tables along the hallway were surrounded by chatting new arrivals. Suddenly I was timid, pushing back the moment when I revealed that this inflated body with twisted facial features hid a former cheerleader and a successful New York realtor. Before I joined the throng, I wanted to freshen up and change clothes.

A migraine threatened to keep me from attending the opening festivities. Lying on a king size bed in my dull room, I imagined other graduates socializing, reminiscing, sharing news. I was curious how life had treated my classmates. I conquered my headache and dressed in a muumuu for the cocktail hour. The hotel bar was clogged with smiling classmates closing in on the big "Five-O." Most wore Hawaiian shirts and a lanyard with their senior annual picture attached to a name tag. Some sported their senior rings.

By the time I was emboldened with a shaker of margaritas, the unmanned registration table displayed only a few name tags. One for Shelley Rebecca Winter lay close to a tag for Rosalinda Wilson. I remembered the heavy girl who stayed on the sideline, eager to chat, anxious to be chosen but always ignored. How callous I had been. Now that I was trapped in a lumbering shell, I understood her frustration. Inside this flabby façade, I was the same person who had played intramural basketball and ran track. A thinner me was on the swim team in the summer. So maybe Rosalinda never did those things, and maybe I was one of those who mistreated her. Today, I was choosing her. Rosalinda would enjoy this reunion even if she had changed her mind about coming. I took a welcome packet and hung her name tag around my neck, ID for admittance to a special group: Oakwood graduates of 1982. Rosalinda Wilson belonged.

I went back to the bar for a Jack on the rocks.

A deep voice next to me said, "Rosalinda, remember me? Frank Scott! I sat next to you in Mr. Albertson's chemistry class."

"Oh, yeah. Good grief, I remember chemistry was so boring." I noticed that Frank was no longer covered with red pimples. He probably noticed my words were slurred.

"You're kidding. I thought you were the only one who was listening," said Frank.

"Ahh, I had to pay close attention because he mumbled."

Frank sat down. "I heard a rumor that you are recently deceased."

"Not yet."

"I'm glad it's not true. Wonder how that got started."

"Excuse me, Frank, I'm meeting somebody in the lobby. We'll talk later. Great to see you." I left the bar and headed back to the registration table. This wouldn't work if people pestered me about Rosalinda's death.

I put her ID down and picked up another one. The lights were low, but I saw the name Alice Elizabeth Tripp. I couldn't remember her. Probably nobody else did either.

I hid in a corner of the bar with my new persona, sipping my whiskey, a watcher out of bounds. I used to be the one creating the action. Classmates emulated me, eavesdropped on my conversations. No more of that. Inside my packaging, I was now invisible.

"Have you seen Jordan? She looks so different, almost svelte." My old cheerleader friends cackled in a nearby clutch, smiles perky, pom-poms sagging in their halter tops.

"That's what happens when you marry money. You can afford a personal trainer and a personal shopper. And a cook and a nanny. You pretty much rent out different parts of your life so you can concentrate on entertainment."

They raised their tinkling voices to hear each other over the din. One of them glanced at me, smiled, looked at my name tag, and returned to her conversation. She didn't know Alice Elizabeth either. And she confirmed what I suspected. All fat women look alike to the beautiful people. They were self-absorbed. I was alone.

I followed a crowd to the roof terrace, the setting for that evening's gathering. I stood at a railing by myself, looking for one familiar landmark. To the north was the Bank of America Corporate Center, the tallest building in North Carolina. To the south was Duke Energy headquarters, probably the second. Both of them huge, and modern. More New York than my genteel hometown, now seen through the eyes of an outsider.

While I hovered by the Polynesian buffet lit by tiki torches, a husky guy in jeans stopped a man wearing a starched shirt and black slacks.

"Tommy, good to see you, buddy. We're getting the team together at Capital Grille for steaks."

I thought Tommy would draw away and decline. Florida Senator Tom Buchanan looked too rich to acknowledge a farmer. I was surprised. He slammed his manicured hand on his friend's broad shoulder. "Dan, the man. I'm ready."

"Bring your wife."

"She didn't come this time. Said she's heard all the replays she can handle." Tommy laughed. "Best time of my life, believe me." They walked away jostling each other like kids.

It had been the best time of my life, too, and I could be reliving it, if I didn't look like a freak. I refreshed my drink and sadly left the roof to hide in my solitary room. Lights out, I opened the drapes and sat in the window, beholding the changed skyline.

Saturday morning I slept late, bruised by the stress of peer rejection. Not only that. The whole year had depressed me. I felt as though an unseen hand had reached down from the sky to unfairly tumble me out of the good times. I sat in bed with my tasteless coffee and youthful memories. If there had been a giant hand that moved me out of action, I must have missed the one that would move me back. Maybe I didn't play the game right. I shook my head. I sounded like Dan. Everything's a game.

No. The only hand that influenced my present circumstances belonged to somebody I had trusted and paid well. Last night on the terrace, Dr. Anthony Papaleo didn't even give me the courtesy of a friendly nod. He glanced at my name tag and looked away. I was too devastated to speak. His attitude seemed to be if he couldn't remember me, he didn't want to know me, and I didn't exist. And he had created my face. A mistake? Incompetence? At this point what did it matter?

I picked up the name tag lying on the nightstand. I examined the annual photo glued to it. Her face was pudgy with small eyes. Alice Tripp, you are nothing to him. Except for her dark hair, she looked like me in my overweight prison. My heart filled with rage.

Anthony's hands did this to me. He needed to pay. Alice and I would be on a team for a game of Payback. Energized, I dressed and went downstairs to the breakfast bar. I needed a strategy. I didn't wear an ID this time so I could observe. I already knew I was invisible.

My opponent came in at nine forty-five, right before the buffet closed. Anthony looked bleary-eyed as though he drank too much the night before. I focused on his hand pressed to his companion's back, directing her path. Those slim fingers. I wondered if he could operate minus one of them. Or two. Chopping off one from each hand would be ideal. Freaky. I smiled my way out the hotel doors to go shopping.

Festivities started with cocktails at five thirty, dinner at seven, and a band at eight. I had time to dye my hair dark brown before I dressed for playing games in a black tent-like dress, pearl necklace and earrings. I had to blend in. My name tag went into my black evening bag along with my ammunition. When I wiped down the room like I had seen them do on CSI, I shivered with excitement. Let the game begin.

I checked Shelley Winter out of the hotel room and rode the shuttle with my suitcases to the airport where I cancelled my return flight and rented a car. I drove back to the hotel.

When I waddled through the lobby, I saw Dr. Anthony Papaleo looking at the leftover name tags on the registration table. I wondered if he saw mine and recognized the name of his client who had been billed enough money to buy his Maserati.

By six thirty the bar crowd had thinned as my classmates made their way to the ballroom. No doubt they wanted to have seats near close friends. Tonight they befriended strangers because everyone had changed. I smiled to myself as I watched the game of musical chairs. We all grew up on party games. When the music stopped, the kid without a chair was a loser. I always fought for my seat. The strong survive. My jetsetter third husband and I had once been invited to Dr. Papaleo's mansion for a political event, an adult game. I had been foolishly impressed with the glitz of the doctor's success in his world of confetti.

The reunion's dinner and dance was a recreation of our prom theme of Shangri-La, another one of my ideas. The better seats were in the center because the band positioned their loud speakers at the side. I found a place with my back to the wall, with good visibility of the popular people. I couldn't believe I was once the heart of that frantic effort to be chosen by people with low self-esteem. Thirty years later, they still sought each other's approval. I recognized who I had been, and I was more satisfied with my mature compassion for the outcast.

From behind me, I heard "Alice Tripp." Over my shoulder, a tall man read my name tag lying on top of my purse. "Remember me? I'm George Eastman. Do you mind if I sit here?"

"Not at all, George." When I turned to face him, I could see a flash of pity, maybe horror. Couldn't blame him. I gave him a lopsided smile. We chatted awhile about how Charlotte had changed. Others sat down, introduced themselves and George fell into the recitation of name, location, children, and job. Nobody asked for my credentials. I probably had the fattest bank account and still failed to impress because it was invisible.

I caught sight of my opponent settling in near the middle of the room, surrounded by giggling, bejeweled women and men in expensive suits. I glanced at my three-carat remounted engagement diamond. That last husband was the reason I took a chance on surgery. He left me for a younger, saucier partner, a clone of me at a younger age. Anthony encouraged me to compete. I couldn't nip and tuck my aging self fast enough. I lost that game, and Anthony tried to console me. I was never good at games anyway. Until Payback.

Only six were at my table, in spite of the available ten place settings. I was concerned I would have to move or participate in conversation, until two couples rushed over. One of "the girls" was my former best friend, Marilyn Jeane Baker. My face rearranged itself into a bright smile. I thought my game was over. Even though I hadn't seen her in ages, I felt Marilyn would look into my eyes and recognize me, and I would have to confess a silly mistake at picking up the wrong name tag. I was almost relieved, ready to change course and enjoy the evening. But Marilyn could barely hide her revulsion and quickly turned to introduce herself to the others at the table. She accepted me as Alice Tripp, whoever that was. Nobody remembered, nobody cared. Maybe she had died, too. I felt dead already.

My diamond ring was the only outstanding detail that might be recalled on the fat lady who left the party early. I put it in my bag. As I did, I grazed the vial of rat poison appropriately named for this game. I had enough to share with the entire table. No, I had to focus. None of these people had harmed me. Hurt my feelings, yes, but they had not been guilty of mutilation, like Dr. Anthony Papaleo. I now considered that his actions were deliberate, that my rejection of romance spawned hatred.

Dinner was the predictable chicken, rice pilaf, and broccoli vegetable medley accompanied by background music. Several couples took advantage of the photo opportunity under the Shangri-La banner reminiscent of our prom night. Two couples from our class had been together at the first prom and now this one. I couldn't imagine such a lasting relationship. The people at my table talked about events that happened in high school, and I longed to blurt out, "I remember that." But I kept silent. Occasionally, someone would try to include me by smiling or asking a question. I really appreciated the small effort, but I didn't belong here anymore. I didn't measure up to the standards of normal. All because of Dr. "Slash" Papaleo.

A former president of the student body was tonight's Master of Ceremonies who recognized the members of the planning committee. They had labored for hours on this event and a current directory of all graduates so we could keep in touch. The lights dimmed, and we were encouraged to party till the sun came up like we used to do. Many aging revelers chuckled, but I felt a lump in my plump throat. I would never be that person again. I clenched my fists, determined that my last reunion would have a spectacular finale.

Waiters freshened drinks, and the band tuned up. I absorbed the music. Suddenly it was prom night 1982 again. My date that night, the one I had chosen over Anthony Papaleo, was here with an attractive brunette. I watched him checking out every table. I wanted to believe he was looking for me, remembering the intoxicating time we had as seniors, preparing to be loosed on the world. He went to a different college, and I didn't see him again until the ten-year reunion when everyone was still young. I should have stayed with him. My life might have been better. Tears blurred my vision.

The stalking phase of Payback began around nine thirty. I migrated to other tables several times, quietly sitting with a crowd, always moving closer to my prey, until I was seated at a table right behind Dr. Slash. I ordered the same drink he had and wrapped a napkin around the icy glass. I made my move when he and his younger friend went out to the dance floor again, where he impressed himself with his non-dance moves, very much under alcoholic influence.

In preparation for attack, I selected a few roses from the centerpiece at my table and the one next to us. Then I went to his table. I leaned over his empty chair, commenting to the two couples seated there that I wanted mementos for my scrapbook. I placed my collection of flowers and my glass next to Dr. Slash's drink. I gave a crooked smile that everyone pretended to indulge before looking away, leaving me a few seconds to select a rose from their centerpiece. I walked away with the flowers and the good doctor's drink. I left my own that looked exactly like his, with an extra ingredient for the attack phase.

I went to two other tables before my retreat out the door, hiding in plain sight as only fat women can. Clutching my victory bouquet, I walked through the lobby past the parking valet and down the block where my rental car waited.

Rat poison causes internal bleeding, and I wondered how Payback would play out. It could end in a heart attack attributed to heavy dancing. Or there might be lots of blood on the floor. Before the commotion broke out, I would reach the state line. Newspapers would solve my curiosity, but it didn't matter. I was a different woman.

I speed dialed the California number in my cell. "Hello, Alice Elizabeth? This is Shelley Winter from Oakland. Remember me? I'm driving home from the reunion in Charlotte. I didn't fit in, and I left before dinner when I heard that Rosalinda died."

I drove the scenic way home chatting to Alice. I could hide or start over.

TRIUMVIRATE

SUZANNE LILLY

"We need to talk."

My mother watched me from her seat at my old wooden kitchen table as I carried in two bags of holiday baking groceries. *Why is it that even though I'm in my thirties, my mother can give me looks that make me feel like I did when I was a young girl caught peeking under the Christmas tree?*

"Mom, is something bothering you?"

"Sit down." My mother patted the cushion on the kitchen chair next to her. She poured some tea from a pot into my favorite mug.

"Did you get the turkey?" I delayed the impending serious conversation with mundane things. I set the bags of groceries down on the counter and began taking out the staples. Brown sugar, flour, pecans.

"Yes, I did, and I put it in the freezer." Her eyes narrowed and she watched me with even more intensity.

Why is she looking at me as if I'm a bug under a microscope? "Thanks for picking it up, Mom."

"I had to move some things in the freezer to make it fit."

"Oh?"

"Yes. It was quite full."

"That's odd. I don't use it except for holiday baking."

"The freezer wasn't full of holiday baking."

Who cares if my freezer is full and what's in it? "Maybe Dan did some warehouse shopping." I avoided the chair next to her, moving past it to put the groceries on the shelves as we talked.

"It wasn't full from warehouse shopping, either." She stood and put her hand over the cans of cranberry sauce so I would have to stop working and look at her.

Fine. I've had enough of this conversational roundabout game.
"Mom, just tell me what's bothering you. Get to the point."

"You know what's bothering me. What you have in the freezer is bothering me."

"What are you talking about? Do I have too much ice cream or something? I'm pregnant, you know. I'm allowed a little excess."

She searched my eyes, deep into them, looking for something. Whatever it was, she didn't find it. "You really don't know, do you?"

"No. So tell me what this is all about." I put the cranberry sauce in the cupboard and let the door slam shut.

"Come with me and I'll show you." She walked to the basement door. "But I have to confess something to you."

I wondered what it could be, but I didn't worry. Since Mom had retired, she'd been getting worked up about little things. Too much time on her hands. *I hope once the baby comes, she'll be too busy to worry about minutiae.*

We descended the narrow basement stairway together, down to the craft and laundry room where the big chest type freezer sat in a corner, next to my sewing machine. The top of the freezer made an excellent fabric layout and cutting surface. I also used it for folding clothes. Multi-purpose appliance, that's what it was.

A plastic laundry basket sat on the floor next to it, filled with frozen food packages, condensation beading on them, beginning to thaw.

"Mom, why did you leave this food out?" I hefted the basket onto my hip and swung open the freezer lid with my other hand.

No smell accompanied the sight I saw, and the waft of frosty air in my face made me think I'd imagined it. Then the air cleared, giving me a full view of the freezer contents. I dropped the basket with a thud. It tipped sideways, scattering frozen desserts and vegetable packets across the tile floor.

My stomach heaved. I grabbed the wastebasket next to my sewing machine and hurled green bile into the pile of red holiday fabric scraps and thread. My head pounded as if someone had hit me with a sledgehammer. I squeezed my temples and concentrated on breathing in and out.

"Is that Frank?" I gagged on his name.

"It looks that way." Mom placed her hands on the edge of the freezer, peering down at the body. "Although with the frost damage on his face, at first I wasn't sure." She moved the quilt that covered his body farther down, uncovering his torso.

Her face and posture remained calm, dead calm, like the still air that precedes a storm.

Waves of panic surged through the wall of pain in my head. *This is a fine fix I'm in.*

"Mom, how did he get in here?" I gripped my stomach and lurched over the wastebasket again as I convulsed through a dry heave.

"That's what I'd like to ask you."

I felt my eyes widen. *Was she accusing me, her only daughter, of stuffing her boyfriend's body in a freezer?* "Mom, I swear to you, I don't know anything about this!"

My mother leaned her back against the freezer and brushed the hair away from my face. "I do believe you. It's obvious you've never seen this before." She crinkled her brow and pulled a pack of cigarettes out of her jacket pocket. A tremor shook her fingers as she flicked the lighter to the end of her smoke. She almost dropped the cigarette. "Like I said, I have a confession to make."

"How did Frank's body get into my freezer?"

She blew out a long blast of smoke as she regarded his cold, gray shape. "If I knew, would I be asking you about it? Anyway, it's neither here nor there at this point in time. The main worry now is you have a dead body in your freezer. What are we going to do about that?"

"Are you thinking we should call the police?" *Please say no, please say no, please, in God's name, say no.*

She turned and flicked some gray ash on her dead lover's face. "Not an option. They'd find out I killed him, and suspect you of covering up the crime by hiding the body."

The empty pit of my stomach clenched and my unborn baby squirmed and kicked. *Does the baby sense my fear?*

"Are you saying you had something to do with this?" I purposely avoided using the word murder, and its cousin homicide. It sounded too harsh.

Frank and Mom's relationship had been tumultuous at best, abusive at worst. He'd been sloshed the last time he'd been to our house. Easter dinner, eight months ago. Then he disappeared. No one missed him, not really. We just wondered where he'd taken off to. When he left, Mom had returned to her former, happier self.

Two jets of smoke puffed out through Mom's nostrils. She eyed my belly, and remembering I was pregnant, she dropped the remaining half of her cigarette into her cold tea. "The last time I saw him was here at Easter. Do you remember I called the taxi for him?"

The front door upstairs opened and closed. I looked at the clock on the wall. It was after five. "Dan's home!" I hissed. "We've got to cover this up!" I bent down and grabbed the packages strewn across the floor. My mother upended the laundry basket of food over the Arctic remains of her dead lover. I tossed the rest on top of that, and jammed the turkey in last. We slammed down the lid just as Dan poked his head through the doorway at the top of the stairs.

"What are you two beautiful ladies up to?"

"J-just putting the turkey in the f-freezer." *Can he hear me tripping over my words?*

"You should have waited and let me do that." He came down the stairs. "I don't want my mother-in-law or my pregnant wife carrying a twenty-pound turkey up and down the stairs. Next time, let me take care of it."

"We didn't want to let the food thaw. Right, Mom?"

She nodded, suddenly mute.

"Well, you missed one." He stepped off the bottom tread, and picked up a stray package of peas. He walked over and opened the freezer lid. The basement air froze in my lungs. I held my breath as he scanned the freezer contents. One corner of the frozen quilt stuck out from under the turkey. His brows crinkled, and he quickly shut the lid.

"Nice bird." He leaned in to kiss me and made a sour face. He must have smelled the vomit in my mouth. "Are you still having morning sickness?"

My mother found her voice. "Why don't we all go upstairs? I'll make Kayla a pot of peppermint tea to settle her stomach." She linked her arm in Dan's and led him back to the stairway.

"I'm going to get some Tiger Balm for my headache." I escaped into the master bedroom and opened the medicine cabinet.

Think, Kayla, think. What happened last Easter?

I replayed the day in my mind's eye. Frank had eaten dinner, and drunk plenty. After a few glasses of Pinot Noir, he was not in the proper Easter spirit. He had started knocking back the port he'd brought me as a hostess gift, and before long he was yelling at my mother, slurring so badly we couldn't understand him. He always ruined our family celebrations with his drunken anger. I had gone into the kitchen to start cleaning up and stay out of the way. My mother had called him a cab, and said she was spending the night at our house. Hadn't Frank left in the taxi Mom called for him? When I came out of the kitchen, he was gone, and Mother was in the bathroom. Dan had been stoking the fire, building up a flame.

"Is he gone?" I'd asked when I didn't see his coat on the rack.

"Yes, the cab just drove away," Dan rubbed his hands together in front of the fire. Last Easter, there had still been a dusting of snow on the ground outside.

My mother had come back into the room, rubbing lotion on her hands. "Good riddance to rubbish."

That was the last time any of us had seen Frank. He just went away and didn't call or text or email. My mother said he never even collected his clothes from her apartment. Later that summer, she threw them in the trash. Life had carried on, much calmer now that Frank was out of our lives.

Until this afternoon, that is.

I smoothed Tiger Balm across my forehead.

"You think I did it, don't you?" I whirled around at the sound of my mother's voice. She'd followed me into the bedroom. "You think I put his body in your freezer."

She was reading my mind. "What am I supposed to think?"

"Well think about this. I love you. More than anything in the world. I would never, ever, endanger you in any way." She grabbed me by the shoulders. "Besides, why would I show you the body if I had killed him? I would have moved it out of here by now. I would never leave it here and put you at risk."

She pulled me close and hugged me. I wrapped my arms around her. I wanted to believe her.

"That only leaves one other person," she whispered.

I pushed away and looked her in the eyes. "What are you saying?"

"The only other person here that day was Dan."

"Mom, I trust Dan! He didn't do this!" I extricated myself from her arms and sat down on the edge of my bed. The sledgehammer pounded on my head again, harder now. I massaged more Tiger Balm on my forehead and temples.

"He's the father of my child. I don't care what you think he did."

"I actually should be thanking Dan." She sat down beside me and her shoulders slumped. "Frank wouldn't leave, no matter how many times I told him to get out of my life. It was only a matter of time. It had to be either him or me."

"Mom, I'm not sure you should be telling me this. You certainly shouldn't say anything to Dan."

She took my hand. "One thing is for sure. We need to get rid of the body. If anyone else ever finds Frank in the freezer, you or Dan or all of us will go to prison."

Not Dan. I need to keep him safe.

"Mom, I have a confession to make. I'm not completely innocent."

Mom sat back down on the bed. "What do you mean? You just told me you didn't have anything to do with this."

"I didn't know Frank was in my freezer. I truly didn't. But do you remember when Dan hurt his back last March? The doctor gave him Oxycontin. I took some and crushed them and put them in Frank's mashed potatoes at dinner."

My mom covered her face with her hands. Now that I'd started to tell her, I had to get it all out at once. The words shot out of my mouth like bullets, firing out my story before I could change my mind. I had to turn any blame away from Dan.

"Don't you remember I plated our food in the kitchen that day? I doctored his potatoes and poured on the gravy, hoping he'd miss the taste of the Oxycontin. He ate so greedily he probably never even tasted anything. I was confused when nothing happened. I thought he must have had the heart of a horse. Then, when he didn't make it home that night, I figured he'd had a delayed reaction. I thought perhaps he wandered off like a rat after eating poison, and collapsed and died on some street corner or alley. I kept checking the papers and the Internet news every day for weeks, but no one ever found his body."

My mother shook her head. "And since he was estranged from his son three thousand miles away in New York, he didn't have anyone to declare him missing, except me. But I had a good reason not to report him missing."

"You're not angry with me?"

"I have a confession to make to you, too. I don't think the Oxycontin killed him."

Mom probably doesn't understand how lethal a large dose of Oxycontin can be, especially mixed with wine.

"I killed Frank." Her voice hitched and she pointed to herself. "Not you. I took a bottle of the dog's epilepsy medicine, Phenobarbital, and dissolved it into a carafe of wine. I made sure Frank was the only one who drank from the carafe. Do you remember I placed it right next to him and poured from the bottle for Dan and you?"

"I thought that was strange." I remembered how she guarded his wineglass and kept prompting him to drink more. "I wondered why you gave him a whole carafe when he always got so ugly with alcohol."

"So I'm the one who killed him, not you." She reached in her pocket and took out another cigarette, but didn't light it. "I figured he fell asleep in the taxi and the cab driver rolled him. Took his money and dumped his body somewhere. So imagine my surprise today when I found him in your freezer."

"If you didn't put the body there, and I didn't..." My words trailed off as we both realized the implications of what I was thinking.

Dan cleared his throat. Mom and I jumped and grabbed each other. How long had he been standing in the doorway? How much had he overheard?

"Sorry, ladies, you're both wrong. Neither of you killed him. I took care of the menace myself." He handed us both a mug of peppermint tea.

"What are you talking about?"

"When Mom went to the bathroom, and you went to the kitchen, I invited Frank downstairs to see my latest woodcarving project. He was so drunk he could hardly stand up straight. Now I know he had a whole cocktail of drugs floating in his bloodstream. It only took a tap on the shoulder to send him tumbling down the stairs. He broke his neck. He was so numb from the drugs he probably didn't suffer at all."

"Why didn't you just tell us? Say it was an accident, and call the police?" I asked.

"I didn't because I saw you put something in his potatoes. I didn't know what it was at the time, but I didn't want to risk losing you if the coroner found whatever it was in his bloodstream." He ran his fingers through his hair. "I hurt my back again hefting his dead weight into the freezer, and when I went to the medicine cabinet, I saw half the bottle of Oxycontin was gone."

My shoulders slumped as I realized what a burden I'd caused Dan. He'd never said a word to me. He'd kept my secret all these past months.

The three of us stared at each other as the meaning of what we'd done together and separately sunk in. We'd become an unofficial triumvirate, passing judgment and sentence on the abuser.

Unanimously.

My mother was the first to speak. "What do we do now?"

"Isn't it a new moon tonight?" I asked. "Why don't we head out on a quiet country road for some stargazing?"

"I'll get some shovels," Mom said.

"I'll go warm up the car," I said.

"I'll get Frank," Dan said. "He always did enjoy an evening drive."

BOB, OLD ONE EYE, AND THE PIRATE QUEEN

CATHY C. HALL

B ob adjusted the stuffed parrot perched on his shoulder. It had been a real steal, at just two hundred and thirty bucks. Too bad Alicia couldn't see it that way. But then, Alicia couldn't see much to like at all about Talk Like a Pirate Day.

"Arr, me beauty, I'll be leaving now to fill me bung hole at Jimmy's!"

Bob winked as he passed his wife. No time for a kiss. He had to meet his friends at the neighborhood bar.

"Do you even know what a bung hole is?" asked Alicia. She didn't bother to look up from the *TV Guide*.

The door slammed louder than usual. "Idiot," muttered Alicia, flipping the page.

Jimmy's always pulled in a good crowd on the nineteenth of September, and this evening was no exception. The joint was packed with patch-wearing pirates; hooked arms and striped shirts kept bumping into one another.

Bob looked around the room, his chest swelling with pride: nobody had a parrot. Still, he couldn't help sighing just a little. Wouldn't it be great, he thought, if a TV news crew showed up at the bar and profiled him for the holiday? Bob the ordinary accountant by day, but on September 19, Robert Blood, fierce pirate captain, his faithful Polly on his arm.

"Avast ye! It's Captain Robert!" The greeting hailed from a rowdy bunch in the corner, breaking up Bob's reverie.

"Tom Timbers!" returned the Captain, grabbing a pitcher of beer as he strode across the bar. "Arrggh," he grunted happily. Nothing beat Talk Like a Pirate Day!

By eight o'clock, Captain Robert was three sheets to the wind, and listing a little to the port side. He'd reveled in the attention that his parrot had garnered, but his joy had been considerably dampened when an overzealous pirate had popped one of the bird's eyes out. He sat with Old One Eye, as everyone had taken to calling the parrot, and he was seconds from leaving—and taking Old One Eye with him—when a pirate queen pushed open the door to Jimmy's.

The fetching enchantress sneered a command. "Ahoy, ye bilge rats! Out of me way!"

The crowd parted easily. She paused at a table or two, but it was clear that her gaze was fixed upon Captain Robert and Old One Eye. She stopped short at Bob's table and with a quick kick of boot to chair, Tom Timbers flipped over, toppling pirates next to him.

The men scattered, and just like that, the pirate queen had a cozy table for two with Captain Robert.

At the other end of the bar, Little Petey and Tom Timbers had plenty to say about the mystery woman who now leaned over a barstool, ordering a drink.

"I wouldn't mind a bit o' that booty," said Little Petey with a leer. He watched the queen's hips sway and her flaming red curls shake as she headed back to Captain Robert, two Singapore Slings in hand.

"Aye, a buxom wench she is," agreed Tom Timbers. "A sailor could get lost in the depths of those…er, uh…" He cleared his throat. "Eyes," he stammered. "Those sea-green eyes!"

Little Petey and Tom's discussion ended suddenly when the pirate queen stood and swiped her jeweled hand across her mouth. She stretched then, slowly, like a cat, and turned, hips swaying as she sashayed down a dimly lit hallway. Three pairs of eyes followed her down the hall; one pair of eyes dilated much too widely.

"All hands on deck!" shouted Little Petey. The alarm on his watch had just blared a shrill siren.

It was time for the traditional singing of the sea chantey. Plastered pirates stumbled to the bar, grabbing song sheets, squinting at the paper. With a signal from Petey, the raucous rendition of "The Pirate Song" began. Thirty lusty-throated men launched into the first of ten verses, and Jimmy's rocked with the noise of off-key singing and clanking glasses. And in the midst of the din sat Captain Robert Blood, laughing his fool head off.

More than an hour later, the singing and toasting finally wound down to a low hum. Little Petey and Tom Timbers ordered a coffee and joined Captain Robert at his table for a nightcap. All that was left of the mysterious pirate queen was the lingering scent of sandalwood and jasmine.

"Ahoy, ye blackguard!" said Tom, shoving his friend.

Captain Robert's legs poked straight out, his head rested on his chest. When Tom's push got no response, Little Petey kicked his foot. "Avast, ye scurvy dog!"

Again, no response.

"Sink me," said Tom, blanching. "I think he's dead."

Captain Robert would get his holiday wish. He'd end up on the news, after all.

The police arrived within minutes, and by the time Lieutenants Hartwell and Valery walked through the door, most of the pirates had sobered up enough to make sense. Of course, everyone felt pretty bad about Captain Robert. Still, a handful in the crowd smiled, murmuring that Captain Robert seemed downright jolly for a man who died of a heart attack.

Lieutenant Anna Valery did *not* smile. And she didn't think it was a heart attack, either. There was something about this guy that made the detective think murder. So naturally, she asked if he was married.

Her partner sighed. "Yes, he was married. Five years, no kids." Lieutenant Kyle Hartwell knew where she was going with this. "It wasn't the wife; it was a heart attack."

Valery wasn't listening. She was inching around the table, examining the body. "It's always the spouse," she said as she continued to search, looking for anything odd, out of place. The stuffed parrot hanging off the dead man's shoulder fit the bill. "What in the world?" she asked.

Her partner shrugged. Little Petey stepped forward.

"Ahoy," said Petey. "That be Old One Eye."

The detectives exchanged a look.

Tom approached the group and introduced himself, speaking in his regular voice. "It's, uh, Talk Like A Pirate Day," he said, trying to explain Little Petey's foolishness.

Lieutenant Valery nodded and stared a little closer at the parrot. The dead bird *was* missing an eye.

She blew out a sigh. She could tell it was going to be a long night.

Captain Robert's body was taken downtown to the coroner's, standard procedure in a suspicious death like this, even if it did turn out to be the heart attack scenario. Which Lieutenant Valery strongly doubted. She wanted to speak to the medical examiner ASAP. She was sure that this was not a death from natural causes, despite her partner's view to the contrary.

"Look, it was a simple heart attack," argued Hartwell. "All the pirate fun, drinking too much. And don't forget that hooker who showed up." He smirked and offered her his notes.

"A heart attack that nobody notices?" Valery made a face.

"They were singing 'The Pirate Song.'"

"And that hooker? She just happened to show up at Jimmy's?"

"Where they always celebrate Talk Like A Pirate Day. She was a *pirate* queen."

Lieutenant Valery rolled her eyes. Only guys could think up a holiday to indulge their pirate side. But it took a woman with a little extra creativity to cash in on it.

It was well after eleven when the two detectives rang the doorbell at the victim's house. Alicia answered, wearing a robe and put-out expression.

"Ma'am, we're sorry to bother you so late." Lieutenant Hartwell swallowed. "May we come in?"

Alicia nodded and led the detectives toward the couch. But Hartwell was a blurter, and before they had a chance to even sit, he rushed into the reason why they were there. "I'm afraid your husband died tonight…at Jimmy's. Heart attack."

Lieutenant Valery expected shock. Even guilty wives could fake shock. But Alicia's knees nearly buckled. Valery reached out and grabbed the woman so she wouldn't fall.

Alicia dabbed at the corner of her eye with a crumpled tissue. "I *just* talked to him. He called from Jimmy's." Both detectives instinctively glanced at the cell phone on the table. They knew the cell phone would be no help. The wife could have been anywhere when she answered that call.

Valery's own cell buzzed, and she walked into the kitchen. She preferred not to speak to the medical examiner in front of the grief-stricken wife.

"Can't say this was a natural death, Lieutenant," said the ME to Valery. "Looks like this guy had a toxic amount of atropine in his system. Found traces in his stomach."

"Huh…" said Valery. She was not surprised.

"It was the dilated eyes made me look for poison," he continued. "Wasn't expecting atropine, though. I mean, people don't usually die from atropine poisoning."

"Why not?" asked the detective. That had the sound of "hard to prove" written all over it.

"An atropine overdose affects people differently. One guy may lose his voice…another guy may get the giggles. Pretty darn hard not to notice. Didn't I hear this guy was at a crowded bar?"

"Yeah," said Valery, "Jimmy's. But there was a whole lot of pirate partying going on. And laughing hysterically can't kill a guy."

"Actually, it can. But that's not what killed him. Atropine poisoning's fairly easy to treat. Just pump out the stomach. But if it stays in the system too long, you got your paralysis setting in. Then it's Davy Jones' locker for the poor guy."

"So how long did it take?" she asked.

"Thirty, maybe forty minutes."

Lieutenant Valery whistled. "Shiver me timbers," she said.

She peered out the kitchen's bay window at a lovely garden, its shadowy flowers lit by the full moon above. All those people at Jimmy's, she thought, but no one had seen or heard anything odd. The pirates had been drinking beer, mostly, and no one else had been even slightly sick. And Jimmy's didn't really serve food, just bar munchies. Valery double-checked her notes, stopping on the bottom of the second page.

Captain Robert had slugged down something on top of his beer. He'd had a Sling. He—and the mysterious pirate queen.

Alicia entered the kitchen then, still sniffling.

"Thought we could use some coffee."

Valery nodded and quickly joined her partner in the next room. "Wouldn't drink the coffee," she said, lowering her voice. She filled Hartwell in on the latest developments.

"But what's the motive?" asked Hartwell. "This marriage is about as ordinary as they come: no secret lovers, no money problems, no nothing. At least, nothing to kill somebody over." Then he hissed the showstopper in a tense whisper, "She *wasn't* at the bar."

Lieutenant Valery's lip curved in an almost-smile. She was remembering little girls—and big girls, too—playing dress up. Her partner would be shocked to know that only last weekend, she'd had an ooh-la-la time as Fifi, the French maid. Wigs, contact lenses, push-up bras, a costume…none of those accessories were hard to come by.

"What if Alicia was that pirate woman at the bar?" she whispered back.

Now it was her partner's turn to whistle. "Are you crazy?" Hartwell forgot to whisper. "Don't you think the guy would know his own wife?"

"Who says he didn't? Maybe he went along for the fun of it." Valery raised an eyebrow. Fifi had had quite a bit of fun.

"And Tom and Pete, they knew the wife, too," said Hartwell. "Don't you think they'd recognize her?"

She shrugged. "People see what they want to see."

Alicia came in and sat down beside the detectives, setting her cup on the end table where it wobbled a moment, off balance. She picked up the cup and quickly placed something black and shiny in her robe pocket. But Lieutenant Valery had seen it. And not for the first time. Valery excused herself once again to the kitchen. She had to make a quick call. She had one more question about atropine.

The ME skimmed the website, humming the pirate song from that amusement park ride. "Yeah, here it is: atropine *can* be found in a plant, in something called Belladonna, fairly common around here. It's the berries that are toxic. They're purple and sweet, when they're ripe."

Valery could feel her heart beating faster. "When's that?" she asked. "When are the berries ripe?"

"September," said the doctor.

"Yo, ho," sang Valery, closing her cell.

When Lieutenant Valery rejoined the others, she asked Alicia for the marble in her pocket. Lieutenant Hartwell stared at it.

"What is that supposed to be?" he asked.

"Evidence," said Valery.

The detective remembered where she'd seen that black marble: Old One Eye, Captain Robert's parrot. Alicia must have picked up the missing eye at Jimmy's tonight, sometime after the bird's unfortunate accident. Probably while the pirate queen had been hanging out at Captain Bob's table.

"I bet we'd find belladonna out in the garden, Lieutenant Hartwell. It's a lovely plant, but I'd stay away from those berries. They make a killer chaser for a Singapore Sling."

Now Lieutenant Hartwell was truly lost. Alicia sipped her coffee.

"C'mon, Alicia, give it up," said Valery. "A red wig, green contacts, and every man in that bar will identify you."

"For crying out loud," spat Alicia, slamming her coffee cup on the table. "I didn't mean to *kill* him."

Lieutenant Hartwell's jaw dropped along with his cup. It always *is* the spouse. He'd never hear the end of this.

"All they had to do was call 9-1-1!" said Alicia. "They could've pumped his stomach in the ambulance! Bob's fine, lesson learned. But no, nobody noticed anything. They were all too busy singing their stupid pirate song! For stupid Talk Like A Pirate Day! I mean, can you believe Bob paid *two hundred and twenty-nine dollars* for that dead bird, just for this stupid holiday? Our *fifth* wedding anniversary was two weeks ago and what did I get? Not even a stinkin' card!"

Alicia fell back against the sofa, her fury spent. She sobbed now as Lieutenant Hartwell started reading, "You have the right to remain silent..."

Lieutenant Valery sighed once more. She figured the pirate queen could very well get off with involuntary manslaughter.

Especially if the jury was packed with women.

WISHING FOR IGNORANCE

E. B. DAVIS

I heard her turn on the faucet. The water sloshing down the drain competed with the sound of my blood pulsating through my veins. I leaned against the stall door to steady myself, slung my large handbag over my shoulder, and emerged from the toilet. She was washing her hands at the sink. After years of research, I'd located and followed her. Should I introduce myself?

I glanced in her direction, smiled, and met her eyes in the mirror. She acknowledged my presence with a nod of her head, crowned in salt and pepper hair. No real warmth. Was she a cold person or indifferent to strangers? Words froze in my mouth. I couldn't introduce myself, not here—in a public bathroom at the mall near my Northern Virginia home.

The mirror reflected her image. I watched her as I washed my hands in the sink next to hers. The oval shape of her face, blue eye color, compact build, and long legs—she resembled me, or should I say—I resembled her. Who was this woman? Her story would fascinate me.

"At least the bathroom is clean," I said, and smiled again hoping to initiate a conversation, but all she did was shrug. She gave no indication I looked familiar.

The woman dried her hands using a blower. Its sound irritated me. Then, she bent under the sink to pick up a Macy's bag and her purse. She slung the purse over her shoulder by its strap in a mannerism akin to my own and left the bathroom. I wiped my wet hands on my jeans and followed her.

Throughout my life people had asked questions for which I had no answers. My personal history was shrouded in secrets, a tangled web of legal documents designed to camouflage the truth. It annoyed and challenged me. Educated in computer science and schooled in research methodology, I had unearthed the truth by hacking into The Agency's personnel files. Only one woman could confirm the facts and provide the human angle not revealed on paper.

Her.

There were many legitimate reasons for finding my birth mother, such as family medical history. Pert, white-clad strangers looked me in the eyes and expected me to spout answers to their questions. Heredity was a factor. Genetics increased statistical significance, they explained, as if I were stupid.

Teachers expected me to know my genealogy or be able to readily access it. As a middle-school student, I never could trace my genealogy as assigned by naïve teachers. It had taken me years to unknot the threads. My unknown past propelled my career at The Agency. Finding the truth wasn't imperative, but it would simplify my life, explaining the mystery and satisfying my curiosity. Had the search been less challenging, my interest might not have been as keen.

Her pace quickened in the stream of people. She walked to the food court, ordered a coffee, and took it to a table with a view of the mall crowd walking through the main thoroughfare. Why would anyone rush to get coffee and then sit down in leisure? I approached the same vendor, ordered coffee, and found a more secluded table from which I could observe her.

She seemed to study the crowd, glancing up at faces. Her attention focused on men as if choosing one. Did she pick up men at the mall? Was this her habit? Following that theory back to my own conception made me shudder. Women outnumbered men in the D.C. area. My research had revealed she worked for The Agency in McLean, Virginia, not far from the mall. Her job position precipitated my employment with the same government branch. A professional woman with administrative overseas assignments. She had never married. Was her love life dismal?

She must have cared enough to give birth to me. My heart longed to believe. Had she loved my father? Were they star-crossed lovers, and I the result of their youthful passion? Had her overseas assignments resulted in an exotic affair with a mysterious man of foreign origin? I'd created scenarios, each more outlandish than the previous. Could my father have been an unscrupulous Monte Carlo gigolo? Or had jealous harem girls tracked my mother through Middle-Eastern bazaars forcing her to leave their country and her lover behind? A shake of my head brought me back to reality and common sense. My heart still wished for a fairy tale.

A few minutes passed. I saw her eyes widen. She rose from her chair, dumped her coffee in a waste bin, and followed a man who wore a blue windbreaker jacket and carried a briefcase. I did the same, trailing behind her, slowing my pace to allow two shoppers to intervene. She placed the Macy's bag under her arm and took out a cell phone. I raced to close the distance between us, eager to hear the conversation.

"Target in sight," she said and paused, cocking her head. I assumed the other person spoke.

"I doubt if he'll do it in public." She looked to the right and left as if assessing those around her.

I dropped back, took a baseball cap from my bag, and slipped it on. Silly of me, but then women notice other women's hair. The call took less than a minute. She replaced the cell phone in her purse and entered Nordstrom. I watched her stop at an accessory counter and pick up a scarf. I scooted to a sweater display to hide. From my position, I could see her head rotate to follow the man's progress as he circled the first floor and exited Nordstrom. She followed him, and I followed her.

The man ducked through a metal door labeled "Mall Personnel Only." She stopped by the door as it slammed shut. After waiting a minute, she slowly opened the door, entered what appeared to be concrete-sided corridor, and closed the door by hand without allowing it to slam.

Having seen how to enter without alerting the previous person, I waited for a few moments before following. Her actions mystified me, but I hoped to learn more. Perhaps when she finished her business, I could approach her, invite her for another coffee, and then, finally talk to her. If she wouldn't disclose the secrets of her life, would she reveal the secrets that limited mine?

I entered the corridor and stopped at the clatter of my shoes on the concrete. Fearing she'd hear me, I took them off, dropped them into my pocketbook, and walked on sock-clad feet. Her footfalls were silent. Had she known to wear rubber-soled shoes?

The corridor turned in a right angle about ten yards down. She turned the corner and left my sight. I jogged to the corner and peered around it. She had disappeared. I panicked thinking I'd lost her, but further along the hallway I saw the man in blue. Her quarry. He was talking to another man in a black Mall Security uniform.

The man in blue handed his briefcase to the second man. After receiving the briefcase, the security guy nodded, a queer little smile on his face. The man in blue frowned and then scurried down another corridor leaving my sight.

The security man pressed an elevator button I hadn't noticed on the wall. A click resounded in the corridor, a door opened, and the woman popped out. As she walked toward him, the man's eyes widened into alarmed circles. With the two of them engaged, I raced to the door that she had exited before it closed and slipped inside a supply closet. I held the door open an inch to watch. Would she notice the door hadn't clicked shut? I hoped after the man got on the elevator she'd give up this charade so we could talk.

The man dropped the suitcase and put out his arms as if warding off a blow. I didn't understand. She hadn't touched him.

I saw a flash of light and heard a muffled pop. The gunshot's lack of volume confused me. There was an echo in the corridor, but it was no louder than a door slam. Red bloomed on the man's black uniform. He seemed to jump backward, then toppled, fell to the floor, his head bouncing off the concrete floor twice. He lay still. She grabbed the briefcase with her empty hand.

I shut the door, inhaled, and leaned against the wall for support as if the gunshot had hit me, too. My jellied legs wobbled. I concentrated on quieting my breathing and stabilizing my muscles in the darkness of the closet. Who was this woman?

The door opened with abrupt light. I froze. She stood in front of me holding the gun. The briefcase was upright on the floor aside her. Would she kill me? She hadn't killed me before. Could I count on maternal instinct or shock?

"Hi, Mom," I said.

"I gave birth to you, but I'm not your mother."

"True." My words shook exiting my mouth, but I persevered. "When did you recognize me?"

"In the bathroom. Did you really think I wouldn't know who you were?" She sounded annoyed. "You're good at your job if only you'd stick to hacking other systems, not The Agency's personnel files," she said, as if she could anticipate my every move. "Did you really think we wouldn't know?"

"No one would tell me anything. I have a right to know." My defiant glaze bore into her, but her face reflected mirth.

"Information is on an 'as needed' basis. No one has a right to know. Your employment will be terminated—one way or another."

That stopped me, fear spread in my chest. *Why?* Then, I realized. "You're not administrative staff?"

Her mirth turned into a snarky smile. "In a manner of speaking." She looked around the door to the corridor. "You're interfering just like you did when you were conceived."

My mouth dropped open. Hurt radiated from my chest. I glared into her eyes. How could I have anticipated her indifference? "That's all I am? An interference?"

"Yes. Inconvenient," she said with a sniff of her nose. "My own failure staring me in the face."

Her attitude ticked me off. "Doesn't that beat all," I said. In an instant, I went from naïve baby to rebellious teenager. Indignant. I put my hands on my hips. "Really. Did you even love my father, or were you just a slut? Who was he?"

"An assignment."

There was a far-away look on her face as if she ruminated memories. I dropped my eyes to the gun she held on me. The barrel had an object attached to the end. A silencer? She cocked the trigger of the gun. In that moment, I understood what had happened after they had spent their lust. A chill traveled from the back of my head down my spine. "You killed him." I didn't think it was a question. I laughed. Bravado or hysteria?

Her jaw tightened. "No—he wasn't *just* an assignment," she said, backpedaling from her professional objectivity. An emotion reflected in her eyes.

"You botched the job, didn't you?"

She flinched at my words. "I was a new agent. Got involved with, formed an emotional attachment to—a target." She bit her lips, hesitated, and looked at the floor. "My target was reassigned to another agent." Tears trickled from each eye and rolled down her face. She wiped them away and glared at me. "Abortion wasn't legal then. I could have requested one, but then I wasn't supposed to sleep with the man. I took a leave of absence."

"They covered up the birth and adoption well."

She nodded. "They'd invested in me." She tried to say more, but she faltered before regaining a professional composure cauterized of feeling. "I matured after that mistake." Her look defied me to contradict her, as if I could. What she hadn't said, her faltering and hesitating, told me the truth. It would save my life.

Encouraged, I sprang at her, pushing at her with both of my hands to grasp her shoulders. She didn't fall, but my attack forced her into the corridor. Trusting she wouldn't shoot me, I erupted out of the closet. Panic crossed her face. I felt exposed until the elevator's ding let me know someone else approached. She turned at the sound. I ran, hoping a bullet wouldn't rip through my back. The storage closet door slammed shut behind me.

I took the corner in a slide and continued running to the metal door, put my hip on the bar, and released it. I glanced down the corridor behind me. It was empty. The normalness of the mall's lights, people, and sounds soothed me.

When she'd hesitated and faltered, I'd found the truth in her eyes. What she'd said was only the partial truth. She'd loved my father, lacked the wherewithal to kill him or me. She gave me up for adoption. By the time of my birth, he was dead—another agent's mission—successful. The regret in her eyes enabled my escape. Had she spared my life now out of love, or would killing me have been another spot on her record? My questions no longer pondered fairy tales. I walked through the mall like an old woman wishing for ignorance.

THE HOT BUNS OF FATE

JENNIFER JANK

Kiki flicked her phone on to check the time again, then flipped it over on the table in front of her. Maybe she should just leave after she finished her tea. Maybe that would get the message across to Sarah, finally. She lifted the huge mug emblazoned with "Hot Buns Bakery" and two suggestively placed rolls, just as Sarah yanked open the door of the bakery. The eager teen boy in a baseball cap couldn't leap to her aid in time. Sarah flashed him a smile, bracelets jangling, blond hair swirling out behind her, cell phone in hand, and Italian leather handbag dangling from her arm. She threw out her arms once she spotted Kiki, narrowly missing the barista who managed to save the double half-caf soy macchiato in the nick of time, and raced to the table.

"Thank God!" Sarah exclaimed, collapsing onto a chair and tossing her bag on the table. "Keeks, I am *so* glad you're here."

Kiki smoothed her pale brown hair and smiled into her chai latté. Sarah was always so enthusiastic about everything: her husband, Mike, killing a spider, her own ability to do a headstand in yoga, a pretty leaf swirling onto her car. Sarah pushed her sunglasses back into a headband, and the misery on her face startled Kiki. Even though Sarah's mascara hadn't run and her makeup was, as always, carefully applied, her eyes were puffy like she'd been crying all night.

"Are you all right?"

"No. Would you be, if your husband... Mike, that son of a...that sneaky... God! He's having an affair."

"How? I mean, how could he cheat on you? I mean, you! How is that possible? Wait a second, are you sure? I mean...are you sure?" Kiki asked. Sarah and Mike were so active in the community and both of them worked, so when could he have been sneaking away from Sarah to have an affair?

"I saw all these text messages. To some student."

What an idiot, Kiki thought.

"And I confronted him. He couldn't even lie about it. God. I started yelling and he, he left." She got up abruptly. "I need some caffeine."

Kiki watched her stalk over to the barista. She and Sarah had known each other in college, or more accurately, had known some of the same people at college. They'd never really been friends until a party, several years after graduation, where they'd bonded over the hilariously tacky décor of their hostess. "Really, a silver David?" Sarah had snorted, champagne glass perilously close to spilling on the artisan hand-woven rug from Guatemala.

"Fig leaf and all, *trés chic*," Kiki had agreed, and they'd laughed. Something about Kiki's laugh made Sarah look at her more closely. "Hey, aren't you..." they both started at the same time, and laughed again.

Fate, mused Kiki, staring at Sarah's flashing hands at the bakery counter without seeing them. Destiny, kismet, whatever, had drawn the two of them together. How else could they have stayed such good friends? But fate must have brought Mike and Sarah together too. Well, that was another story altogether. They'd been married at least ten years, maybe fifteen, Kiki thought. *I'm old. We're old.*

Sarah sat back down with her iced tea, and Kiki asked, "How old is she?"

"Early twenties. Of course. Couldn't you guess?" Sarah snorted. She took a deep breath, pasted a grim smile on her face, and said in a singsong voice, "So that's my news. How's things going for you?"

Kiki flinched, and despite her own pain, Sarah gently patted her hand. This time it was Kiki's turn to take a breath. "Passed over for tenure again. Because a married man is more stable than a single woman."

Sarah's eyes widened. "No! They didn't tell you that!"

Kiki waved her hand. "Of course not. But there's no other reason that Warrington Weasel, excuse me Weasel the Third, who's never even been published in *American Journal*—I mean, there's no reason for it, just Mrs. Weasel. Every last professor in the department who made tenure is married."

Sarah downed her tea. "That's awful. You know what? We need something stronger than tea."

Kiki opened her mouth to object, and then realized she didn't want to. She couldn't remember the last time she got drunk—she was far too cautious to jeopardize her career. Ha, what career? "Let's go."

"It'll be just like old times. Remember when you had that place on York?"

"You mean the one that didn't have a sink in the bathroom? The one where I brushed my teeth in the kitchen for four years?"

"Yeah, wasn't that the one where you ended up with that sailor from Fleet Week?"

Kiki laughed. She'd almost forgotten the guy, but he had been hot in his sailor suit with that tight butt, no doubt about it. Sarah had been out of town, so Kiki hadn't even had to consider what would happen when he saw pretty blonde Sarah, with her pretty curves. That had been a very good week.

The two of them left Hot Buns and Sarah waved to the barista. She turned to Kiki as they walked across the street to O'Finnegan's Pub. "I'm at Hot Buns all the time. It's terrible, I know I shouldn't, but they have great tea."

"Well, O'Finnegans has…um…" Kiki started.

"Terrible beer?" They sat at the bar with their pints so they could get refills quickly. Just like the old days.

After several drinks, neither of them was feeling any pain. Kiki looked at Sarah. "Will you take Mike back?"

"Are you kidding? I love him. I mean, I'm so mad I could cut up his entire wardrobe with a rusty nail, but we can work through this. I can't go through dating anymore, Kiki. It's too crazy out there."

"Tell me about it," Kiki mumbled.

"Well, you seem to handle it all right. I do not know how you do it." Sarah waved her glass, nearly sloshing the contents over Kiki, the bar, and the bartender. "Here's to you, dating girl, and your dating ability."

Was she condescending or drunk? Kiki frowned at her nearly empty glass. "Is that why you'd take him back? Just to not be alone?"

"No, I have you for that, silly!" Sarah giggled. "But seriously, I love him. And his…you know. He's good in bed."

Kiki did know, but she wasn't drunk enough to say it. "You wouldn't have married him otherwise."

"Is that why you keep dating? Cause you can't find a guy who's good enough in bed?"

"Sarah!"

"Sorry, just asking." She giggled again. "I don't know why you never got married. But maybe you're supposed to be single. Just Kiki!" She gestured, and a bowl of nuts went flying. "Oh! Midnight already? Gotta go. I gotta go first though." Another giggle.

Kiki blinked in fuzzy alarm. "You're not leaving are you? I mean, you're in no shape to drive. And I'm in no drive to shape either. I mean, I can walk from here though."

Sarah laughed. "Look who's talking. No, I can now afford cabs. Or rather, Mike can afford my cabs." She managed to leave without further accidents, blowing Kiki a kiss at the door.

The next morning Kiki crept in to the kitchen and swallowed some aspirin, waiting for the beast who had taken up residence on her tongue to evacuate. Oh yeah, that's why she didn't drink. She groaned and held her head, wondering what Mike did at times like these—comfort Sarah? Cower in his study? Not even realize it was happening? She had dated him years ago, but not for very long, because he met Sarah, and then it was goodbye Kiki.

She had dated a few guys who were mesmerized by Sarah, though not all of them, to be fair to them. And to Sarah. It wasn't her fault she was drop-dead gorgeous and she, Kiki, was merely attractive. It was hard to be friends with someone like her though. Sarah didn't even try and she had men draping themselves all over her. Sarah and Mike got serious fast, and Kiki comforted herself, thinking that she and Mike wouldn't have lasted long anyway. For one thing, his massive ego—it was a state secret that he was allergic to peanuts. She couldn't figure out why he was so tight-lipped about it. He wouldn't even have told her about it, but she had made PB & fluff sandwiches, and after he threw a temper tantrum, he'd had to admit why he wouldn't eat them.

Oh yes, even back then she could tell that Mike was going to have some issues when he hit middle age, and this ridiculous affair seemed like proof. He'd date this child, this infant, and when he got it out of his system, he'd go back to Sarah. Kiki found it impossible to believe that this girl could be better looking than Sarah. Younger, maybe. Sarah was vain, but not enough to shoot deadly poison into her forehead. Would he bring the child to his Rotary club meetings? Would she host poker nights at her miserable little apartment? Kiki knew what those off-campus apartments were like. She taught girls in their twenties, and they couldn't even figure out how to have a friend over without asking their parents what to do. Mike liked independence, or at least he had when they were younger. She went into her office to grade papers, briefly wondering if his fling had written one of the essays on her desk. She decided, from the poor quality of the papers, that the cheater had to be in her classes.

Later that night her cell phone rang with Sarah, sobbing, on the other end, so upset that Kiki could barely understand what she was saying.

"Mike wants a divorce!" Sarah finally shrieked, and Kiki simply held the phone in her hand, shocked. "He's moved out to be with her. He doesn't want to be with me anymore, he'd rather be with some stupid brat than me." She trailed off into more sobs.

Kiki already had her keys in hand and was putting together an overnight bag. "I'm coming over." Mike was actually leaving Sarah? Had she been so wrong about them? What had she missed? Because the last time she'd seen him with Sarah at a faculty party, he'd been unusually attentive to Sarah, holding her hand, nuzzling her. Had it already started then? What a jerk.

Sarah answered the door, still wearing her outfit from work, a pinstriped suit that still managed to show off her curves. Kiki ordered her to change into something more comfortable and wash her face. Sarah shuffled upstairs and Kiki looked around; the bottle of wine was almost empty, but luckily nothing was broken. Sarah had been known to throw things during breakups.

"She knew he was married," Sarah wailed later on, after ice cream had been eaten. "God! Going after a married man. Well, she'll find out. If a man cheats on his wife, he's going to cheat on the infant too. I don't even know her and I hate her guts. I could kill her, I seriously could."

"No you couldn't," Kiki replied.

"Something should happen to her. Something should happen, and then Mike would come back to me. How could he? What is wrong with him? Just because she's younger than me? Just because she's young, he wants to end our marriage?" She cried again, but more softly, having worn herself out. Kiki walked her up to bed and then went to the guest room. Sarah didn't need to ask—they'd done it before, when either of them had been dumped.

Mainly it had been Kiki, of course, she thought as she sprawled in the king-size guest bed. Idly she wondered what would happen to the house. Sarah would probably get it, since Mike was the one cheating. It was a big house; both Sarah and Mike made a lot of money and didn't have any children to spend it on. Kiki couldn't afford a house like that on just her salary.

Sarah's face was puffy the next morning, but she seemed to have cried herself out. "I just wish there was something I could do, you know? I mean, other than wipe him out in the divorce. It's just so unfair."

"Yeah, too bad you can't just take him out," Kiki said, dumping syrup on her pancakes.

Sarah snorted. "I don't know, like, cut out the crotch of all his pants. Burn his suits, shear his ties. You know, that kind of thing. I need to talk to a lawyer."

"A mean, nasty one that chews up jerks for breakfast and spits out nails for lunch."

"Speaking of which, hopefully Mel is available," Sarah said dryly. They'd both known Mel in college and she had been a barracuda then. Rumor had it she only got more toothy with age.

Driving home, Kiki couldn't imagine what Sarah was going through. A devastating breakup with a boyfriend was one thing, but a public divorce was something else. How humiliating for Sarah, she thought, not without a small tinge of satisfaction. Now she might understand what it was like to be a lesser mortal. And frankly, better Sarah than her, dealing with him. Even when Mike was cheating on Sarah with her, last year, he'd never suggested that he would divorce Sarah for her. He seemed to think their affair was a fun way to reclaim his youth.

Kiki hadn't dared—had she?—to think that maybe, just maybe, Mike would realize his mistake. His life with Sarah, all a mistake. She was better for him than Sarah was, more attentive. Sometimes she fantasized about telling Sarah, about confronting her about the affair, just to get even with her for all those times when they were younger and the guy left her for Sarah. It would have been even more satisfying with Mike, to really rub Sarah's nose in it, though Sarah had never done that to her. Kiki knew she wasn't particularly noble, but in the end she hadn't been able to tell Sarah. They were friends, for one thing. And then the affair ended. She had too much pride to make it difficult for Mike. If he thought it had been just an amusing way to pass the time, well, he could think that and she was the only one who needed to know it wasn't the truth, wasn't even close.

And then! This. He'd given up her, he'd given up his wife, for what? A much younger woman, what a cliché. Pathetic, really. Kiki hoped the girl would figure it out soon, like maybe as soon as Sarah's lawyer had chewed him up and left him hanging in a terrible, cricket-infested apartment. Maybe the woman would realize what kind of man-boy he was and dump him flat on his aging behind. Kiki found herself rooting for the woman, hoping she'd do some damage to Mike.

But what if she didn't? What if she just kept hanging on, taking the strings-attached dinners and little presents as her due? What if she let Mike keep thinking with the little head?

Kiki couldn't let him get away with it. Dump her, but then move in with some other woman who wasn't Sarah? No, he had to be punished. He wasn't the first married man to cause her trouble, and he wouldn't be the last, but she didn't have to sit around and take it. The lawyer could punish him monetarily, but that was all. Sarah could talk about giving him wedgies, or whatever she'd been yapping about at breakfast, but Kiki felt that the situation needed a stronger touch.

She rummaged through her kitchen cabinets, and sure enough, there were the peanuts. She took out her mortar and pestle—she had a food processor, but it felt more real, more effective, to be mashing the nuts up by hand. She imagined Mike's face in the bowl as she repeatedly stabbed with the pestle, grinding and grinding, until the peanuts were a fine powder.

She remembered that he loved lemon meringue pie with the graham cracker crust, and she had a serious talent for desserts. She didn't need too many peanuts, but it wouldn't take many in any case. Good thing she was a saver—she went through her closet until she found a bag from Hot Buns. When the pie was done, she thought she might just have made the best pie ever. She licked the beaters just as she'd done as a child. Poetic justice, really, she mused. She put on her dishwashing gloves to handle the pie case, and then the bag, which she stowed in the refrigerator.

The Internet just made life so much easier, didn't it? Mike's teaching schedule hadn't changed. He wouldn't be there early, and neither would anyone else. Just to be on the safe side, she searched for the blond wig from Halloween when she'd gone as Barbie. Kiki was surprised at her lack of hesitation. It wasn't like she'd ever done anything like this before. Well, not exactly like this, anyway. College was a difficult time. But now she handled her responsibilities like an adult, and if she was the only grownup in this situation, well, that was the way it was.

Kiki sauntered up the steps of the college, blond wig anchored by her hat, holding the bag with her gloved hands. As if to tell her that she was doing the right thing, the universe was cooperating with chilly weather, making it easier to hide herself, easier to avoid students who would rather skip class than venture out into the cold. She'd typed a letter that morning, as if the pie was from a starry-eyed student. She encountered no one in the building as she delicately placed the bag just outside his door and exited by the back door. Just in case.

She picked up a cupcake at Hot Buns on her way home. A righteous duty, quickly done—red velvet was so tasty a reward.

"He's dead!" Sarah sobbed into her ear, later that evening.

Jeez, what a pig. He must have gobbled the thing down when he arrived for his ten o'clock class. Served him right. Aloud, she replied, "Sarah! What happened?"

"I don't know," she wailed. "He didn't show for his class and one of the students found him dead on his desk! It's awful! I mean, I thought him cheating was the worst...but now he can't ever come back to me." She dissolved into sobs, and Kiki comforted her before Sarah's call waiting beeped. Kiki slept very well that night.

She agreed that, of course, she would accompany Sarah to the morgue, a few days later. She felt like wearing her forest green dress, which she knew showed off her eyes, but reluctantly went with black. No need to share her feelings with the rest of the world. Sarah looked stunning in black, of course.

After they sat for a few minutes in a bleak waiting room, Kiki noticed a uniformed officer approaching. He was very well built, and she enjoyed his approach before realizing he might have other things on his mind. Sarah, who had cried on and off, didn't notice him at first, then grabbed Kiki's arm.

"Mrs. Latalle?"

"Yes?"

"We've had to hold your husband's body here a few days pending the tox results."

Sarah looked blank. "Tox results?"

"Yes, in the event of sudden death for someone your husband's age, standard procedure is to request toxicology results. It appears your husband died of anaphylactic shock brought on by peanuts."

"Why was he eating peanuts?" Sarah exclaimed. "He knew he was allergic to them! Why did he do that?"

"I suspect he was unaware that he ate the peanuts, ma'am. They were apparently in a pie, a pie in a bag from the Hot Buns Café. Where you were seen the night before he died."

Uncomprehending, Sarah stared. Kiki squeezed her hand and did not smile.

"Mrs. Latalle, I am placing you under arrest for the murder of your husband." He began to read her rights as he cuffed her. Sarah was too stunned to do more than ask Kiki to talk to Mel. Kiki promised she would. Then she turned and walked out of the morgue, feeling the benediction of the sun, a happy message from fate.

THE DISAPPOINTMENT OF HEAVEN

DAVID K. AYCOCK

You know you're not looking too good when even the scruffiest wino at the soup kitchen is giving you the eye. But I had a really good excuse!

"Holy frijoles, girl! What happened to you?" A large, incongruously dark man in a Santa suit paused mid-ladle.

I was killed in a car crash when some methhead crossed the centerline and hit me head-on?

"Merry Christmas?" I hazarded.

"Right," he drew out his response. "Merry Christmas." He looked dubious, but shrugged and forged ahead. "So how can we help you, sister?"

How, indeed? I thought back to all the Christmases I'd dropped coins or stuffed a couple of bills into red kettles in front of Walmart or the grocery store. I'd never imagined ever being on the other side, but here I was, feeling a wave of gratitude welling up inside me and beginning to leak out of my eyes.

"I take her, Oscar," a voice suddenly beside me spoke as an arm draped cautiously across my shoulders. A cool hand gently took my chin and turned my head to the left. Dark, concerned eyes in a round, nut-brown face sought mine.

"You hurt, *chica*? Need a doctor?"

"No," I sniffled. "I'm okay. Just a little grungy, I guess. Thanks."

"We got a chower in back. You wanna use it? Maybe I can find you some other clothes, *si*?"

"*Si, gracias,*" I nodded.

"*Por nada, chica.* You come." The woman guided me to a hallway beside the kitchen and on to a bathroom halfway down on the right. "Here is towel, an' soap, an' champoo," she said. "You get cleaned up. I go find you some jeans an' a chirt, okay? But maybe I not find no underwears? I see what is there."

She disappeared, pulling the door shut behind her. The bathroom was small, surprisingly clean, the shower a freestanding metal box with a plastic curtain. Standing under the heavy, hot spray it seemed indistinguishable from a shower in a high-dollar hotel. Heavenly. No, better than heavenly. This was purifying comfort I could revel in on simple, human terms. Heaven had nothing that could even match it.

His name was Kenny Orlang, a known drug trafficker and sex offender. I met him right after the accident. In fact, he was waiting for me when I got to heaven. Apparently he was killed instantly. I didn't die until I was scraped out of the wreckage. Air bags. Just like that, thirty-one years came to an abrupt end. Two loving parents lost their only child, two beautiful daughters lost their mommy, and my husband, the heart of my heart, lost his sweetheart and wife of more than ten years.

"Dude," Orlang said. "Like, I'm so sorry! Hey, like please forgive me, okay?"

What could I say? There we all were—in some mystical, disembodied sense—me, my killer, and right behind him your basic heavenly host. God rested one metaphorical hand on Orlang's left shoulder, the grace of forgiveness fulminating in the aura of the divine.

"I don't think so, you bastard."

Everyone burst out laughing. It must have been the mother of all punch lines. He laughed so hard, Jesus wept.

I seemed to be the only person who didn't get the joke.

The laughter subsided into chuckling and headshaking as the throng began to disperse. Soon I was left standing alone, everyone else having wandered away, quite amused by the wacky Mrs. Knox. This was not what I had expected.

I used to joke that God was going to have some explaining to do when I got to heaven. What a disappointment. God's answers didn't seem to match any of my questions. I came away unsatisfied from every encounter I had with Him. I don't know if it was because I was dense, or because He was.

And the constantly changing, sycophantic entourage that flocked around him, basking in what I perceived as a vacuous omniscience, made me nuts. If this was heaven, I wanted none of it. There was no way I was going to endure this torment of eternal bliss. So I left.

I don't think anyone even noticed.

When I came back, I was suddenly and uncomfortably aware of several things. My remains, such as they were, must have benefited from the skills of a mortician who did taxidermy on the side. I could feel the welts of puckered tissue along the seam lines that tracked across my arms and torso. So, it was definitely a corpse I had come back to, quite dead, stitched together, and made-up to look like a wax fruit version of me. But I felt a heartbeat. Pumping what? Don't they drain your blood when they embalm you? A wave of nausea washed over me and passed. There was a permeating coldness and a sense of confinement, and it felt like my mouth and eyes were glued shut. The darkness was like the deep and absolute absence of light in a cave. Or a grave. I realized where I was, and freaked.

Stark terror elicits a pretty primal response; a mind-numbing paralysis one-hundred-eighty degrees and seven seconds away from frantic flailing and trying to scream, manic sobbing, a gradual subsidence into whimpering helplessness, then an abyss of despair as dark as, well, the inside of a casket.

Was it hours, days, or only minutes? I couldn't say, but at some point I realized I had become very still, barely breathing, an effort forced through clogged-feeling nostrils.

Breathing what? my awareness asked. That got my attention.

At that time, I had no idea how long I'd been dead. They don't do "time" in heaven, another disconcerting and annoying detail that exasperated me. So how long does it take to exhaust the oxygen supply in a closed coffin? I did a little math and figured I'd been out of air for a long time. So what was I breathing?

Calmer now, I began to explore the darkness, feeling around. I gingerly touched my face, eyes, nose, and mouth. My eyes and mouth really were glued shut! I guess you can't have eyes popping open and jaws sagging agape in the middle of the eulogy. After some painful tugging and stretching, I managed to tear them open. I could feel some kind of fluid running down the sides of my face, blood I hoped, but had no idea how that could be. There was an awful chemical taste in my mouth. I kept turning my head to either side, spitting something out, gagging.

My nose still felt clogged, though. Well, being inside a coffin is a little like being inside a car at night. No one can really see you performing a little nasal excavation. I dug around and came out with what felt like more than a yard of cotton batting. Gross. I crammed it into a corner, breathing easier.

The laughter startled me, an uncanny, unnerving cackle in the pitch black of the coffin. It seemed the sound of incipient madness. It was mine. I was laughing at a joke in which I was the punch line.

It had just occurred to me that I was thinking about how I was going to get out of that box, a box that was probably locked, probably sealed in a concrete burial vault, and probably buried under a ton of dirt. It was hilarious to think I was going anyplace. Oh, clever me, escaping heaven only to trap myself in my own grave. Would I simply lie there until I died? Again? Apparently not since I had long since used up the air supply and was still breathing.

Oh, what a funny joke, God. Ha, ha. You got me! I guess you win big fella. I'll go along quietly now, be a good little girl. You can let me out now.

Yes, now would be good, fine with me! Good joke! Look, I'm laughing! I get it now!

Hello! Anybody listening? Anyone there?

Hello?

Hello!

In a flash I went from a state of manic hilarity to being completely pissed. If I had been nearing madness, now I was just plain mad, thrashing out with a fury I had never known before. I was shocked into sudden stillness when I realized I had bashed out the right side of the coffin and had slammed the lid against the top of the concrete vault.

I flashed on *Buffy* and *Friday the 13th* re-runs—visions of undead ghouls exploding out of splintering caskets or erupting mud-caked from rain-sodden, unholy ground. Is that what I had become, a monster from beyond the grave, a zombie, a fiend? A surreptitious tongue checked for fangs but encountered nothing a toothbrush couldn't handle. Maybe I could just stay there in the dark and never have to find out. I could do that, couldn't I? I felt myself getting weepy again.

After sobbing into the darkness for a while, a familiar stubbornness began to reassert itself. I didn't ask for this. I didn't ask to be killed by some dope freak. I didn't ask for an afterlife bereft of reason. I wanted my life back. I didn't come back just to spend eternity in a coffin. Damn it, I wasn't going to take this lying down. Well, not for long anyway.

I scrunched myself sideways bracing my back against the unbroken side of the casket and used my feet to finish kicking out the busted side. Then I turned around and kicked out the opposite side using the exposed sidewall of the concrete vault to brace against. I was on a roll now and worked methodically until I had collapsed the coffin around myself and managed to crawl on top of the lid. Now there was nothing between me and freedom but three inches of concrete and six feet of soil. Scratch that. The burial vault took up a good two feet of the depth of the grave, so I only had four feet to go. I felt myself grinning crazily.

Figuring what worked for one box might work just as well for another, I braced my back against the left side of the vault, planted my feet against the other, and pushed. And pushed. And pushed some more, straining the muscles in my legs until I could literally feel them burn, thrumming with strength. Some part of my mind was prattling on about giving it a rest and trying again later, but the rest of me wasn't listening. This had become an elemental, tectonic duel and I knew I was unbreakable.

The crack and grind of shifting stonework came from the wall behind me as I felt it begin to bow outward. A silt of crumbling concrete mixed with dirt began to patter the top of my head. Then the other wall abruptly gave way beneath my feet, compacting six or more inches into the side of the excavation. More dirt tumbled into the cavity beneath the concrete lid of the vault.

I relaxed my assault for a moment as I repositioned myself a couple of feet down the sidewalls, re-braced and started pushing again. This time the sides moved more easily, too easily in fact. Before I knew it I had shifted the concrete walls so far out there was nothing but the shorter end walls holding up the lid. I heard a crack in the slab above me and realized half-a-second before it did so that the roof was about to come down. I rolled to my right as the slab sagged under the weight of the dirt covering it and found myself curled into a ball under the concrete tent formed by the broken lid and the inwardly canted end wall. A slurry of loose soil rattled for a bit, then there was only the pant of my own breathing.

Still grinning in the blackness, I squirmed around and located the cool talus, following its slope to the point of entry, pawing the loosed soil back and between my legs like a cartoon dog. Soon I was squeezing through the gap between the slabs and into the newly formed cavity above. Then I was scrabbling and burrowing like some massive mole giddily pleased with itself, auguring my way a handful of dirt at a time toward the surface.

It was a cold shock when my hands finally crashed through the last six or seven inches of dirt and grasped fistfuls of something crunchy and icy wet. Snow? I dragged some to my mouth and tasted the muddied froth, my eyes squinting against a frigid finger of wind probing the sudden tunnel. Gradually a dim filter of lesser darkness defined the hole above me, and I realized it must be night. Another few minutes of heaving, pushing and digging and I had head and shoulders poking out into a whirling maelstrom of cold, wet flakes that quickly plastered the left side of my face. Twisting around I could see the bulking shapes of tombstones looming in the half-light cast by the muted glow of streetlights. I heard the rasp of the scuttling snow and, further away and behind it, the sound of vehicles trundling through a drifted roadway.

I hauled myself up by elbows and forearms, slithering out of my hole and flopping onto the snow, sinking a good eight inches into the drift that had formed against the headstone. I lay there, suddenly stunned by what I had done, a tingling of apprehension flitting through my mind. Now what?

I had no idea of what to do next, or the consequences of what I had done would be. Chagrined at my belated consideration of the question it sank in that dead people don't usually come back. It wasn't the natural order of things.

I had quit heaven in a fit of pique, more bent on leaving than on going anyplace in particular. That my "spirit" had simply returned to its old home made sense. I mean, where else would it go?

The question lingered in my awareness, generating an uncomfortable chain of doubt. I sat up in the snow and turned to regard the snow-covered gravestone beside me.

My husband, Kevin, and I had never intended to be buried. We had agreed that when the time came, whatever we hadn't willed to science would be cremated.

The accumulated snow clumped off easily enough as I brushed my hands across the stone and soon I had cleared enough away to let me peer into the shadows and make out the inscription there.

MOLLY SPRINGER
MAR. 12, 1994 - DEC. 13, 2014
Soldier, daughter, sister, friend

I was still sitting there, staring unseeing at the once again snow drifted gravestone, when it dawned on me it was no longer cast in shadow. A soft, blue-tinged light had infused the air, steadily gaining in intensity. The sound of silenced wind emphasized the stillness.

Blinking in mild surprise, I shifted my gaze above and beyond the mound in front of me to see other snowy humps scattered or lined up all around. The hum and rattle of traffic sounds and the hint of movement outside a distant, white-flocked hedge brought me back to the moment.

I leaned forward, reaching to wipe away the fresh accumulation from the face of the stone, but paused, seeing for the first time the hands at the ends of outstretched arms, hands and arms I didn't recognize. And yet, they responded to my intentions.

That same strange name was still there when the snow had been brushed aside. The marker was unmistakably associated with the grave from which I had just emerged.

"Oh, this is too weird," I whispered. I wasn't me.

I looked down at a smallish body, barefoot, dressed in what must once have been a rather plain white dress. Now it looked like muddied rags. I touched my hair, a ratted and grungy-feeling, bobbed cut cupping my cheeks, my face puffy and raw. I must have looked like death warmed over.

Well, duh, I thought.

Standing up, I saw a gate in the hedge wall and started toward it, but something kept niggling at me, something that wasn't quite right. Besides me, I mean. Then it hit me. It was the trees, snow-draped palm trees lining the driveways between the plots. Snow and palm trees didn't go together. I began to suspect I wasn't in Colorado Springs. When I got to the gate and peeked out, I knew it for sure. The sun was rising over open surf behind a cloud-barred sky. On the other side of the boulevard that ran in front of the cemetery, kids were rollicking in a snowy strand of park that rolled down to the water.

I was just about to hoist myself up and over the gate when I heard a vehicle approaching from the right. I noted the familiar clank and rattle of snow chains. A moment later a patrol car drove into view, and I pulled back a little, trying to conceal myself better. It was an instinctive reaction, but as soon as I did it, I knew it made sense. I wasn't in any position to provide a reasonable explanation for my presence there, or my appearance. As it was, the driver never even glanced my direction, his attention being drawn by the kids playing in the snow across the street. But his passing did allow me to snag another clue as to where I was. Slightly obscured by road grime and icy spray, but still readable, I could make out the words "Corpus Christi, Texas."

Once he had passed, I scrambled over the gate. I could see what looked like a business center farther along the curve of the shoreline, and I headed that direction, thinking I'd look for a Salvation Army outfit there, maybe get a change of clothes and something to eat. Then I would begin to think about what to do next.

The woman must have returned without my hearing her. A worn but fresh pair of jeans and a plaid flannel shirt, along with a pair of boy's boxers had been left on the edge of the lavatory. The pants and shirt were a little on the large size, but felt wonderfully cozy, and the boxers unfamiliar but not uncomfortable. She had also brought a pair of fuzzy gray socks and low-sided, black and white Keds that fit pretty well.

Sporting my new look I made my way back to the dining hall, following some totally tantalizing aromas. I was suddenly ravenous.

The hall was still doing a pretty brisk business, most of the tables filled with dedicated feasters. The woman caught sight of me and waved me over to an empty spot.

"Hey, you feel *mas* better, no?" she smiled.

"*Tambien que una chica,*" I smiled back. "*Muchas gracias.*"

"*Siete se.* Eat."

The dozen or so others seated at the long table nodded and smiled their welcomes, passing bowls and platters my way. The expressions on their faces had changed from the looks of mild distaste I had seen when I first came in. Now there were appreciative gleams in many of their eyes.

"You clean up pretty good," one grizzled character informed me, wiggling his eyebrows.

What could I do but give him a big smile and wiggle my eyebrows back?

The man sitting on my left, a younger, strong looking man with thick dark hair and a matching mustache introduced himself.

"Name's Yancy, Ben Yancy. And what might your name be? Me and the boys here are mighty pleased to have you sprucin' up our table today. We consider it a rare opportunity."

"Knox," I began, and then realized I really didn't know how to answer that question. My return had been a lot like lightning going to ground and taking the path of least resistance. Was I still Laura Knox, or was I now Molly Springer? According to the headstone back in the cemetery, Molly would have been dead for a little less than a month. It was plain, blind luck that popped me into the corpse of a recently deceased young girl. I imagined her sudden return from the grave would cause joy for some, fear for others, and consternation for everyone. And once they noticed that the person inside didn't match the packaging, there was no telling what the fallout would be. As for Laura Knox, she would have been killed some twelve years ago and a thousand miles from Corpus Christi, but the same problems would confront her.

"Opportunity," I finished, echoing Ben's comment. "Opportunity Knox."

"Opportunity Knox," Ben grinned at me. "Well hello and welcome!"

BESS HARDING, MYSTERY QUEEN

KAREN MOCKER DABSON

Bess gazed out the kitchen window, admiring the way the fresh breeze fluttered her new curtains. Their yellow checks waved on either side of the bow window and framed a lush view of the backyard, still green in early September. She ignored the gaggle of breakfast dishes and cereal boxes before her and took in the scene. Asters and mums bobbed in the wind and bordered the play set and patio with their colorful dance. The smell of sun-warmed pavers floated through the window and flavored her last sip of coffee.

As she placed the cup in its stained saucer, the telephone jangled. Her hand jerked, and the remaining drops slopped onto the Formica tabletop. *Oh dear*, she thought. *Don't let one of the kids be sick or hurt. Not this early in the school year.* Bess reached for the wall phone, but before she could say hello, Posey bawled down the line.

"Bess, is that you? Have you heard what's happened?" Posey panted with anticipation.

Bess rolled her eyes, knowing a revelation from the excitable Posey could be as significant as a broken fingernail. "Hello, Posey, I'm fine. How are you?" Bess smiled into the phone.

"So, you haven't heard then."

"Heard what?"

"Brainard's gone missing!" Posey shouted down the line.

Bess shot up in her chair. The skirt of the chenille bathrobe slid from her knees, and her hand clenched the phone. "What? How do you know?"

"Carol just called and said he hasn't been at school for three days. They can't find a trace of him at home or anywhere." Carol, the school secretary and Posey's best friend, was no doubt licking her lips as she spewed her suspicions about Brainard into Posey's ear. Hal Brainard, young, good-looking, and friendly, ran the school library. Voted most valuable staff member of 1965, everyone liked him except Carol. He'd dumped her after two dates last year.

Clearly, Posey wanted to wallow in the gory details of supposition, but Bess cut her off. "Er, thanks for letting me know, Pose," she said and slowly hung up the phone. The loss of Hal, if it was one, felt personal. He'd been terrific with her seven-year-old Todd after the kids' dad had vanished eighteen months ago, and she worried about how her son might take this latest news.

She had been about to get her day started, but now Bess slumped back into her chair and stared at the blank wall opposite the table. Her chest ached, and she realized her brain buzzed with white noise, displacing any ideas she might have had. Instead, questions zipped through her mind. *What could have happened? Wouldn't he let someone know where he was going? Did he leave a trail?*

"Oh!" Bess pounded her temples. "Why can't I be a Miss Marple or think like Poirot? Where would Sherlock Holmes start or Inspector Alleyn?" She addressed these remarks to the window seat where she had devoted many happy hours imbibing her favorite sleuths' tales while roasting a chicken or baking a cake. "One thing's certain, they're always dressed by the time they investigate."

Pulling herself together, Bess hurried into the bedroom and donned a black sheath dress. She tied a red silk scarf around her head to hold back the mass of blonde curls that usually fell into her eyes and planned her next move as she slipped on her black pumps. "Must look the part," she murmured as she grabbed the leather bag that held her notepad.

She glanced at her watch. A good half-hour remained before the school principal left for lunch, but as she clasped the knob to exit the house, the doorbell rang. The vibrations sent an alarm up Bess's arm, and she jumped back. She peered through the sidelight by the door, but the glass block only revealed a wavy male figure in dark navy attire. She opened the door a crack.

"Elizabeth Harding?" A gold badge flashed.

Bess shook her head, confused. "Um, yes, yes, that's me."

"City police, ma'am, you'll need to come with us." The police officer eyed Bess from head-to-toe as she opened the door wider. He shot a glance at his partner. "Were you planning on going somewhere?"

Bess hesitated only a moment, then said, "Are you arresting me or something?" Out of the corner of her eye, she could see Mrs.

McGilliken standing on her front porch. "Because, yes, I was going somewhere."

"No," the officer said, "but we have some routine questions we'd like to ask you down at the station."

Bess looked at her wrist again. "How long will that take?"

"That's nothing you need to worry about right now. Come along."

Bess's eyes swept the neighborhood. More neighbors had congregated on the street. *Curiosity seekers*, she thought, *and not one offering to help me*. She shrugged. "All right, but let's make it quick. What's it about, anyway?"

"We've received information that you were the last person to see Hallerton Brainard alive."

Bess rode in stunned silence to the station.

Three hours later, the cops had allowed Bess to phone her mother. "Honey, you sound tired."

"It's been a confusing afternoon, Mom," she said. "They keep bombarding me with questions, the same ones, but with a slightly different tack each time. They're seeking Hal's whereabouts, and have gotten a lot of false leads apparently."

"Well, haven't they found any clues at all?" her mother said.

"Right now, they're thinking he either met with foul play or committed suicide," Bess said, "but frankly, they don't seem to have any evidence. I told them I couldn't think of any reason why Hal would take his own life. He seems to be a happy, content—I mean, really well balanced—sort of guy. And I'd be astonished if he had any enemies." Bess sighed. "But look, Mom, what I called about is to ask you to go to my house and look after the kids when they get home from school. I don't think I'm going to be home any time soon."

About four that afternoon, two plainclothes policemen took the place of the two uniforms that had detained Bess. They began a different line of questioning.

"So, Mrs. Harding," the burly one said, "can you tell us why a housewife with two school-age kids would be dressed to the nines at 11:00 a.m. on a weekday?" Before Bess could answer, he spoke again. "Would you say that was," he paused, "usual?"

Bess set aside the urge to roll her eyes. "I had some business to attend to," she said, "and I always dress for business."

"I see. And this business, it wouldn't happen to be out of town, would it?"

So that was it. They thought I was going to skip. She stifled a laugh. *This is like being trapped inside a bad soap opera.*

"Look, guys, you're right. I am a homemaker, and I am a mom. But I'm also a writer, a free-lance journalist." She eyed them directly. "That makes me a pretty fair researcher, and today, I was simply going out to conduct some research. If you looked in my purse," and she was sure they had, "you would have found my notebook. You can see that's where I record all of my data and interviews."

The man who used too much Brylcreem on his hair slapped a small datebook on the table. "Never mind that," he growled. "We did see your notepad, but we're much more interested in this." He flipped to a page in the calendar. "Beginning about six months ago, it looks like you did go to a lot of meetings—with a certain H.B. Care to tell us about those? What were you writing about then, huh?"

"That wasn't work," Bess blurted before she could stop herself. "Those dates have nothing to do with what you're investigating today."

"*Au contraire.*" Brylcreem spat out the French words with a coating of sarcasm. "They have everything to do with it. It seems that nobody spent more time with Hallerton Brainard than you this past half year. You can't explain that away, lady."

A dull crimson crept upward from Bess's jawline until it burned her eyes. Damn them. She had hoped to keep her personal life away from their prying questions. Hadn't her poor children suffered enough? Air huffed out of her nose.

"I can, actually," she said.

"Can what?"

"I can explain what those entries mean, even though I think they're entirely none of your business."

The two men waited and watched, their eyes prepared to disbelieve her words.

"More than a year and a half ago, my husband deserted us, leaving no note, no money, no nothing." The men exchanged looks. "My younger son, Todd, was brokenhearted. Eventually, that played out in bad behavior at school." Bess bit her lower lip in remembrance. "Mr. Brainard always liked my son, and one day, he offered to help. We took him up on it, and it was incredibly good for Todd." She pointed to the little book. "Those dates you see, those are the regular times that Mr. Brainard came over to pick up Todd. He'd take him fishing or bowling. Sometimes they just watched TV together and talked." She studied her hands for a moment. "That's all I have to say, except, you see, we had every reason to want Mr. Brainard around."

A patrol car dropped Bess back at her home about nine o'clock that evening. She gave her mother a hug, and then went to check on the boys. Paul slept soundly on the upper bunk, but when she leaned down to kiss Todd on the cheek, he reached his arms around her neck and whispered, "I'm glad your home, Mummy."

She nuzzled his cheek and said, "Me, too. Night-night, baby. Sweet dreams."

A steaming cup of cocoa sat on the kitchen table waiting for her. Bess's mother asked, "Would you like anything else, honey?"

"No, thanks, Mom, this is great."

Her mother settled in the chair opposite her. Bess filled her in on the police station experience. "God, I hated telling them about Hal's help with Todd, but worse, I realized that—well, I could just hear them thinking, 'strange that her husband disappeared on her and now this other guy.' Oh, Mom, they made me so mad."

Bess pulled at her curls. "I could tell they didn't believe a word I said." She snorted. "I think there's a real possibility they'll even try to pin this on me. Save themselves from any further investigation."

Her mother reached out for her hand. "What are you going to do?"

"I don't know." Bess squeezed her mother's fingers. "I'm working on it."

Thunder clouted above the street, and the morning rain drilled the metal roof of her Plymouth sedan. With windshield wipers flashing at full tilt, she could dimly make out the entryway to Hal's duplex, and she parked in front of it. *At least this miserable weather is keeping everyone off the streets*, she thought.

Bess eased quietly through the door of 313 Putnam Place. Awhile ago, Hal had given Todd a key as a gesture of trust even though it was unlikely the boy would ever visit on his own. Now she relocked the door behind her, drew the curtains, and switched on the lights.

If only this were a suspense story on television, she wished, *then Hal would've been sitting in his armchair when I turned on the light, and all would be revealed.* But the only thing that greeted her was his tidy, well-ordered living room, minus a spattering of notes and papers on his desk that the police had no doubt mussed.

Hal had organized half of the room as a library, and Bess initially searched the shelves for any signs he might have left. Her hands, gloved in soft, gray cotton, brushed over the volumes. With some precision, the books stood in lines, each the same distance from the edges. Her lips tightened as she searched the upper shelves—more neatly aligned books and no clues—yet something pricked at the back of her mind. Her eyes slid to the bottom shelf where Hal's Encyclopedia Britannica resided. The grouping rewarded her gaze. One volume, near the middle of the series, wrecked the symmetry by sticking out a half inch from the others. She stooped to pull out the miscreant. It was the volume titled *Q*. A quick leaf through its pages did not reveal much, so she replaced the book in line with the others.

Bess investigated the rest of the apartment rapidly. She slipped her hands down the crevices of upholstered furniture, flipped through record albums, and patted down the contents of drawers. The kitchen equaled the other rooms in neatness. Numerous cupboards and drawers depicted the methodical mind of their owner. Only a round carton of Quaker Oats, forgotten, held a lonely vigil on the counter.

There remained one last place to look—the cluttered desktop. The sole indicator of something amiss, Hal would never leave the desk in such a state. With her gloved fingertips, Bess picked up one paper and then another, but they only represented the ordinary correspondence of daily life—an electric bill, a coupon for laundry detergent, an advertisement for tires, a postcard, a donation request.

Beneath the sheaf of papers lay a blotter with tear-off sheets. It bore the imprint of Hal's heavy hand as he wrote out bills or answered a letter. Bess tilted the blotter under the lamp for a closer examination. A faint circle carved its way over the smaller scribbles on the pad. She could swear it was a large *Q*.

Bess sank back into the driver's seat of her car. She'd stuffed the top blotter sheet into her handbag and re-scattered the other papers over the desktop. Now she contemplated the meaning of the letter *Q*. No doubt it was a message from Hal—one the police would not get—but what did it mean?

The downpour cloaked the car like a thick cape. Bess started the engine anyway. She would feel safer considering her options in neutral territory. A block down the road, she noticed a set of headlights in her rearview mirror. She pulled into the parking lot of a drugstore, and the vehicle drove by. Bess wiped her forehead. Easing the Plymouth to the rear of the building, she glided to a stop between two delivery vans.

Immediately, her mind crowded with ideas. *The Q is for Queenie, something the cops would never guess.* Hal teased her often about her passion for mysteries, calling her the Mystery Queen. This had devolved to Queenie, and then to Q, especially as they became more acquainted. Her skin trembled a little as she remembered the way he used to draw *Q*'s on her arms, on her back, and on—well, other places.

She re-focused. *The Q's were on the encyclopedia, the oats box, and the desk blotter. Did they stand for knowledge, hunger, communication? Were they connected, or was it just the letter Q Hal was trying to get across, putting it in three places to make sure I saw at least one of them?*

Bess took her notepad from her purse and drew three *Q*'s on the first sheet, labeling them and dotting lines from one to the next. She considered the paper. Surely, Hal intended to send her some kind of message. She made lists under each label: Encyclopedia—knowledge, information, to know, some *Q* subject, out of line; Quaker Oats—oats, cereal, cylinder, breakfast, nutrition, religion; Blotter—message, letter, trace, impression, writing, hidden, invisible.

The lists frowned at her from the page. If anything, they served to confuse her further. Her brain felt like mush. Bess licked her lips. "All right. I'll put you away for the moment," she said to the paper, "and take another look when I get home."

She was walking in the front door when memory smote her like a mallet. "Oh my God," Bess said, "could he possibly mean Sherm?" Suddenly, the *Q* hints seemed to point directly to her ex-husband. *Someone I know. Someone with a Quaker background. Someone who became invisible long ago. Someone Hal would want to warn me about.*

Bess covered her mouth with her left hand and peeked out to the street through a slit in the living room drapes. A car idled at the curb across the way as the rain streaked its black finish. *Could Sherman Botts and his bad temper have resurfaced?*

A chill streaked across the back of her neck. Did she dare call the police, or would they scoff at her fears? The telephone rang, stopping her heart. She picked up the receiver, but said nothing.

"Bess. Honey, is that you? It's Mom."

"Oh, thank heavens, Mom!"

"What's wrong?"

"Mom, could you come here right away," Bess said, "and bring a few of your friends? I think somebody's watching the house. There's a strange car parked out front."

"I'm on my way. Lock the doors, Bess, and close all the curtains. Bye!"

80

Bess curled on the sofa hugging her knees. How had life blown so far off course in twenty-four hours? She tried to focus but the lack of clues baffled her, and fear acted as a mighty distraction.

When at last her mother arrived with two friends in tow, Bess had resolved to take action. "Mom, I'm going to check out the car across the street, and I want you to watch. If anything happens, call the police, no matter what."

"Oh, Bess, you can't, honey. It's too risky."

She knew her mom would protest, but Bess was determined. "I need to shortcut this mystery somehow, Mom, and this seems like a first step. I feel stronger now that you're all here." She pasted a smile on her lips.

Bess went out the back and circled the block to approach the black auto from the other side of the road. Under cover of the rain, she arrived at the driver's door unnoticed. Bess yanked at the handle. The car door swung wide, but no one was inside. Hastily, she turned off the ignition and pocketed the key. Backing away, she looked all around, but could not see anyone on the street. A slight thump put her on the alert. The sound had come from the trunk, and now she slowly unlocked it and raised the lid, her eyelids half shut. Sherman Botts looked up at her through bleary eyes. He was trussed like a pig, and a big bruise ripened on his cheek.

"What in the world?" Bess threw up her hands. Then she noticed her mother waving wildly from the front stoop. "I'll be back," she said to her ex-husband and hurried over to the house.

"Mom?"

"I think I've solved your mystery. Come inside."

"Okay, only we need to call an ambulance. Sherman's injured and bound in that car trunk over there."

"Don't worry, I'll take care of him," said a tall, handsome man.

Bess flew into Hal's arms. "You're alive, you're alive!"

Hal held her tightly. "Are you all right?" She nodded. "Heck of a gamble to take, Q." He stroked her hair, and then her face. "I only meant for you to find out who was causing all the trouble, not go after him."

Bess smiled.

Later, after they'd handed the case over to the police and were sipping coffee on the sofa, Bess said, "I had to do something. But what really happened?"

"What do you think, mystery queen?" Hal asked.

"Well, I've thought about it all day, and I believe Carol was behind everything. A woman scorned, you know. I think your encyclopedia hinted that somebody stepped out of line and that the Q you indicated wasn't just me, but Queen Qaarifa of Ancient Egypt, remember? She was the one that Romana Nostra—that mystery writer you like— invented who cruelly eliminated any lovers who crossed her.

"But Q was also for the Quaker grandparents of my ex-husband, Sherman, so I guessed he was involved. Even though we weren't together any more, I knew he wouldn't like you being in my life, so that made him the perfect shill for Carol's plans. I imagine she paid him, and she would get a two-for-one if she could hurt both of us.

"The last Q was a little more difficult, but I think you were trying to tell me that you had to disappear in order to foil Carol's plans. It wasn't about Sherm being invisible, it was about you. I just wish you could've told me, but now I see it was essential to create a mystery that took me by surprise. Plausible deniability, right?"

Todd scampered into the room and crawled onto Hal's lap. "You've got one smart mama, my man," Hal said, "and one with a great imagination."

He gathered them both in his arms for a long, group hug, and ignored Bess's muffled, "What do you mean?"

THE BUTTERFLY DRESS

J.D. FROST

I wasn't really stalking her. That clingy, white dress covered with butterflies drew me in tow. She stepped out of a Caddy ten feet ahead of me as we walked through Wechler's old parking garage. The sound of her heels popped off that concrete like rifle shots. Those butterflies, outlined in different colors, swelled and flexed, as if they would surely fly.

She adjusted her wide-brimmed hat as she stepped from the garage. The sun hit her like a spotlight. That dress swung like the Captain's Ride at Beachside Amusements. I surrendered my plans to waste my day at Cherry Street Park across Ocean Boulevard. Then she broke that marvelous rhythm, stepping into Sapore di Sol, a café in the cobblestone courtyard at the head of the alley.

I slipped into a trinket shop across the way. I fingered a bookmark but kept my eyes on her, thinking she would take a table. Instead, she slalomed through the cafe's umbrellas. Their wedges colored like lemon and coconut lit up in the sun. She pulled a folded bill from her bag and gave it to a waiter near the drink station. It quickly disappeared into his front pocket. She followed him but then, as if she had some kind of built-in radar, pointed those big black sunglasses straight at me. I dropped my gaze and flipped the bookmark. How does a woman always know when a man is looking? The answer certainly wasn't in my hand. You are what you read, the bookmark said.

When I dared to look back, the waiter poured coffee into a large foam cup, fashioning her a drink. A frappe, I thought, something cool in the heat. She seemed to lecture him. He nodded several times, then placed a menu on a table in the middle. She said something but didn't sit. She took the frappe, swayed past a couple of tables and walked out the other end of the alley. It was only another fifteen feet to Ocean Boulevard.

I hurried after her. I spotted familiar faces in the park across the street. Everyone there or any who might walk by seemed bland compared to the beguiling woman. Early lunch-goers cluttered the sidewalk on Ocean. I searched for the dress. All I knew was she had turned left.

I trotted and it paid off—I would've lost her. Up ahead, through the flow of lawyers, laborers, and losers, I saw her dip into Delvaney's jewelry store. I pushed through a trio of idiots going the wrong way and followed her inside. She strolled along the glass case on the left, her finger riding its edge. I went to the right and sidled to where the counter made a corner.

A mousy girl in a skirt and a short-sleeved sweater planted herself in front of me. A sweater in the summer, even in the early summer, makes my skin crawl. She offered to help. At least she asked, in so many words, if I needed help. Her expression said something else, something like: Get lost, I want to go to lunch. I assured her I was only looking, but she wouldn't take that. She remained anchored on the opposite side of the corner. Just to keep from feeling weird, I pointed at an elegant watch.

"May I? For my girlfriend," I said.

On the other side of the room, Miss Butterfly had asked to see several bracelets. The salesman, between fumbling and pushing up his black glasses, placed the boxes side by side on the counter. I didn't need a loupe to know at least two of the pieces were covered with diamonds. Light from the window behind me danced over the rows of stones, and they sparkled like chop on a Sunday lake. She sat the cup on the counter and bent over the bracelets. The top of her dress dropped ever so slightly. That space sucked in the clerk's eyes...and my own. She didn't seem to notice. After we'd both taken our fill, she straightened. Her right hand moved as if to point. She tipped the frappe. The go cup laid on its side. Its contents raced across the counter.

The already flustered clerk's hands flew up. He ducked, pulled a cloth from beneath the counter, and trapped the brown liquid before it spilled over the side. He turned his back and pulled another cloth from an adjacent counter. I watched Miss Butterfly's left hand flick across the display. She dropped a bracelet on the counter and whisked away the string of diamonds faster than a shell can hide a pea. Her hand disappeared into the purse and was just as quickly beside her face. He surrounded and wiped at the puddle. She apologized repeatedly, even placed one hand on the clerk's arm. In a voice that easily carried across the store, she declared herself too rattled to shop. She promised to return when her nerves were settled.

I hovered over the watch, but my eyes slid to the left as she walked out the door. I straightened and looked at Mousy.

"Maybe I should look at a bracelet."

With her prickly temperament, I wouldn't have guessed it, but Mousy must've been on commission. She didn't call to the man. He had cleared the counter and was busy arranging the bracelets below. She squeezed past his behind. I indicated the piece left by the woman. The sweater girl lifted it and placed it on a black cloth. I didn't have to look closely. It was cheap, like something from a county fair. The settings were—cartoonish. I thanked her and walked out.

The lunch crowd had grown. Men and women in all combinations strode arm in arm and all were in each other's ear. I'd never been one to step out of the park into that flow, but what I had witnessed in Delvaney's emboldened me. I reached the cobblestones. She was at the middle table. She had removed the hat. She was finger combing her dark hair. All the other tables were taken, not that I was about to bother with them. I pulled the chair opposite Miss Butterfly and sat. Her lips parted but she didn't speak. Instead, she flipped the sunglasses up and took me in with luminous blue eyes. The flash of anger in them ebbed and left only a mild curiosity.

"The tables are taken," I said. "I thought you might like some company, a way to unwind, someone to talk with. You look like a woman with a great deal to share."

"I can have you thrown out, you know," she said.

I looked left and right. Without mentioning that we were already outside, I leaned onto my forearms. "You mean like call the police?"

She hesitated, then her eyes widened. "That was you across the store."

I assured her it was me. I complimented her hand speed and her daring.

"You didn't call to the clerk," she said.

"You are a *very* beautiful woman."

As I said it, I wondered why a woman like that would steal? Did she need money for drugs? She didn't look it. Wouldn't her husband give her anything?

"Don't be a dolt. What is it you want? A confession?" she asked.

"You *are* beautiful. And not just this day. You are a fantasy on a loop. I've seen you every night for what seems like forever. And now you are here, in the flesh."

"I'm married."

"Wouldn't he buy you a bracelet like the one in your pocket?"

"I'm not your fantasy. You have no idea to whom you are talking." She looked around, maybe for a policeman.

"Maybe I do. Your husband is a generous man, I'm sure. But not like me. You see, I would give anything…or forget anything to have you."

"You're vulgar. Despicable." She drew her lips into a knot and looked to the side. Finally, the color in her neck faded. She cut her gaze back to me. "All right. If you're up to it."

There were the details, the matter of where and when. I wasn't about to take such a woman to my junk-strewn apartment. We made the arrangements. At her suggestion, we would meet that very night. I insisted on seeing her driver's license. My threat meant nothing if she walked away still a stranger. She took the license from her purse and snapped it on the table as if dealing a card.

Sarah Lynn Collins. I memorized the address as well. She countered, asking to see mine. I didn't weigh the possibilities at that time; with no hesitation, I unfolded my wallet. She looked at it through the plastic window.

"Robert Glenn," she read. She flicked her lips, leaned back, lifted her purse, and was gone.

I spent the afternoon grooming myself. Under the threat of blackmail, she could hardly turn me down. Still, I wanted the night to be the best it could be.

That evening, I waited in the hotel lobby for her. She walked in, wearing the same butterfly dress. Her hair was different and she wore a deep red lipstick. We didn't touch. She walked beside me and we stepped into the elevator.

The ocean was a block away. I stood by the window of our fourth floor room. I could see the white foam almost glowing on the breaking waves.

"Click off the overhead," I said.

Light from the street lamps and even the moon came through the barely open slats. Stripes fell across the room.

"Slip out of that dress."

"I thought you would grab me, tear my clothes off."

"I don't want to grab you. I want to watch you," I said.

She pulled at a zipper. The butterfly dress fluttered to the carpet. The strips of light from the blinds fell across her perfect shape. Maybe she visited a gym or ran. No matter, her beauty was a gift.

I inhaled the scent of gardenias, like those in Cherry Street Park, as she neared me. She tasted faintly of butterscotch, not as if she had eaten butterscotch but like the thing itself.

I wanted to slow down time. I wanted to see the second hand creep between marks. But like a bite of the sweetest cake, those minutes melted away.

She rested her forearms on my chest. Her face only inches from mine. There was a smile. It was the smile she had given the clerk in Delvaney's. "Was it better than the fantasy?" she asked.

She had me reacting, not thinking. I breathed, "Yes."

"Do you realize what you have started," she said.

She kissed me with passion that can't be forced or bought or faked. She stood and said brightly, "I think we should celebrate. Some fruit. Grapes. Wine in bed. I saw a market on the way in. It'll only take me a minute."

I watched her slide into the butterfly dress. She grabbed her purse and disappeared through the door. I felt good but edgy. I wanted another chance. At worst, I wanted to sit down at the table with her again. I picked up my watch from the night table, which was silly. I didn't know what time she had left. I thought of looking for her, but I had no idea where. A knock came on the door. Had she forgotten her—

"Police!" a voice said before I reached the door.

I halted in mid-step.

"Just a moment."

I had one leg in my jeans when they entered.

"Robert Glenn, place your hands against the wall."

He pushed me up. I placed my hands on the sheetrock. My pants hung around my right ankle.

"What for?"

"Give me your right wrist, Mr. Glenn. You're under arrest for theft. Shoplifting. However you wish to say it."

It didn't dawn on me at first. He finished cuffing me. "I haven't shoplifted anything."

He dropped out of sight behind me. I craned my neck to see what he was doing.

"And I suppose you have no idea how this got here."

He pulled his hand from beneath the bed, the corner where the dress had lain. He held up the bracelet, the one Sarah Lynn had stolen from Delvaney's.

"I didn't put that there," I said.

"It seems your girlfriend is upset that you're stealing jewelry for another chick."

"She's not my girlfriend."

"If you say so, but I think she still carries a small torch. She did say it wasn't entirely over."

MOVING ON

PAULA GAIL BENSON

Misty took careful steps as she crossed the parking lot. Since the old Thrift Warehouse closed, no one had cared for the surface. The ruts and holes became more pitted, with grass sprouting and ground reappearing. She normally felt steady on her feet, but the slightest crumbling edge of asphalt or unexpected gradation could send her tumbling, and that was never pleasant when you carried all your belongings in a frayed, black, handmade backpack.

So, she watched where she walked, and strained to listen for anyone who might sneak up on her in this isolated spot. Only after she started around the side of the building, did she stop and gaze up at the boarded, ramshackle Victorian on the hill across the street. The "for sale" sign had begun to look as forlorn as the house. The yard was a jungle of undergrowth with one redeeming feature that made her smile.

It was the last weekend in June and the crape myrtles were in their glory with outshoots of blossoms at the end of each branch like bridal bouquets designed by God. Already their explosions of gentle violet, brilliant fuchsia, and perfectly white blooms outshone any possible upcoming Fourth of July fireworks displays.

She took a deep breath, hoping to inhale the sweet fragrance in the deepening twilight and lessening humidity of another sweltering day. The other homeless opted for air-conditioned shelters if they were fortunate enough to be admitted, or headed for the river, where, if they could not be cool, at least they could be wet.

Misty didn't need water when she could have this place all to herself. By lying perfectly still below the branches of blossoms, beneath the undergrowth, on a layer of pine straw blanketing the slope, Misty could convince herself that she had regressed to her former life as Elizabeth Siddal, model for Sir John Everett Millais's picture of

Ophelia. He painted Shakespeare's character floating alone, so relaxed in comfort and peace, that Ophelia never noticed her garments soggy and pulling her into the depths.

Suicide is wrong, said the devil voice in Misty's head.

Maybe it's blessed relief, the angel voice responded.

Or perhaps Misty mixed up who said what. The voices in her head often grew so noisy and confusing, that she tuned them out like buzzing insects and let them fight things out among themselves.

She grew up in this currently abandoned house. After her parents died and other family members took over, she chose to live on the streets instead of an institution. Mr. Tobias, who used to run the Thrift, had always been kind to her, never minding if she slept at the back of his building and often leaving her blankets or clothing from his stock.

His daughter's picture was in the paper today. Misty found a discarded copy in the coffee shop and carried it under her arm. Erica Tobias, engaged to be married this weekend, stood before the purple fronds of a wisteria tree. Perhaps a weeping willow would have been more appropriate, since her daddy wouldn't be there to give her away. But the colors in the newspaper photo would blend with the undergrowth and crape myrtle blossoms. Misty could drape it over herself, while dreaming she floated again in chilling bath water as Millais painted his Ophelia, and she would be cool, calm, and content.

Oh, Jeez. Get a grip on yourself, Lizzie girl.

My nerves were so jittery, I almost ran into the bedraggled woman. I would have for certain if I hadn't slammed on my brakes as soon as I drove around the Thrift and saw her. She had just been standing there, holding the portion of today's paper with the engagement picture and looking at the old house on the hill.

I guess we were each so absorbed in our own worlds that the near collision scared us both witless. When I halted, she was no more than a foot away from the headlight on the driver's side. Her frizzy gray curls reached below her shoulders. Her wide eyes and unlined face made me decide it was life conditions instead of years that aged her. She stared at me, no more than a minute, although it seemed longer. Then, she put her hand up, as if the headlights' beams hurt her eyes. Or maybe to hide her face so that I wouldn't remember her features.

Too late. I was cursed with one of those eidetic memories, like Dan Brown's hero Robert Langdon. Sometimes I just wanted to get images out of my head. One from inside the old Thrift would never stop haunting me.

Already, the woman was scuttling away, moving sideways at first like a human crab, then angling to scramble back around the corner of the building. I put the car in reverse, backed up, and roared down the road.

Today was not your time, the devil murmured.

Or maybe you just missed the opportunity, the angel replied.

Banishing the voices, Misty leaned against the building until she heard the car skid away. She looked around the corner, making sure the way was clear, then clambered across the street until she plunged into the nurturing embrace of the jungle terrain.

About ten minutes later, I returned, made another circle around the building, and, when I was sure I was alone, parked in the back, my heart still pounding in my chest. The woman had disappeared. I turned off the ignition and leaned back in my seat, willing myself to take regular, quieting breaths.

By the time the drug dealer arrived, I had managed to get out of my car and stood leaning against the driver's door with a hefty oversized clutch handbag wedged under my right shoulder. I wore the lightweight blue and green dress with caplet sleeves, knowing it revealed the bruises on my forearms I got when Duke and I boxed at the gym the other night. He apologized over and over, saying the wedding guests would know I'd been brawling. I shrugged it off, telling him my maid of honor jacket would cover any telltale signs.

Now, I flaunted the bruises on purpose, hoping the dealer would comment about them. Wishing, because I didn't dare pray, that her taking notice would open up the avenue I needed.

The dealer had driven up in a cream VW bug just as the lone street light blinked on. She parked several car lengths from me, and called me on her cell with her car motor still running. Despite the heat, my hands and arms trembled as I reached to get my phone from the clutch and answer the call.

"Rethinking where you wanted to meet now, Lizzie?" Her sultry voice matched the weather.

No. The place had never been in question for me, even though she urged me to make it more public because nobody suspected buys to take place out in the open.

"Let's just get it over with," I said and disconnected.

She gave me a smirking smile, turned off the engine, and picked up her bag from the passenger seat. In a slow motion, she opened the door and rose from the driver's seat. Her shiny straight black hair was parted in the middle and flowed down her back. She wore a black shell and skirt, but the jacket was bright chartreuse, almost neon. In contrast, the bag was a large suede emerald green hobo.

Not what I had expected or remembered. When she used to huddle as Cade Blaine's shadow, she went by Sissy Reid, and looked like she had just crawled out of a grease pit. Now that she had taken over his trade, she called herself Isis, which at least incorporated some of the letters from Sissy, and dressed like a candidate for businesswoman of the year. I wondered if changing her name to Isis helped her create a new identity. Maybe successful dealers equated their status with iconic rock stars. Or perhaps desperate junkies found it easier to remember single names.

Isis approached me with confidence, looking like a femme fatale from a noir movie, itching for confrontation. I felt ready to grant her wish. Then, I noticed a newspaper caught in the undergrowth across the street. Had the homeless woman taken refuge there? I didn't want any witnesses.

Pointing at my shaking arms, Isis said, "You got it bad."

"Oblivion's the only way I make it through."

"You've internalized your problems when you should externalize."

She had become an analyst. Maybe that would make this easier. "Why do you say that?"

"I see the bruises"

"So?"

"I've been where you are."

Maybe. Or, maybe not. "Let's just finish this deal."

"Fine with me. Internalized problems just send me more business."

My nerves made me lose focus, jump ahead, and ask too quickly. "Have you ever killed anyone?"

Her smirk returned. "Why do *you* ask that?"

Get control over yourself, Lizzie girl, I told myself. "You said you'd been where I am. I wondered if that was how you took care of it."

"Let me see the cash."

Get a grip, Lizzie girl. Go slowly.

I opened the clutch and took out the stuffed envelope. One hundred twenty-dollar bills. My entire savings.

Her blood red nails flicked through the stack. She looked up after the count when she was sure it was all there. Placing the money in her purse, she then withdrew a sandwich-sized baggie and handed it toward me.

I needed more.

"Prime stuff," she said, wiggling the baggie when I didn't reach to get it.

"Tell me how you solved your problem."

"You can't copy my fix."

"Maybe I can learn from it."

As I reached to take the baggie, I saw the glint in her eyes. She wanted to brag about her achievement. Cade had taken the credit for too long.

"Please," I begged. "I won't tell."

She was wavering now. Eyeing the baggie and thinking how zonked out of my skull I'd be once I'd consumed it. Too spaced out to be listened to or believed.

"Let me put it to you this way," she started, pausing to lick her upper lip before continuing. "What you do is to take 'your problem' out of the picture. It's hard to hide a body. Better to leave one out in the open if you can convince 'your problem' to take the fall."

"You mean, you killed someone else and got 'your problem' to take the blame?"

She frowned. For a moment, I saw Sissy reemerge. Not the scared druggie who fed her habit from Cade Blaine's supply, but the battered girlfriend who couldn't take another day of abuse. "My man was the biggest badass in the territory. He walked around with a piece, even waved it in people's faces when they owed him, but he was all talk and no action. One night I asked him to get me a soda. Instead of buying one, he broke in a building to steal one. Made me hold his big gun while he picked the lock. Never worried about a security system. Only, he didn't know the owner was still inside."

"Did the owner catch you?"

"We caught him. He hid from us, but we heard him knock something over. My man called him out, made him get us the soda, and forced him down on his knees, threatening to shoot him." She paused. "Since I had the gun, I just made his word good."

Now I had what I wanted. I shoved the baggie into my clutch. "Uncle Toby didn't knock something over. I did. I was with him in the Thrift that night. I still hear his voice telling me 'Stay hidden, Lizzie girl. Let me handle this.' He stepped forward to deal with you to protect me."

Her face paled. "Cade's been convicted of the murder."

"I heard you tell him he could take the credit that night. And, of course, his bragging about it helped to get him caught. But, I'm betting you made the anonymous call to tell the police where to find the gun. Convenient that it was wiped clean of all but Cade's prints. How did you manage that?"

"You can have the money back. Here." She reached in her bag and withdrew the envelope I had given her. "You have to understand, I had no other way out."

I reached to take the envelope and returned it to my clutch. "Unfortunately, when you solved your problem, you created another one. Tomorrow, my cousin Erica's getting married without her father to give her away. This is my wedding gift to her."

From the clutch, I pulled out my gun with the silencer. Isis stood with her mouth open as I fired. She dropped in a surprised puddle. The newspaper and surrounding foliage on the hillside shook worse than I did.

Misty just wanted to sink back in time and resume her past life as Elizabeth Siddal suspended in freezing water. A bout of pneumonia would be better than what she faced here.

What good was remembering a past life if you couldn't regress to it when the present one became unbearable? Why did a life have to end before you could move on?

Well, Lizzie girl, it's done. Only, my first thought looking at Isis' blood seeping into the broken asphalt was that Uncle Toby wouldn't approve. I imagined him waiting for Isis at the pearly gates with an apology. Or more likely, looking down upon her in a fiery hell.

Uncle Toby's opinion didn't matter. Erica would be appreciative. And, it was her present. Her closure.

Somehow I got the gun back into my clutch and turned to walk across the street.

Misty heard the footsteps approaching and knew she was a goner. When the shooter stood directly beside her, she felt something drop onto the ground. Twisting to see the item, Misty found a baggie filled with drugs.

"They're yours if you want them," the shooter said.

Misty sat up, shaking her head furiously. "I got too many folks yapping in my brain. That stuff just distorts the conversations in stereo."

After retrieving the drugs, the shooter placed a white envelope in Misty's hand.

"Then take the money and forget," she said.

Misty's fingers curled around the envelope as she watched the shooter return to her car and drive away. For the first time in a long time, the voices were silent.

THE PHOTOGRAPH

SUSAN E. THOMAS

"I'm going home."

"Already? But you said you'd help me fix up that old desk my Mom gave us."

"Sorry, babe, but I'm just not feelin' it. Can't you do it?"

Cass sighed. "All right, Jay. I guess I'll see you tomorrow, then."

"K." A quick peck on the lips and Jay left.

Cass turned to the monstrosity of a desk her mother had given her for the apartment she and Jay would share after their wedding. The walnut, roll-top desk had seen years of neglect, sitting beneath a large window until the stain faded and the varnish cracked and shriveled. Though some of the drawers didn't sit quite right, the body was largely undamaged and the roll-top moved smoothly. It had been in their family for years, Mom said, and deserved a little TLC.

"Well, I guess it's just you and me."

After a great deal of shoving and grunting, Cass had the desk sitting on a layer of newspaper. Placing a stack of sandpaper and a toolkit nearby, she went to work rubbing away the old varnish and buffing out small dents and scratches. When her arms tired, she turned to the drawers. Three drawers moved easily, but the fourth stuck.

Cass wiggled and tugged, fearing she would rip the hardware off the drawer, but then suddenly it gave and came flying out. She landed hard on her buttocks with an "umph." The drawer landed upside down nearby.

Well, that was stupid.

Cass moved to her knees and rubbed the pain from her backside. Reaching for the drawer, she noticed something peeking out from underneath.

Uh, oh. Did I break it?

A piece of thin wood lay beneath the drawer, but the drawer looked to be intact. Cass picked up the pieces and realized that the extra piece of wood was, in fact, a false bottom. Once concealed between the pieces, an old photograph now lay before her.

It's Mom.

Cass picked it up and looked into Julia's much younger face, immediately recognizing the eyes and features of the woman who raised her.

And...she looks happy.

Cass's mother stood behind a seated man, who held a baby on his lap.

Wow! Dad looks really different without a beard!

Cass's father had passed away only two years ago. Her mother explained it as liver failure. Though technically true, Cass knew he had finally drunk himself to death.

He looks happy, too. Odd, if Mom hadn't been in the picture, I wouldn't have recognized him. Oh! That must be me!

Cass's eyes shifted to the baby sitting on the man's knee. She looked to be eight or nine months old. Soft, plump cheeks framed a laughing mouth and bright, shining eyes. Her father's strong hands held her about the middle, but...

Cass sucked in her breath and stared.

What? How is that possible?

The hands who held her child-self, distinctly visible in the photograph, could not possibly be her father's hands.

Who are you? And what are you doing with my mother? And me! You're not my father. My father had all his fingers.

"Mom, please stop telling me to drop it. You know that's not going to happen. Just answer the question. Who is the man in the picture?"

Cass sat in Julia's small drawing room holding the picture. Julia turned away. A tear ran down her cheek, meeting her neck at the jawline. Cass softened.

"Mom, please. Please tell me."

"That man is your father, Cass." Julia swallowed and wiped away the moisture beneath her eyes. "Your real father."

"Where is he?"

"He passed away not long after that picture was taken." Julia finally turned to face her daughter. "I'm sorry I never told you about him, my dear, but that was another life. When he died, well, I...I wished I had died, too. But, I had you to think of. We had to move on. So, I put that life behind me."

Cass stared into the smiling eyes of a man she did not recognize but suddenly longed to know. She had always wondered where she'd gotten her red hair and dimples.

"You look happy," Cass said, eyes on the photograph, tears welling in her own eyes.

"I was very happy. The happiest I've ever been."

Cass nodded. She loved her dad—the man who raised her—but he was a tormented soul. Living in fear of his drunken rages had not been easy for Cass, but life with Bill had nearly destroyed Julia. Now that Bill was gone, Julia had only just begun to discover herself again. Cass didn't want to cause her mother more pain, but she had to know more about the man in the photograph.

Was he kind? Did he and Mom love each other? Did he love me?

"Will you tell me about him, Mom?" Cass whispered.

Julia's eyes softened. Her lips eased into the barest hint of a smile, and she reached for the photograph.

"His name was Asher Clemens. We met and fell in love the summer of 1985. We married the following spring. You were born a year later. We were so happy! Your...father...worked as a mechanic and general fix-it guy in Manley Hot Springs, Alaska, where we lived. He often repaired the vehicles and generators for the people of the Koyukon reservation, but he had to get there by plane.

"When he told me he and his partner, Steve—a pilot, had planned a trip for October, I was worried. The weather can get quite bad that time of year. But, Asher felt the situation was urgent. He was determined to go.

"He left the morning of October 2, 1986. It was a Thursday. I kissed him goodbye. He gave you a squeeze and said, 'Bye, Cee-Cee. Take care of your Mom for me.'"

"Cee-Cee?" Cass asked.

"Yes. That was his nickname for you. Back then, your last name was Clemens."

Cass smiled.

"We never saw him again," Julia continued. "The next day, some officers came to the house and told me his plane had gone down in the Yukon-Koyukuk wilderness. Three weeks passed with no more word. Then they finally confirmed that he'd been killed and buried in a small cemetery on the reservation. By then, the money had run out, and I was out of options. I moved back to Texas. Bill started coming around. I knew he wasn't good for me, but he had a good job, so... Well, the rest you know."

"Except one thing," Cass said. "How did my real father lose his finger?"

Julia smirked. "That was your fault, actually."

"What? But, I was just a baby, wasn't I?"

Julia laughed—the first laugh Cass had heard from her in a long time. "Yes. He was supposed to be watching you, but some poor soul came by needing help—as they often did. Your dad never could say no. He sat you down in the grass while he fidgeted with a stalling engine. Well, he had his hand in there, messing with the things, when some bee decided it was time to sting you. You let out a holler and he jerked. The belt caught the index finger of his right hand and—well, that was the end of that."

"Jay," Cass said, speaking into her phone, "why are you fighting me on this? Can't you see it's important to me?"

"But we're getting married in less than two weeks! Cass, I know you've always longed for a better father figure, but it's not like you really knew this guy. How's visiting his grave going to fill that hole?"

"You know how little family I have. My dad—Bill, I mean—well, I guess I just need to know God had something good in mind for me, you know? And, if He did, shouldn't I honor that? Mom said she never got the chance to visit his grave or say goodbye. It's too painful for her, but I need to go. I want to connect with my past before I take the next step into my future—our future."

"But why now? Do you know how selfish you sound? You know I'm too busy to deal with this wedding stuff! Besides, shouldn't I be enough for you?"

Yes, you should be...but, you're not.

"How can I make you understand?" Cass asked. "I just need some closure on this and then—"

"Enough, Cass! You can't go! Maybe we can go up in a year or two, but..."

"Not later, now. I need to go now."

The line went silent for a while, but then Jay said, "Well, then go. But, if you're not back by the twelfth, consider the wedding cancelled."

This is not the way I was hoping to connect with my father.

Cass again felt the small plane engine sputter. She gripped the armrests of her tiny passenger seat, knuckles white. Getting to the small town closest to where her father's plane had gone down proved adventurous in and of itself. But lost bag, odd seatmates, and unforeseen expenses aside, Cass was glad she'd come.

Now, if only we don't hurtle out of the sky in a fiery death spin.

"Welcome to Manley Hot Springs. Will you be needing a ride to the roadhouse?"

"Yes, please," Cass answered the airport attendant. "And, could someone recommend a good trail guide for me?"

"Sure, I know a fella. Name's Samuel. Here, I'll write down his number for you."

"Thanks so much!"

The next morning, Cass waited expectantly in the Manley Roadhouse's quaint sitting room for the trail guide.

"He's the son of a friend of mine and the best guide west of Fairbanks," the round-faced, blue-eyed man had said. "Knows every nook and cranny of the Yukon-Koyukuk, if it can be known. Charges a reasonable fee, too. Just don't be fooled by his youth."

Cass, at twenty-eight, still felt young and inexperienced from time to time, so when a child of about seventeen approached her and spoke to her with the confidence of a man twice his age, she could barely contain her surprise.

"Hello, my name is Samuel. Are you Cassandra Jackson?"

"Y…yes, I am," Cass answered, shaking the young man's offered hand.

"Glad to meet you. I'll be your guide for as long as you need me. It's seventy-five dollars a day. Gas and meals are extra. You said you're looking for some old cemeteries?"

"That's right."

"Sounds good. I know a few places we could go, if you're ready." He smiled. His dark hair and skin, black eyes, slightly rounded face, and high cheekbones were characteristic of an Alaskan Native. Cass liked him instantly.

"Great! Let's go, then!"

They did not waste time searching the public cemetery in town, since Cass had already paid the innkeeper to drive her there the evening before. Before leaving Texas, she had checked its online registry to no avail, but decided she might as well take a look for herself, anyway. No luck. So, Samuel first drove Cass to a couple of places he knew that were likely unrecorded, but held grave markers nonetheless. One was located in a small field behind an old ranch house owned by a lady he knew. Another was in a narrow, open lot at the far end of a lonely road.

As Cass walked amongst the stones, Samuel waited at a distance, evidently sensing her need for privacy. Cass was glad for the space. It helped her imagine what life might have been like had her father lived. But she also heard Jay's voice in her head, condemning her.

Maybe he's right. Why do I need this so much? I never really knew this man.

The stones and wooden markers she found were so old and weathered that many of the names were no longer legible. But, of those she could read, the names of both whites and natives lay intermingled, reminding her that, in death, all find equality. She thought of Bill—the man she had always just called "Dad."

I was angry with you for a long time, Dad, but now, I just hope God finally chased away your demons.

The first day yielded no results, but on the way back to town, Samuel encouraged her not to lose hope. From her description of where she thought the plane crashed, he believed he knew where they might have buried him.

"You can only get to it by boat," he cautioned. "It's an Alaskan Native cemetery deep in Yukon-Koyukuk territory. I've never been there, but I know where it is. It's usually for Natives only, but if he was a friend to them, as you say, they might have made an exception."

"Yes, he was. Ended up giving his life to help them, as it turned out."

"Then, I'll meet you here in the morning," he said, as he dropped her off at the roadhouse. "Say about five? Don't worry. It's summer, so it'll be plenty light out. Be sure to dress warmly, anyway. I'll bring food."

The motorboat rental cost more than Cass wanted to spend, but at least she didn't have to pay for a driver. Samuel proved to be as capable a river guide as he was a trail guide.

"How did you learn all of this?" she asked, admiration showing clearly on her freckled face as the wind whipped at her red hair.

"I've lived here all my life," he said, which wasn't much of an explanation given how young he was. But then he continued, "My dad homeschooled me—mostly out here. We'd take our lessons out on the trails and he'd teach me everything from math to English to science while we camped, fished, and hiked. All the while, I learned the lay of the land and its history, too."

"He sounds like an amazing guy," Cass said, hiding a twinge of jealousy. Her dad never even bothered to show up at her softball games, let alone take her camping or fishing.

The trip was a long one, but the time passed quickly. Along the way, Cass learned a great deal about Alaska and the Koyukon tribe from Samuel, who claimed to be one of them. He told her about the land and the people and regaled her with the Distant Time legends. They spotted river otters, martens, and a variety of river fowl. Samuel knew all their names.

"It's just around this loop of the Tanana River," he said near lunchtime. "It's probably a little overgrown, but I brought a machete. Just don't wander off and keep an eye out for bears."

Bears?

Samuel brought the boat near a grassy shoreline and hopped out. He pulled it halfway up the bank and extended a hand to help Cass find her footing as she disembarked. He then retrieved his shotgun.

"Here, hold this," he said, shoving it to her. "If you see any bears, shoot."

Cass swallowed hard.

Samuel reached for his machete, removed it from its cloth sheath, and began hacking away at some of the overgrowth along what had once been a footpath.

The cemetery was a bit farther from the shore than Cass had hoped, but they finally entered a clearing where the grass was dotted with markers—some decorated with Native beads and ornaments, others bordered with short, white, iron fences.

Cass moved from stone to stone, reading the lines etched there, sometimes having to rub off lichen to make out the words and dates.

Could his gravestone be one of these unreadable ones? Twenty-seven years is an awfully long time—especially in a climate as rough as this one. She sighed. *I might never find it.*

Just then, Cass spotted an undecorated stone at the edge of the clearing. She moved toward it and knelt down.

There he was. Asher Clemens. July 25, 1963 - October 2, 1986.

She sucked in her breath and her right hand moved unbidden to her lips.

Dad? Is that really you?

A powerful feeling descended on her—a sorrow and longing she did not know she possessed. But another sensation stirred—the awakening of the part of herself who had been valued and loved by a father.

I'm here, Dad. After all these years. I'm here to finally meet you...and to say goodbye.

Cass sat in the grass for a long moment, staring at the words, realizing her search was at an end. From what her mother had told her, they had no family in Alaska, so what more was there to learn? She suddenly felt very alone—both in the joy of her discovery and in her grief. She looked up.

"Samuel," she called. He sat at the far end of the clearing, playing with a long stalk of grass. "I found him. Thanks to you. Want to see?"

"Sure," he smiled. "If you're sure you don't mind."

"Not at all."

He approached the marker, but then stopped and backed away, an indiscernible look on his face. "What?" he said. "That's not possible!"

"What do you mean? This is my father's grave. It's what I've been looking for this whole time."

"Asher Clemens? Your father's name was Asher Clemens?"

"Yes, why?" Cass asked.

"That's... That's *my* father's name."

"What? Wait. This is too weird. It must just be a coincidence that they have the same name. Besides, my father died a long time ago—long before you were born." Cass reached into her back pocket. "Here, I have a photograph of my father. Take a look. You'll see."

She held it out, and he leaned forward to look. He gazed at it for a long time. Cass almost laughed.

Surely this boy's father must be native. How long can it take to see that the man in the picture is as white as I am?

"It's him," he said, in a barely audible whisper.

"What?"

"That's him," he repeated. "The man in that picture is my dad."

"Samuel. You must be mistaken. That man is dead. His grave is right here. He died back in 1986."

"No, he couldn't have. Because when I was three years old, this man adopted me." He gestured to the photograph. "And, he's not dead. He's very much alive."

Cass stared, wide-eyed at the boy before her, unable to speak.

"That picture," Samuel continued. "The baby is you?"

Cass could only nod.

"And that must be your mother... Julia, right? Dad once told me a story. A long time ago, he had a wife and daughter. One day, he went to help the Koyukons fix a generator. A storm was coming, and they were afraid. But, his plane went down in the wilderness. His friend, Steve, was killed, and Dad was badly injured. My people found him and nursed him back to health over many months. He became a part of the tribe.

"When the authorities finally found the crash, they made a mistake. A report was sent back that Dad, not Steve, had died in the crash. After an accident like that and a couple of months in the wilderness, I'm not surprised the body was falsely identified. In fact, I think Steve must really be buried here." Samuel gestured to the grave. "Anyway, when Dad was strong enough to return home, his wife and child were gone. He searched and searched, but never found them."

No. Mom remarried so soon afterwards...changed her name...and mine. No family to point him in the right direction. We just disappeared.

"But now, here you are!" Samuel said with wide-eyed wonder.

Tears sprung into Cass's eyes. "Yes, here I am."

Cass allowed Samuel—her new, very excited, little brother—to take her hand and lead her to the field behind his home, where he said his father would be working on their tractor's engine. As they rounded the corner and passed a row of flowering hedges, Cass spotted a tall man leaning against the front end of an old tractor, one foot balanced on a thick tire tread. Reddish hair, now streaked with gray, poked from beneath a broad Stetson.

"Give 'er a go, Joseph," he called to a dark-skinned man who sat at the controls. The engine flared for a moment and then died.

"Dad!" Samuel called, making use of the brief silence. "Dad! We have a visitor! You'll never guess who it is! It's amazing! You'll never guess!"

Asher looked up and his eyes met Cass's. A flicker of emotion crossed his features and then he just stared, long and hard, not moving a muscle—not moving his boot from the tractor tire—not moving his hand from the tractor's surface...his right hand...a hand missing an index finger.

"Cee-Cee?"

"Hi, Dad. It's me! I've come home!"

PICKLED

EDITH MAXWELL

I'll never eat a pickle again.

I had agreed to throw an evening party for my friend Louie at my country store, Pans 'N Pancakes. Louie successfully defended her doctoral thesis in anthropology on Tuesday, so a bash seemed in order. But a dead guy in my pickle barrel wasn't supposed to be on the menu.

I'm getting ahead of myself. Last night several dozen graduate students and faculty from the Anthropology Department drove the fourteen miles from the university out to the village where I now live. At Pans 'N Pancakes I normally make gourmet breakfasts and lunches for locals, tourists, and even some academics, in a village where nobody locks their doors. And it was a perfect place for a party.

"Louie, you are positively glowing," I told my BFF after giving her a big hug. And she was, in wide silk pants and a brilliant hand-painted silk tunic. A couple of years older than my twenty-five, she had worked really hard to earn her doctorate and deserved a fantastic celebration.

I had set out trays of mini-quiches and mini-meatballs with toothpicks, several dozen hand-sized pizzas fresh from the oven, and a hot artichoke dip. Louie had brought platters of veggies with humus and a dilly dip. I'd ordered dozens of mortarboard-decorated cupcakes for later.

George and I poured champagne all around to the group, whose ages ranged from younger than me to nearly retired. George was an ABD like I am—All But Dissertation—except he was still enrolled in the program. He had returned a few months ago from a year away doing his fieldwork on amulets in West Africa. He should have been writing up his research, but he'd confessed he was feeling blocked.

Mitch led the toast. "To Dr. Louisa!" He beamed and clinked his glass with hers. Mitch, Louisa's dissertation adviser, had only last year secured tenure, largely because of his published work on divination and curses in several desert cultures. The man had luscious lips, a teddy bear body, and a Casanova eye. He'd tried to hit on me more than once in the past.

The guests echoed the toast, as did I. The Moët went down really nice.

"Professor!" Louisa's ex-husband Berto Faraldo raised his glass with a smile.

I was surprised to see the slim Italian in the group, even though I knew Louie had settled into a wary post-divorce peace with him. If she didn't mind Berto being here, I didn't care. And he was a grad student in the department, after all.

People mingled, munched, and switched from bubbly to microbrews or wine, with the few teetotalers pouring cups of local cider instead. Berto set a bottle of rum on the table and added a healthy slug to his cider. Holding a cup of red wine, Louie's visiting sister browsed the shelves full of antique cooking tools: cast-iron Dutch ovens and skillets, moon-shaped choppers, meat grinders, a long-handled sandwich press. Besides pancakes, omelets, and burgers, I sell antique cookware along with just about everything else under the sun. Which includes fat pickles from a vintage barrel, my signature garlic-pepper pickled cukes. This autumn was my first in the store and the colorful leaves had cooperated nicely, bringing tour buses and all kinds of city dwellers who wanted a taste of an old-fashioned country store. I was happy to provide it.

George hooked up his iPod to a couple of tiny but powerful speakers, which was enough to get the dancing underway. He had assembled an eclectic playlist that included LCD Soundsystem's latest album, some Congolese dance numbers, Lady Gaga, a little Euro pop, and the YMCA song. Anthro types like to dance.

George grabbed my hand. "Come on Robbie." We'd had a flirtation a few years ago. He was a fun and energetic lover, but our life goals hadn't really meshed and now we were casual friends. Pretty soon almost everyone present was on the dance floor, that is, the dining section of the store, shaking their booties surrounded by tables and chairs stacked along the walls. My academic thesis—looking at the concept of "talent" and why some cultures hold up talented musicians as a kind of special class while in other societies everyone is considered able to play music—was still valid. Every single person dancing here tonight had a bit of talent to offer, just like the Indonesian villagers I'd lived with while I did my field work. Maybe I should have finished that doctorate, after all.

At one point, Berto, in his signature tight-cut pants the color of baby olives, swept Louie into a drunken dancing embrace. Mitch wanted to cut in, but Berto didn't let him. Berto tried to pilot Louie around the floor until he stumbled and tromped on her sandal-clad foot. George threw him a look of disgust. Louie was sober enough to gently pry Berto off and steer him to a chair, throwing me a raised-shoulder glance that read, "What can I do?" I only hoped the Italian wouldn't lose his dinner on my floor.

Mitch took Louisa's hand in his, and they started dancing as a couple. For a guy that round, he sure could move, but his other hand gradually drifted south from Louie's lower back. She ever so firmly lifted his mitt off her butt before she spun away to dance solo.

Despite the late hour at which the party broke up, I was awake before the birds this morning. I had breakfast to get underway and the cleanup to finish. I'd gone upstairs to bed before everybody departed last night, leaving Louie, her sister, and a few others clearing up much of the damage.

"I'll make sure somebody drives Berto home," Louie had said.

I needed to prep for today's breakfast: whole-wheat banana-walnut pancakes, herb-cheese biscuits with my special gravy, apple muffins, and omelets to order. This was peak color weekend, and I was looking forward to an overflowing cash drawer by Monday. At least I had a short commute to work.

I ran through a shower and clattered down the stairs at six thirty. First things first. I fired up the oven and started a pot of coffee, as much for me as for customers. I pulled a pan of biscuits out of the freezer, popping them in the oven the minute the beeper said it was preheated. Customers went nuts over biscuits drowning in gravy. I wanted to get the furniture back in place, too, so even if somebody arrived before food was ready, they'd have a place to sit. As I reached for a chair stacked a little higher than my five-foot-three could manage, I glanced to my left. My hands let go. The chair toppled and crashed onto my shoulder. I didn't even notice where it landed, because my eyes were on a jackknifed Berto with his head in the pickle barrel, arms splayed out to the sides, those green pants nearly splitting at the rear. He looked for all the world like he was bobbing for apples. Except he never came up.

I froze, remotely aware of a stinging in my shoulder. What was he doing? Why... *Shee-it*. Nobody could survive a head submerged in pickle juice.

The officer was all business with her questions fifteen minutes later, despite the fact that I'd dined with her at her cousin's house a couple of months earlier. Such is small-town life. I'd asked her when I'd called, all breathless and panicked, if I should try to take Berto out of the barrel but she'd said to leave him be.

We occupied two chairs, facing each other knee to knee. She'd forced me to lock the front door and keep the sign turned to Closed. I wondered how much business I was losing. On a Friday morning, I always had a decent breakfast crowd.

"So, Ms. Jordan, you're sure you have no idea how the victim came to have his head in your pickle barrel?" Wanda Bird looked up from her iPad. We might live in a country village, but we have a well-equipped public-safety team. Her tablet was a lot more up to date than my ancient little laptop.

"No. But I never lock the doors."

When she shook her head in disapproval, not a hair escaped the bun her red tresses were locked into.

"Does anybody use locks around here?" I asked. This town is the kind of place where, if I forget to put the ZIP code on a letter, I call Raylene at the post office and ask her to do it for me.

She ignored both my familiarity and my question. "Who might have wanted the victim dead?" She'd already grilled me on who had been at the party, what time they had left, and how I knew Berto.

The timer on the oven dinged. "Hang on a minute." I dashed over and pulled out the biscuits. Sliding them onto a cooling rack, I inhaled their crusty cheesy aroma, although it didn't sit as well as usual, considering that Berto was dead a few yards away. I doubted if any customers were going to have a chance to munch down one of the little baked treasures. On my way back to my chair, I spied an empty hook on the wall of cookware. Little cogs whirled in my brain but they didn't settle into a clear picture.

"I have no idea who would do that to Berto," I said as I sat again. I really didn't. "Louie won't even kill a mosquito now that she's a practicing Buddhist."

"Louie?"

"Louisa Murray. I told you. My friend who the party was for. Berto's ex-wife."

"Nobody else?"

"No." I couldn't conjure any enemies for Berto. "When can I reopen? This is a super important weekend for my business."

Wanda shrugged. I had happened upon a couple of guys talking at the post office last month who made it sound like pretty near every crime case in the village ended up cold. Unsolved, that is. Did I have even a shred of hope that she'd figure this thing out?

As Wanda asked me another question, her fellow officers extracted Berto from the barrel and laid him on a sheet of plastic on the floor. The watery green liquid dripping from his high brow made me feel like upchucking the breakfast I hadn't eaten. They turned him onto his front side.

"Sergeant?" One of the guys gestured. "Looks like a swelling on the back of his head here."

"Right," Wanda said. "Make sure we get a picture of that." To me she added, "Probably got it when he fell in."

To myself I added: *he "fell" in headfirst. How would that produce a bump on the back of his head, exactly?* Man, it could be days, weeks before she let me reopen.

One gloved officer investigated Berto's pockets. He extracted a key ring. I stared at it.

The police—photographer, medical examiner, fingerprint experts, the whole gang—got out of there by early afternoon. I'd lost the morning and lunch business and had given away the coffee and biscuits to the cops. Wanda had insisted on securing a strip of yellow police tape across the front door. Maybe it seemed cold, but if one of us didn't figure this thing out today, I'd lose a weekend of lucrative autumn income that I could not afford to do without.

"Now, don't you be revealing details about any of this, you hear?" Wanda set her hands on hips that had been reluctantly conscripted into pants cut for a man. "No talking to anybody."

I studied my left pinky cuticle without answering. Wanda and her buddies left through the back door. The folded leather triangle attached to the ring wasn't Berto's. I knew exactly whose it was.

After I completed a more thorough search of the premises than the cops had accomplished, I figured I could resolve the situation faster than the village authorities, especially if they thought Berto just fell into the barrel. What did they have that I didn't? Training, sure. But possibly I had some talent at investigating, too.

If I could muster my inner brave heart and solve this murder before them, I could get that tape off my door by tomorrow morning and salvage my weekend income from busloads of leaf-peepers. I shoved a key piece of equipment from my fieldwork into my bag and steered my Mini Cooper through picture-perfect fall color toward the college town.

I faced him, swallowing my nerves. He'd already killed once. Both my life and my livelihood depended on playing this like a talented performer. He'd invited me in, poured me a beer, offered me pretzels. I sat on his couch, avoiding the side piled high with academic journals. He sat opposite in an overstuffed easy chair, a display of grimacing Dogon masks on the wall behind him.

"I saw your grigri. On Berto's key ring."

His smile faded. "What are you talking about?"

"Berto is dead."

"What? Faraldo?" He jumped to his feet, pacing to the curtained window and back.

"Yes. He was killed in my store, and I saw your Tuareg grigri on his key ring when the police took it out of his pocket. That little leather triangle." I was pretty sure he was faking that surprise.

"Don't be ridiculous. Anybody could have a grigri."

"A Tuareg amulet? Like the one on your own key ring?"

"How do you know I gave it to him?" Sweat jumped out on his forehead. He blinked fast.

"You didn't like him. You told me that. And his research was better than yours."

"And?" His voice rose. "If I didn't like him, why would I give him something?"

"Come on." I let my voice soften. "We're old friends. Or at least colleagues. I know you believe in the power of a grigri, that it can carry a negative spell. Isn't that the focus of your research?"

He sank onto the chair opposite me. "You know it is."

"It made sense to me that you gave him the grigri. After having it cursed, of course." I reached out and laid my hand on his. "I don't blame you. He was too much competition for you."

He gazed at me for a moment. He nodded. "He's, he *was*, so much smarter than me. And did you see how he was still after Louie? God, I couldn't take it anymore." He squeezed my hand. "I love her. But you won't tell, will you? The police probably think Berto was simply drunk and fell."

"Right. He fell into the pickle barrel." I drew my eyebrows together. "I wonder how his head happened to land at that exact spot?"

He snorted. "The idiot was so drunk. Everybody there saw how sloshed he was. He only needed a little nudge with that disk on handles you have. What kind of crazy cooking thing is it, anyway?"

"It's a cast iron sandwich press. The handles are so you don't burn yourself while you're making a grilled cheese." I rose. "Hey, thanks for the beer." The amber liquid in my glass sat untouched, but he didn't seem to notice.

He walked me to the door. He grabbed my arm. His fingers pressed into my bicep harder than necessary. "You won't tell, right?"

I tsk-tsked at him. "We go way back, you and me. Would I do that? Besides, they seem to think it was an accident."

After I delivered my mini digital recorder to Wanda and told her what I'd heard George say, she said an illegal voice recording wasn't admissible evidence. But when I presented her with the plastic bag containing the antique sandwich press, which had to have both George's prints and Berto's DNA on it, she sent an officer out to bring George in right away. Looks like I had some talent, as it turned out. I didn't owe George anything.

With any luck, I'd be back in business before nightfall. I had pancakes to serve tomorrow, after all.

Dictation of Death

Lisa Ricard Claro

Emmaline Townsend yawned and repositioned her headphones for comfort. She glanced at the job box in the bottom right corner of her computer screen and her lips curved in a satisfied grin. Dr. Clemford's dictation would be her last, and after typing nonstop all afternoon, she was ready to call it quits. Her shoulders ached, her wrists tingled, and her left butt cheek was so sore she'd taken to leaning sideways to ease the pressure.

Medical transcription, she thought, *is not for sissies*. Thank God for Friday.

One more yawn and she was ready to roll. She positioned her fingers over the keyboard, brought up the doctor's personal template, and dropped her foot to the pedal. And there he was, her favorite doc, his Sam Elliott voice oozing into her ears like melting chocolate with a dash of jalapeno. Too bad he looked like Homer Simpson. Also too bad he'd just retired. She would miss him. Any day now, he'd have his dictations caught up and she wouldn't hear his voice again.

"This is William Clemford, MD, providing the consultation dictation for patient Gerald Cohen, medical record number 215788TRC, birth date September 8, 1935, date of service—hold on. Where the hell is—" Papers shuffled. "—oh, heh, heh, here it is. Sorry, Emmaline. Okay. Date of service is—hey, how'd you get in here? The office is closed. What do you think—now hold on just a minute. Put that away. You put that away, now. You don't want to do this. I'm your—please. No. Please!"

Bam! Bam-bam!

Emmaline gasped and stopped the playback, fingers frozen over the keyboard, heart pounding, eyes widened to the size of pizzas. Fear prickled her senses, but she depressed the pedal once more and strained to hear more of the digital recording. Her breathing quickened and she closed her eyes to concentrate.

She heard a person moving about, papers shuffling, a door closing, more moving about, and then someone picked up the telephone. Emmaline held her breath. The person on the other end breathed into the phone, inhalations labored. After a few seconds, the line went dead. Emmaline jumped when the end-of-job beep rang in her ears.

It was just a recording. The heavy breather wasn't there in real time. Of course he wasn't. He was long gone by now. She checked the time of dictation. One-ten this afternoon.

"Holy cow." She set the playback and listened again. No doubt about it. She'd just witnessed a murder.

Detective Miguel Rivera, known as "Hollywood" to friends and coworkers, gulped down the last of his coffee and checked his watch.

"Hey, pretty boy. You've only been here an hour."

Rivera glowered at his partner, Sonja Redstone, whose desk abutted his, putting them face-to-face. She stared him down across the width of their two workspaces and laughed when he flipped her off.

"Someone's cranky."

"I hate this shift," he said. "It goes slower than eight to five."

"Since when have we ever worked eight to five?" Sonja grabbed her thermos and nodded to Rivera. "You want more sludge?"

He mumbled an affirmative, grabbed a file from the cold case box next to his chair, and yawned. It promised to be a long night.

A minute later Sonja returned and set Rivera's mug, still empty, on his desk.

"Captain says we caught a case." She lifted her Glock from her desk drawer, punched in the magazine, and holstered her weapon.

"Thank God." He mirrored his partner's movements and flashed a crooked grin. "Maybe tonight won't be so bad after all."

Emmaline paced in the small office of Speedy Gonzales Transcription Service, awaiting the arrival of two detectives. She had called her boss, Yolanda Gonzales, to report the incident, but Yolanda was on vacation and hadn't answered her phone. *Probably sitting in a hot tub sipping piña coladas*, Emmaline thought with yearning.

Why, oh, why, did she have to be the one to hear that recording? Why did Dr. Clemford always neglect to pause the recording when he was interrupted while dictating? If he had just pressed the star key to pause, she wouldn't have his last words and those gunshots reverberating in her brain.

Emmaline knew personal things about the doctor due to his habit of not pausing his dictations when he was interrupted. It wasn't unusual for a thirty-minute dictation to be delivered to the transcribing system, only to discover that the recording contained only five minutes of actual dictation and twenty-five minutes of the doc chatting it up with whoever had wandered into his office. Due to this, Emmaline had learned all sorts of private things about the doctor over the years. She knew his mother's name was Gertie, that he hated artichokes, loved rhubarb pie, paid a genealogist to trace his family tree which uncovered the surprising discovery of multiple half-siblings (his father was quite the philanderer), and that he had a cancer scare just last year.

Emmaline held the information in strict confidence because she considered herself a professional, and because she believed that, in a weird sort of way, the doc entrusted her with it.

Nervous energy kept her moving, but she paused at the window and separated a couple of slats on the blinds to peer out to the parking lot. A piece-of-crap sedan screaming "government vehicle" pulled into the space nearest the office and its headlights went dark. The car doors opened and a man and woman exited the vehicle.

Her gaze skimmed over the woman—attractive and middle-aged with graying hair—and then stopped on the man. Her jaw dropped.

Holy cow. Is that guy a cop?

Emmaline abandoned her post and ran to the bathroom to fluff her hair. He might be here to question her as a witness to murder, but that didn't mean she couldn't look her best, did it? How many chances did a single, twenty-nine-year-old woman—*oh, fine, thirty-two*—get to meet the man of her dreams? Never, that's when. Would anyone blame her for taking advantage of the situation? God knew Dr. Clemford wouldn't mind. Maybe it was the doc's way of reaching from the Great Beyond to thank her for her years of outstanding service.

She ran back to the door and opened it. God help her. It wasn't a trick of the light. The man was gorgeous, with dark hair, cheekbones chiseled in stone, and sleepy eyes the color of Columbian coffee beans. The expensive ones that hinted of chocolate and hazelnut. And a touch of cinnamon.

"Ms. Townsend? Hello." The female cop waved her hand in front of Emmaline's face. "Over here, dear." She held up her shield for inspection.

Heat crawled up Emmaline's throat and into her face. From the annoyed-but-amused tone of the female cop's voice, and the sardonic curve of the man's lips, Emmaline knew she wasn't the first woman to fall victim to his charms. *But, oh, what a way to go.* She fanned her face with her hand.

"What? Oh, sorry." She forced her gaze to shift. "Is it hot in here? Sorry. I'm, you know, kind of in shock."

"I'm Detective Redstone, this is Detective Rivera. We understand you think you witnessed a murder?"

"Well, yes." She tucked her hair behind her ears. *Should've colored the roots this morning, damn it.* "Dr. William Clemford. He dictated around one o'clock today, so by the time I heard it, several hours passed since it happened. Did you go to his office? Did you find his body?"

"You do transcription here, Ms. Townsend?"

Holy cow. His voice caressed a sexy accent that sort of matched his eyes. It sounded the way her favorite coffee beans tasted after they weren't coffee beans anymore but had been brewed into a delectable beverage. *Oh, yum!*

"Ms. Townsend?"

"What? Sorry. Shock." Emmaline caught Detective Redstone rolling her eyes. "Yes. I'm a medical transcriptionist. You could say I'm a professional listener. So, um, I began the job and it started like normal, but then someone interrupted, and Dr. Clemford didn't press the star key. The star key puts the job on hold. That way he can, you know, do whatever, and it doesn't keep recording. Only he didn't hit the star key. He never does, he always forgets. So it kept recording." Emmaline shuddered and rubbed her arms to make the goose bumps go away. Maybe she really was in shock, one minute hot, the next minute cold—or worse, maybe it was early onset menopause. Holy cow. That would be worse than shock. That would be—

"Ms. Townsend?" Rivera's sexy coffee-voice flowed like silk and interrupted Emmaline's train of thought. "You still with us?"

Emmaline nodded like a bobblehead.

"You know the doctor personally?" Rivera asked.

"We met once, right after he became a client. He wanted to know who would be handling his work. He's a nice man."

"I'm sure the recording was a shock, but we need to hear it," Detective Redstone said.

Emmaline ushered the detectives into the transcription room. She queued up the job and handed the headphones to Redstone. The detectives listened and exchanged a look.

"I see why you thought you'd heard a murder," Rivera said. "Is this the only dictation you received from Dr. Clemford today?"

Emmaline looked from Rivera's face to Redstone's. "Yes. What's wrong? Other than someone murdering Dr. Clemford, I mean."

"That's just it, Ms. Townsend." Rivera's dark eyes turned toward Emmaline. "Contrary to what one might infer from this recording, Dr. Clemford was not the victim of a shooting. He is, in fact, very much alive."

Emmaline sat at her workstation and stared at the screen. She queued the job and closed her eyes to listen again. Somewhere in this recording was a clue, something to explain what she heard, even in the face of Dr. Clemford himself telling the cops it must have been a macabre practical joke.

To the detectives' credit, they had allowed Emmaline to pepper them with questions before they departed, the answers to which all led back to the same conclusion: No dead doctor, no case.

After Emmaline's 911 call, paramedics and police officers had been dispatched to the scene. The office was found to be clean and tidy. No blood, no body, no crime.

Redstone and Rivera had also been through the non-crime scene. They did so in the company of Dr. Clemford and his wife, Nancy, who had abandoned their posh dinner at the best Sushi restaurant in town in order to accommodate the emergency situation, or lack thereof.

"Let it go, Ms. Townsend," Redstone said on her way out the door. "This was just someone's idea of a tasteless prank."

"But it isn't," Emmaline said aloud in the quiet of the empty office. She'd been listening to Dr. Clemford's voice five days a week for more than five years, and the voice on the recording was his. So unless Dr. Clemford pranked himself, gunshots were fired in the doctor's office that afternoon. And maybe there was no dead body, but something sure smelled bad.

"You're brooding, Hollywood. What's got you stewing?"

"The Clemford case."

"There is no case. We talked to the doc, interviewed his wife, walked through the office." She shrugged. "The guy's not dead. Let it go. It was just a prank."

He tugged on his lower lip and frowned. "The gunshots on that recording sounded real."

"Maybe the doc was in on the joke and was just too embarrassed to admit it."

Rivera grunted and keyed the doctor's web address into the search function on his computer and settled in to learn a little more about Dr. William Clemford.

Emmaline trudged into the Speedy Gonzales office the next morning. It wasn't her practice to work on Saturdays, but when she checked the transcription system from home she found twelve new dictations in the queue, six from Dr. Clemford recorded late last night, long after his spectacular non-murder.

Emmaline snugged the headphones into place and queued up the first of Dr. Clemford's dictations.

"This is Dr. William Clemford, dictating for a patient named, uh, Bruce McBride. The patient has, uh, prostate cancer. Uh, PSA of 6.3. Uh, Gleason's grade, uh, 7. Uh, 3 + 4 = 7. He had a prostaticectomy on—"

Emmaline lifted her foot from the pedal and stared at the computer screen. She rewound the dictation and listened again. Since when did Dr. Clemford, a urologist, mispronounce the word prostatectomy?

A niggling shiver worked its way up her spine. She ignored it and continued the dictation.

"—on June, uh, uh. In June. He has an, uh, ISSP score of—"

What? Emmaline listened again, and the shiver rippled to her extremities, lifting goose bumps across her skin.

"IPSS," Emmaline whispered. "It's IPSS."

"—score of, uh, 12. His AUA score is—" A female voice speaks in the background. "—just a minute, just a minute." A click pauses the dictation, and another click resumes the dictation. "Okay, uh, where was I? Oh, uh, review of systems."

Emmaline stopped the dictation. To any other transcriptionist, this recording would be nothing more than an ageing doctor muddling his way through a report, but Emmaline knew better. The voice sounded like Dr. Clemford's, but the delivery was wrong. The cadence was off, the humor nonexistent, and the dictation format skewed. In the most telling clue of all, the star key had been used to pause the dictation, something Dr. Clemford had failed to do even once in all the years he was a client of Speedy Gonzales.

The doc had retired, but she knew he was spending Saturdays in his office boxing things and preparing to close the office for good.

Maybe it was time she met Dr. Clemford face-to-face one more time.

Emmaline walked into Dr. Clemford's office and peered through the sliding glass window at the front desk. "Hello?"

A middle-aged woman appeared from the hallway. Dressed in designer jeans and a low-cut top, her big hair and blue eye shadow were a throwback to the '80s. She held her lips pursed as if she'd just sucked a lemon. The woman picked her way across the carpet on stiletto shoes and slid the window open.

"The door should have been locked. Dr. Clemford is retired."

Emmaline held up a ceramic pot containing a robust philodendron. "I'm from Speedy Gonzales. We do Dr. Clemford's transcriptions. I was hoping to see him in person."

"Speedy Gonzales. *You* called the police yesterday."

Emmaline offered a sheepish smile. "I'm really sorry about that."

"A prank," she said. "I'm Nancy Clemford. You can leave the plant with me."

"I'd like to give it to the doctor in person," Emmaline said. Mrs. Clemford raised her brows and, desperate, Emmaline blurted a lie. "Before he passed, my father was a patient of Dr. Clemford's. Please. It would mean so much." She made a mental note to apologize to her dad for killing him off.

The doctor's wife sighed, pursed her lips again, nodded, and disappeared down the hall.

The door from the back office opened, and Emmaline plastered on a smile and braced to face the doctor.

"Hello. My, uh, wife, uh, Nancy, tells me you're from, uh, Speedy-Guns-or-Less." He held out his hand in greeting. "It's a pleasure to meet you."

Emmaline shook his hand and struggled to maintain her smile. She hoped the doctor would recognize her. They had met only once, but he spoke to her by name in his dictations. How could he be confused now?

"We met once," Emmaline said, unable to hide her consternation.

"Your father was a patient?"

"That isn't what I meant, sir. I'm Emmaline Townsend. I do your transcription."

"Ah, yes," he nodded, but it was clear he had no clue. "How are you, Emma?"

Foreboding raised the fine hairs on Emmaline's arms and at the nape of her neck. The man's voice, his looks—they were Dr. Clemford's, but...not. How was that possible?

Something, Emmaline thought, *is very wrong.*

Emmaline backed up, her eyes widening. "I'm sorry for bothering you. I really should go now."

Nancy Clemford's eyes narrowed. "I don't know how, but she knows. Lock the door. We'll have to take care of her."

The man rushed to do the woman's bidding, pushing Emmaline out of his way. Emmaline threw the potted plant at his head and it connected with a sickening thud. The doctor—or whoever he was—dropped like a stone. Emmaline lunged toward the door, held back by the missus who kicked off her stilettos and ran across the room to clutch Emmaline's shirt in her fists.

Emmaline grabbed at the door, screaming for help, but her sweaty hands slid off the brass knob. Mrs. Clemford pulled her backward by her shirt, and Emmaline dragged the two of them forward again as she lurched, using the full force of her body weight.

The door swung open and both women hurtled forward, colliding with the solid body of Detective Miguel Rivera.

Rivera caught Emmaline in his arms and disengaged Mrs. Clemford with no more than an angry scowl, a feat that Emmaline found impressive and, really, quite sexy.

Not the time for that, Emmaline, Dr. Clemford's voice said in her head. Right.

"That's not the real Dr. Clemford." Emmaline indicated the imposter on the floor. "And she knows it." She glared at Nancy Clemford.

"Arrest this woman," Mrs. Clemford said. "She broke in here and attacked me and my husband. We were only protecting ourselves."

"Actually, ma'am, I've uncovered some interesting facts in the last twenty-four hours. I also obtained search warrants." Rivera's lips curved into a smile. "Guess what we found?"

The woman's red lips puckered in a two-lemon pinch.

Emmaline heard the whole story from Detective Redstone who had joined Rivera in the all-night search for more information about Dr. William Clemford. Their first break came with an article in an online magazine penned by the good doctor himself. He detailed his experience with genealogy, and discovery of multiple half-siblings. The most interesting finding was a brother of the same age who, in Clemford's own words, "could be my twin."

The theory of events unfolded in rapid succession after that. Armed with the genealogy information, the recording of Dr. Clemford's murder, the discovery of multiple communications between Nancy Clemford and the "twin," and what appeared to be insurance fraud, Rivera had convinced his poker pal, who also happened to be his favorite judge, to sign search warrants in the case. A subsequent search of Nancy Clemford's vehicle yielded all the evidence necessary for an arrest: the body of Dr. William Clemford, rolled up in an oriental carpet soaked with blood.

"What you did was foolhardy and dangerous," Rivera told Emmaline as he walked her to her car. "You might have been killed."

"But I wasn't," Emmaline said. "You showed up in the nick of time."

Rivera smiled. "Go home and get some rest, Ms. Townsend. You've earned it."

Emmaline thought of inviting him for coffee, but her heart pounded too hard and her tongue tied up. Instead, she settled for a glass of pinot noir alone on her living room couch. Two sips in, her cell phone rang. She didn't recognize the number but answered anyway. "Hello?"

"Thought you'd like to know they ratted each other out and took a plea. You don't have to testify."

Emmaline gasped and blurted, "That's great! So, um, would you be interested in celebrating with a glass of pinot noir?"

"You didn't even ask who this is," the voice scolded. "Do you always invite random callers into your home for alcoholic beverages?"

"I'd recognize your voice anytime, anywhere, Detective." The moment the words popped out, she squeezed her eyes shut and gave herself a mental head slap. *Holy cow. Way to sound like a stalker, Emmaline.*

Rivera laughed. "Next time I call I'll change it up, try to trick you. For now, thank you, yes. I'd love a glass of pinot noir."

Emmaline punched the air with her fist. He said *yes!* "You can try to trick me, Detective, but you can't fool me. I'm a professional."

THE ZOOKEEPERS

EILEEN DUNBAUGH

S unrise. Mid-October.
Marilyn Harris runs a brush through her hair, while in the kitchen down the hall her son slumps behind a plate of eggs, thumbs on the Nintendo in his lap.

"Five minutes, pal," she says, coming into the kitchen. The eggs look like life rafts in the sea of ketchup he's poured around them.

"Do you hear me?"

He makes no comment.

"You aren't ready in another couple of minutes, Jimmy, I'm taking that thing."

Her arm angles across the countertop for the name tag that identifies her as a Cavendish County Sheriff's Deputy. She pins it on, picks up handbag, keys, and coat, and starts for the door. Jimmy follows at a pace that dares her to enforce her threat.

He hops into the back of the minivan, where it will be hard for her to speak to him. She takes a deep breath before she says, "I'm sorry, Jimmy, but your dad can't pick you up today."

No comment. His Nintendo beeps.

Neither of them says a word as she drives, but her hand on the steering wheel, a white stripe where her ring used to be, makes the accusation plainly enough.

If he would just speak to her—shout at her if he needs to, but get it out—she thinks she could begin to bridge the gulf between them. But he doesn't, and she can't free herself of a defensive reflex where his father is concerned, so she sticks to routine. "After school," she says, "you'll have to ride with me till I get off work. Or maybe, if it's a slow afternoon, Suzanne will play cards with you."

They've turned into the parking lot of the middle school now and he jumps out of the van.

"Be *right here,* Jimmy, three o'clock," she says.

He puffs out his lips—he's heard her—but his eyes glide away across the grounds.

"Hey, what's with the sour face?"

Harris stops and turns back to the glassed-in cubicle at the entrance to the sheriff's department.

"You look like something's bugging you."

"Not really. Nothing other than Jimmy."

"Same old?"

"If you mean pretending I don't exist, yeah."

"Ah, he'll get over it, Marilyn." The jolly face comes farther out of the cubicle. "Gotta be hard on him."

"Yeah, well, he was never an easy kid, but now he's downright impossible—you should see the way his eyes slither around."

Suzanne makes a zipper sign and points behind Harris. She leans back in her chair and closes the sliding-glass window.

Harris makes an effort to smile at her boss. It's their busiest time of year; the town's bed and breakfasts are all full. Yesterday he'd warned her that her shifts would be longer.

"No problem, Bud," she'd said. But now she avoids his gaze.

The tourists who come here are not the sort to cause trouble, but they bring their share of emergencies—car accidents, food poisonings, heart attacks.

Sprawl is limited by the surrounding mountains, allowing the town to remain much as it was generations ago, protected, as the sheriff likes to say, by "the jewel of small-town law enforcement"—his own three-person force.

This time of year, though, he is vigilant.

"We ought-a run by the parking lots for the arboretum and the nature trail," he says. "Make sure no one's taking advantage of an unlocked Bimmer."

"Zoo's open, too," he adds with a snort.

Whenever the sheriff speaks of the zoo, or the elite prep school that houses it, he punctuates what he says with a snort, for the school has discouraged patrols of its premises despite persistent rumors of vandalism and theft.

"You want me to run by there too?" Harris says.

"*Hell no!*" he roars. "Leave 'em to their preppy pie in the sky, that's the way they want it."

Once the sheriff has turned into his office, the face at the cubicle pops out again. "Since we're talking about Jimmy, Mar, do you need to leave him with me this afternoon?"

Harris's head bobs.

"Don can't take him, huh? Is it the *girlfriend?*" Suzanne mouths the word, then adds: "Don't give it another thought. Jimmy doesn't seem all that bad to me. We get along just fine."

While Harris is on patrol in other parts of town, three tourists stand on a bridge overlooking a duck pond. The wind catches the hair of one of the women. Close beside her, bent and frail, is an older woman. A mother and daughter.

The mother turns to a man whose hair is thinning and streaked with gray. She points across the bridge to a sign that says "Warren School Zoo" and gives prices for admission. Advancing in that direction, the man catches up to a younger woman, who swings the camera strapped over her shoulder to her opposite hip and slips a hand with two diamond-studded rings into the belt loops at his back.

There is no one in sight as the family of tourists makes its way up the path and through the door of the first building: no one to take money or issue tickets. The Warren School Zoo is run on the honor system.

The local newspaper's Activities section, provided at the bed and breakfast where the family has rooms, describes this facility as a center for the study of rare and endangered species, run by students of the boarding school. At this hour, classes must be in session but it's odd, they remark, to find their access not only to the school but to the zoo unmonitored.

In the vestibule of the first building, they drop donations into a clear plastic box and hang back for a moment. The daughter wrinkles her nose at the air from the inner doorway.

They move into the first room warily. On the left, figure-eight loops of snakes, piled one on top of the other; on the right, lemurs snuggled together on a branch, heads tucked down almost out of view. The mother makes a pillow with her hands, as if she too would like a nap. Her daughter smiles at this, hooks a hand around her elbow, and guides her under a black curtain into a room that houses nocturnal creatures, mostly bats and rodents. They're restless as they move along, until, around a corner, they encounter something the identifying card calls a "Slow Loris," which moves like a dancer suspending momentum.

They stand transfixed as it travels up to nose them at the glass, then reverses back up the branches into the deeper darkness behind. By the time the long gray arms and black-ringed eyes have disappeared, leaving visible only the white patches of its small underbelly, they've lost their apprehension. The wife uncases her camera and looks around. But there's no light source above or behind.

Forgetting the picture, the family pivots as one toward the far end of the exhibit, expecting another exotic creature. But there they find only the familiar *"homo sapiens juvenalis,"* the mother jokes—a boy who startles them by slipping out from behind a service sink shielded by a black curtain.

Their laughter is cut short when the daughter's hand goes to her chest. The mother is beside her instantly. "Oh dear! Use your inhaler." She reaches for her daughter's bag.

"It's nothing," the daughter says. She raises her voice for the benefit of the boy, who is letting in light from an open back door: "We didn't see you there, you startled us."

The daughter-in-law rolls her eyes. At the bed and breakfast the night before, as her sister-in-law sat in the common room "sucking on her inhaler," she had taken the hotel's owner aside and told her not to worry: "It's all over-dramatized."

The owner, thirty-something and dressed in tight-fitting leggings, had smiled and winked.

The boy at the zoo hears—his neck stiffens—but he doesn't reply. He disappears before they can say anything more.

The tourists retrace their steps to the front of the building and continue along the path that joins this wooden rotunda to several others. Fenced and netted enclosures surround each of the houses.

The day is cold and damp, but the clear light is low enough now to hit the yellow and red leaves of the maples from behind, lending a pleasant golden glow to everything. The mother looks at her watch, sees that it is nearly three, and casts a glance behind her, as if to see whether she might spot the boy from the service area.

At three o'clock, on the other side of town, Officer Harris is sitting in her cruiser, tapping the steering wheel as she scans the paths leading to the front of the school. The other children have all boarded buses or been picked up. But Jimmy is nowhere in sight. After fifteen minutes, she mutters a word she's told Jimmy she'll wash his mouth out for saying and pilots the car to a permanent space.

Outside the car, she hesitates, hands on her thick leather belt and holster. Jimmy's latest taunt is "butch," something he picked up from his father. The boy clearly recognizes the value of the word as an insult, even if he doesn't understand its meaning.

She closes the cruiser's door with an emphatic bang and starts up the path. A teacher is cleaning up inside a classroom, door open to the walk.

"Jimmy here?" Harris says, poking her head in.

The teacher stares at her. "Jimmy? …I thought he'd already been picked up. You know, I bet he's down at the creek. I had trouble getting him to come in at recess…"

At the zoo, as the sun declines enough to create more shadow than color, several students seem to materialize out of nowhere. They flit past the family, weaving around them on the paths without acknowledgment, carrying buckets, sniggering, passing comments.

In front of an enclosure with long grass in which several emus pace the son says, "Looks like they're guarding the wallaby squatting there—see it?" The wife nods, then leans close to her mother-in-law and whispers: "What kind of parents send their kids to a place like this?"

The mother raises her eyebrows. "What do you mean?"

"There aren't any *adults* here."

"Of course there are!"

But in fact, as they'd driven through the campus of white clapboard schoolhouses and sports fields, only a few figures on the horizon were large enough to be adults. And it was possible those were only big high-schoolers, like the one with the blond hair who has passed them on the paths several times already.

"They're in the school buildings," the mother says. "You wouldn't expect them to be hanging around outside."

"Well, there can't be many of them," her daughter-in-law insists.

The mother frowns and adjusts her jacket. She knows her daughter-in-law thinks she's overly solicitous of her grown children.

They move on to a cage of miniature pandas, where their pairing shifts—the mother next to the daughter again; the son back with his wife. The mother is pulling the neck of her jacket close around her throat now and looking, periodically, toward the exit. But her daughter isn't ready to go. They continue on to two small fields surrounding outcroppings of rock. In one of these a Japanese Serow—a bony, goat-like creature—stands at the top of the uppermost projection.

In the neighboring compound, the rock juts into empty space—until around its flank lopes the unmistakable low-crouched form of a wolf. And then another…and then another. The intake of breath from the two women is sharp and simultaneous.

The mother is shivering now, and pulls her sleeve back to check her watch. The daughter puts an arm around her and surveys the nearby exhibits. They find the others on a bridge that bisects an aviary for birds of prey. The daughter-in-law has her camera out and whirring, the sound causing a falcon to fly. She clucks her satisfaction at the picture this allows her to take, and after rotating her to aim toward the other side of the bridge, her husband claps his hands to startle a great horned owl into flight. The owl proves immovable, but a hawk, previously sullen on its perch, suddenly swoops to within inches of her lens.

As the son and his wife plead time for just one more picture, the mother and daughter bounce on the balls of their feet and shrink into their coats. Instead of following the flights of the birds, their heads scan left and right at more distant movement, tracking the increasingly frequent loops of the zookeepers on the paths.

"These kids probably want to close up," the mother says, and the daughter emphatically waves the others towards them.

A small building seems to offer a shortcut to the parking lot. "At least you'll be able to get warm for a minute," the daughter says as she ushers the mother inside and holds the door for her brother and sister-in-law.

Through the large windows on one side of the building, the mother sees the blond boy. He passes the entrance and steps onto a deck, followed by a dark-skinned boy with dreadlocks. By the time they disappear from view, a teenage girl has fallen into file. Then a boy with lank brown hair and skin spotted with acne—the boy they'd seen in the service area of the first rotunda. The mother signals her sightings to the others, who urge her to "just relax and get warm."

Rubbing hands and hugging themselves to press the warmth of the building into their clothes, the family zigzags down the corridor. The cases here are small and set at eye-level. A dusty tarantula at the front of one glass case causes the daughter to step back and turn to the opposite wall, where a chameleon is pasted almost invisibly, except for the pulse at its throat, against one side of its tiny room.

Halfway down the hallway a break in the wall on one side gives access to a service area behind the cages. A muscular arm, a puffa vest, blue jeans, and a blond head fill the space, but soon slide beyond the sight line of the hallway, replaced by three other moving figures, similarly there and then gone.

The mother checks her watch again and presses her hand into her son's back. Her daughter and daughter-in-law have their heads together at one of the cases.

In front of the reassembled family, the four zookeepers emerge from the service area. The blond trails a broom, and several paces behind him, the boy with dreadlocks rolls a bucket with a mop. The girl and the boy with acne come behind, rolling garbage bins. They brush by the little family silently. The blond passes so close that the daughter's purse swings from a bump of his arm.

The family pauses to let the students pass, and then the daughter opens the mouth of her purse wider as they too turn for the exit. The other three watch as she shakes the purse to bring her car keys to the surface. Suddenly, her eyes go wide with confusion—

By the time Officer Harris tracks her son and herds him back to the parking lot, the radio inside the cruiser is squawking like an enraged crow.

From the open door of a beat-up Volkswagen a couple of spaces down, the teacher who spoke to the deputy earlier hangs onto her car's doorframe. "Sounds like someone's trying to get you," she says. "I didn't know if I should call someone."

Harris is already keying the lock. "It's all right," she says, waving the teacher off.

Suzanne's voice sputters deafeningly through static: *"There* you are! Another two minutes I'd've had to call Bud."

Harris pushes the talk button. "What's up?"

"Incident at the zoo."

"It looked like a bracelet at first," the mother tells the EMS worker, "pink and yellow."

But then the thing had moved! Writhed like a baby. Her daughter had instinctively grabbed it to throw it from her purse, but a spasm stopped her. She fell back against the wall as the six-inch ribbon of snake propelled itself to the floor and into the shadows of the service area.

The rest of the family had stood frozen, until the daughter-in-law let out a shriek, pulled her phone from her pocket, and began punching at it, unable to find the right numbers.

"EMS is there. Medics say it might be a heart attack," Suzanne's words thunder through the speaker.

By now the teacher has reversed out of her space and puttered out onto the highway. Harris is relieved; bad news is discouraged in this town that thrives on its leaf tourism.

"Everything's under control then, right?"

"Would I be paging you if it was? Family is off the wall. Telling the EMS guys, 'They meant to hurt her.' Something about the kids..."

"Cripes," Harris says. She rotates in her seat, eyes scanning the parking lot beyond her open door. "They headed for the ER?"

"Yeah."

"Okay, I'm taking Jimmy with me."

The boy has wandered about five yards from the car. He's carrying a jar of worms she told him to leave at the creek. When she'd found him, he'd continued digging as if she weren't there. Her "Let's get going" was ignored long enough for it to appear to be his idea to move. Now he's using a stick to tip the worms onto the asphalt—

"Stop that!" she shouts. She's on him in a second, but he shoulders her away. "Get in the car! Now!"

At the hospital, she doesn't have to struggle to get Jimmy out. The anger that charges the small waiting room radiates all the way out to the curb.

A man in a blue blazer with an emblem on the pocket is protesting and gesturing.

"They *knew* she had asthma. That boy with the acne knew!" a woman is shouting back, shaking a hand that flashes diamonds. "He startled us at the first exhibit. She nearly had to use her inhaler."

Harris doesn't need to ask why they're there.

"Let's find a private place to talk," she says when they have all identified themselves.

"My husband and mother-in-law are in with her," the woman says.

Harris has them shown to a staff lounge with plastic chairs, a Naugahyde couch, a Coke machine. As they wait for the others, the deputy sees that the sky outside the window is starting to be shot through with red fire.

A nurse finally leads in an elderly woman and a middle-aged man. The woman sits on the couch, her son hovering near.

At Harris's request, the mother slowly lays before them the events of the afternoon.

"It was a prank. That snake wasn't poisonous," the school official injects into the silence that follows her words.

The mother struggles against the softness of the couch, straightening enough to look him in the eye. "A prank? All right. But I saw them watching from the far end of the corridor, and when they saw my daughter fall and saw we were having trouble calling for help, do you know what they did?

"That blond boy swiveled around and continued out the door. And the other kids may have been wide-eyed for a moment, but they fumbled with their buckets and bins and followed right behind him."

Harris has been stealing occasional glimpses at her son as the old woman speaks. His Nintendo has remained in his school bag. He isn't fidgeting or swinging his feet or kicking the chairs.

"They're children," the man in the blazer says, with an open-handed gesture.

The mother directs her next words to Harris, as if, with that remark, he's made himself irrelevant.

"They're almost adults," she says. "And they should be held accountable."

There is silence for a moment and then the mother adds, "You have to wonder how they got that way." Saliva escapes from her mouth in a thin stream, giving her a look of venomousness, and this time her gaze is a laser directed at the school official.

He isn't the only one who flinches, though. Harris glances at Jimmy again...and wonders. Most nights as he waits for her to close up the station and hand over to the state police, he's into some kind of mischief. But now he isn't acting up at all; his eyes are locked on the old woman, and his body is still.

Too still.

A nurse appears at the door to the lounge, followed by a doctor who is pulling off neoprene gloves. At the sight of them, the family is paralyzed with fear. Harris can see it, and she can tell too, from the doctor's face, what he is here to say.

"I'm sorry," he begins.

The mother moans and starts to rock forward.

Harris glances at Jimmy and sees a slow smile begin to crease his face.

AT STORM'S END

HARRIETTE SACKLER

By the time Marcie Freeland left her boutique at two o'clock in the afternoon, the hurricane had struck. Torrential rain and gale force winds made it nearly impossible to drive the short distance home. Marcie would have moved inland during the storm, were it not for concern about her mother. Marcie loved her mom, but she was consumed by Alice's neediness. Being the daughter of an alcoholic had drained Marcie's energy and taken its toll on her well-being, not to mention her social life.

Roads were flooded. Marcie inched along through water that rose halfway up the car doors. Her neck and arms ached with tension as she attempted to maneuver and cursed like a sailor when she realized that her brakes were no longer working. She managed to turn right into a parking lot and bring her car to a stop against a curb. She knew she couldn't drive again until the brakes dried out. She wasn't close enough to walk the rest of the way, so she would just sit and wait.

Almost two hours later, Marcie pulled into the garage under the luxury condo building. When her dad had succumbed to brain cancer, he left his wife and only daughter with the resources to live their lives in comfort. Alice had received the lion's share of the estate, and Marcie inherited sufficient funds to start her business. It was tragic that her mother had turned to alcohol to numb the pain and loss she suffered when her husband passed.

Marcie took the elevator to the fourth floor to check on her mother before heading to her own twelfth floor apartment.

"Mom? It's me," Marcie announced as she unlocked the door and stepped inside. She was met with silence. Chances were Alice was sleeping, sprawled on the sofa or in bed.

The living room appeared as it always did. Several glasses and a half-empty bottle of gin littered the coffee table, along with a disorganized array of newspapers and magazines. Marcie didn't doubt for a minute that her mother had ordered enough liquor from her favorite store to get her through the storm. Drapes were closed over the windows and balcony door. The kitchen was in order, except for the collection of unwashed dishes in the sink. The bathroom was dark and empty. Marcie checked her mother's bedroom, which was also vacant. Alice wasn't in the apartment.

Marcie was confused. Her mother rarely left the apartment unless it was with her daughter. This wasn't the way it should be.

Was it possible that her mom was visiting someone in the building? But who? After the summer season, half the condo owners closed up their apartments and left the beach community until late spring. She was certain that most of the year-rounders had evacuated inland until the storm's end.

Marcie tried to quell the anxiety growing in her gut. She'd knock on every apartment door, hoping that her mom had sought the companionship of another resident.

Starting on the first floor, Marcie went from door to door. No luck until 6D. Seth Adams, a freelance writer, lived at the beach when he wasn't chasing a story in another part of the world. Marcie and Seth shared a cordial relationship and had even gone to breakfast together a few times.

"Hey, Marcie, good to see you. Come in."

"Hi, Seth. By any chance, have you seen my mother today? She's not in her apartment. I can't imagine where she'd be."

"No I haven't seen her. Where've you looked?"

"Well, I just made my way up from the first floor, but you're the first person I've found in the building."

"Listen, Marcie, you've got six floors to go. Let me grab my keys and I'll help you out. Your mom didn't head for your apartment?"

"Thanks, Seth. No, she doesn't have a key to my place. I've told you about her drinking problem and, in truth, my place is my special refuge."

"I'm with you. Believe me, I know about the need for privacy. Okay, I'll take seven, eight, and nine and you cover the top three floors. Let's meet back here. Hopefully with Mrs. Freeland in tow."

They both returned to Seth's apartment half an hour later without any success. Only three apartments were occupied. But no one had seen Alice Freeland. Marcie felt her anxiety mounting.

She pulled her cell phone out of her jacket pocket and dialed 9-1-1.

"Oceanview Police Department. Officer Black speaking. What is your emergency?"

Marcie told the officer about her mother's apparent disappearance.

"Ms. Freeland, it takes forty-eight hours for an individual to be considered a missing person. But, given that we're in the middle of a hurricane, I can send someone out first thing in the morning. Tonight all our personnel are responding to injury calls. In the meantime, why don't you contact Oceanview Hospital and St. John's emergency shelter to see if she's there. If you don't have any success, call back in the morning and we'll send a patrol car over. I'm sorry, that's the best we can do."

As suggested, Marcie checked with both the hospital and the church, but came away empty. Where was her mother?

She turned to Seth, who was watching her with concern. "I'm going to spend the night at my mother's apartment. Maybe, maybe, she'll walk through the door and this will all be over."

"Okay, Marcie. Please call me if you need me."

"I will, Seth. Thanks for your help."

Marcie spent the night, pacing, crying, and wondering if her mother had slipped beyond alcoholism into even more serious mental illness. After her dad's death, she'd moved them down to the beach, hoping that the slower pace of life and beauty of the surroundings would lift her mother's spirit. But no such luck. Marcie had consulted with mental health agencies, and even met with an attorney to try to find a way to get Alice into treatment. But, since her mother wasn't considered incompetent or dangerous, there just wasn't anything to be done.

Marcie must have dozed off at some point. When she opened her eyes, gray light filtered into the apartment. Her watch read 6:05. Her head throbbed and her body felt stiff and achy.

She called 9-1-1 again and reported that her mother was still missing. A patrol car would be dispatched to the building no later than eight o'clock.

While she waited, she went into the kitchen and made a pot of high test, hoping the coffee would help chase away the cobwebs in her head.

With cup in hand, Marcie opened the curtains that covered the balcony door. The rain had eased since last night and was now a drizzle. The sky was dull and gray. She unlocked the door and stepped outside. The wind was still fierce, and Marcie held on to the balcony rail. She looked to both the left and right but not a soul was on the beach.

Marcie glanced down at the building's outdoor pool. Furniture had been removed and a canvas tarp covered the water. Marcie's eyes were drawn to a corner of the pool enclosure where some familiar-looking cloth was caught on the fence. She stared. Then she screamed.

Marcie turned and ran toward the front door, the cup she was holding crashed to the floor. She didn't bother with the elevator, just took the stairs to the lobby at breakneck speed, and raced out the door leading to the pool. As she drew closer, she saw that the piece of cloth was her mother's robe. Alice's crumpled body lay underneath. Blood covered her head. Marcie leaned over her mother, pleading with Alice to wake up.

She pulled out her cell and called Seth's number. After three rings, a sleepy voice answered.

"Lo?"

"Seth, it's Marcie. I'm down by the pool. My mom is here, and I have to get her inside. Can you help me?"

"I'll be right there."

In a matter of minutes, Seth was beside her. He gently moved Marcie aside and bent down next to Alice. He checked her pulse, and then shook his head.

"There's nothing we can do for your mom. She's gone. I'm so sorry."

Marcie looked into Seth's eyes. No, he had to be wrong.

Seth called the police. When they arrived only minutes later, Seth suggested that he take her up to his apartment. He told the police they would be in 6D.

Marcie was inconsolable. He set her on his couch, covering her with a blanket to help quell the shivering that wracked her body. He brought her some brandy and held the glass to her lips as she gulped it down.

An hour later, the police knocked on Seth's door.

"I'm Detective McManus and this is Detective Myers, Mr. ..."

"Adams. Seth Adams."

"Mr. Adams, the coroner just left, and Mrs. Freeland's body is being transported to his office. Ms. Freeland, we're very sorry for your loss. I can tell you that, based on the coroner's preliminary examination, it's his opinion that Mrs. Freeland suffered a severe fall that caused multiple bone fractures and head trauma."

Detective Myers addressed Marcie in a soft voice. "Ms. Freeland, I know you've just suffered a terrible loss, but we'd like you to tell us everything you remember from yesterday and this morning."

"Yes. Yes. Of course."

Seth excused himself and left the room.

The two detectives sat down in armchairs across from Marcie.

"We want to be as brief as possible, and then let you be for today," Detective McManus said.

Detective Myers removed a small spiral notebook from the inside pocket of his jacket.

"Can you tell us exactly what happened? We know this is difficult, but we have to ask."

Marcie haltingly recounted yesterday's events. She told them about the hurricane preparations both she and her assistant manager had worked on until they both left the shop at two o'clock. She recounted everything that had happened after. Bouts of tears interrupted her.

When Marcie had answered all the detectives' questions, they rose from their chairs.

"Again, Ms. Freeland, our condolences for your loss. We do ask that you come down to the precinct tomorrow to sign the statement we'll prepare from the information you've given us. Will 10:00 a.m. be convenient for you?"

Marcie wiped tears from her eyes. "I'll be there."

That night, Marcie sat in her living room, staring into space.

She'd miss her mother, but she also felt a sense of relief. After all these years, Marcie would finally be able to have a life of her own.

Already in her late thirties, might she dare to hope that she could someday have a husband? Children? An existence without the responsibility of constantly tending to Alice's needs? But for now, Marcie had to focus on the present. In death, her mother still needed her.

When Marcie arrived at the police precinct the following morning, she was greeted by Detective McManus, who ushered her to an interview room and offered her coffee. She'd never been at the station before. As a matter of fact, she'd never been in a police station anywhere. It looked a lot nicer than the portrayals she'd seen on television. When Detective McManus returned with a mug of steaming coffee for her, he sat down across the table.

"Ms. Freeland, we received the coroner's report this morning. There's something to be said about living in a low-crime area. The autopsy confirmed that your mother died from severe trauma due to a fall. The injury to her skull resulted in a brain hemorrhage that was the cause of death. She also evidenced what might be interpreted as defensive wounds to her hands. Your mother died somewhere between the hours of noon and four o'clock the day of the hurricane. The toxicology report is pending."

During what felt like hours, Detective McManus asked Marcie so many questions, her head began to ache. He wanted her to tell him about the relationship with her mother. Did Mrs. Freeland have life insurance? Who would inherit her assets upon her death? He asked about Marcie's business. Was the store doing well or having financial difficulties? Had anyone seen her parked car during the time she stated her brakes had been compromised? Could anyone have entered her mother's apartment without permission?

It didn't take long for Marcie to comprehend that the police considered her a suspect in her mother's death. It terrified her to realize that her answers to Detective McManus' questions could only heighten their suspicions. While Marcie had inherited a significant amount of money from her dad, she'd invested most of it in her condo and shop. Her mom had received the larger portion of the inheritance. While Marcie's shop was holding its own, it was a far cry from being considered a moneymaker. Yes, when Alice Freeland passed away, Marcie would be the beneficiary of all her mother's assets. No, her mother's front door locked automatically when it closed, and she was not in the habit of opening the door to strangers.

"Detective McManus, in spite of all her problems, I loved my mother. It would never have occurred to me to hurt her. Yet it seems that I'm under suspicion for causing my mother's death. Am I under arrest?"

"Let's not get ahead of ourselves, Ms. Freeland. You've got to understand that your mother died under unusual circumstances. There was no evidence of forced entry into her apartment. According to your own statement, the balcony door was locked when you arrived to check in with her. And, forgive me, there are two hours between two and four o'clock that your whereabouts are unaccounted for. No corroboration. No witnesses. You're not under arrest, but at this point, you are a person of interest. Now, if you would read over the statement you gave us yesterday, and sign it if it meets with your approval, you can leave. But, your mother's apartment is off limits. We'll be checking it out for anything that might help in our investigation."

Marcie read and signed her statement and left the station, numb from head to toe.

The first thing Marcie did when she reached home was to call Seth. She told him what had transpired at the police station.

"Marcie, when someone dies under ambiguous circumstances, family and friends are the first to be questioned. It's just standard operating procedure. Believe me, I know. I've written enough stories about murder investigations. Just hang tight and let the police do their jobs. By the way, Detective Myers paid me a visit this morning. He wanted to verify the time you came to the door the day before yesterday and what happened after. All the information he'd written down in his notes was correct. I'm sure the other residents of the building who spoke to you will confirm it also."

"I guess you're right. I've got to focus on funeral arrangements for my mom right now. Her body is being released to the Oceanview Funeral Home today."

"I'll be at home. Keep me posted."

After the call to Seth, Marcie lay on her bed, staring into space. What had happened to Alice? How could she have fallen off the balcony if the door had been locked? And how could Marcie prove she was stuck in her car for two hours during the time her mom likely died? Would she be charged with a crime she didn't commit?

Marcie spent the following day at the funeral home arranging for a private graveside service for Alice. The few relatives they'd been in touch with had been notified. Several people Alice had befriended in Oceanview assured Marcie they'd attend.

Marcie had stopped by the shop to be sure it hadn't sustained any damage during the hurricane. She was grateful that everything was in order. The store wouldn't reopen until after the funeral.

Back home, Marcie heated up a frozen dinner and picked at it without much appetite. After showering and throwing on a nightshirt, she crawled into bed.

She was awakened by knocking at her front door. It was ten o'clock, well past the time for visitors. Marcie quickly put on her robe, ran to the front door, and looked through the peephole at Detective McManus. A chill ran through her body as she opened the door.

"Detective, why are you here at such a late hour? Have you come to arrest me?"

"Please excuse me, Ms. Freeland, but we've uncovered new developments in your mother's case. May I come in?"

Marcie nodded and ushered him in. She sat on the sofa and indicated a chair for him.

Detective McManus took out his notebook. He flipped through the pages until he located the one he was looking for.

"Did you know that your mother had an account with Grape of the Vine Wine and Spirits?"

"Yes, of course. She set up that account to be able to phone in orders and have them delivered."

"Well, it seems that your mother called in an order in anticipation of the hurricane. It was delivered the day of her death."

"I'd assumed she'd do that. But how did you find this out, Detective?"

"We found a receipt on the top of her living room desk."

"And?" Marcie wanted him to get to the point.

"We paid a visit to Grape of the Vine and spoke to Tim Post, the manager. He told us that he remembered your mother's call, but told her that he only had two employees who were helping him prepare for the storm. He didn't have a deliveryman and couldn't get the order to her. A fellow who sometimes helped him out with odd jobs overheard the conversation and offered to make the delivery on his way home."

"I didn't notice any liquor bottles on the kitchen counter when I went to check on my mother. But the truth is, I had no reason to check in her liquor cabinet."

"Mr. Post gave us the guy's name and address, and we went to check him out. He lives in a dump near the lower end of the boardwalk. Luckily, he was at home. Couldn't get his story straight. We decided to bring him in. He just seemed odd. Nervous. Wouldn't look me in the eye. Just seemed off."

"Did he kill my mother, Detective?" Numbness once again worked its way up Marcie's body.

"He did, Ms. Freeland."

Marcie gasped. "Why? How?"

"Let me finish," Detective McManus said. "First thing we did at the station was check to see if he had a record. Pay dirt. Theft. Aggravated assault. Bunch of petty charges. We Mirandized the guy, and the jerk didn't even ask for a lawyer. He started bawling, apologizing for what he did. Said things got out of hand. He didn't mean for it to happen."

"What happened to my mother?" Marcie pleaded.

"When he got to the apartment, your mother opened the door and let him in. She thanked him for making the delivery in such nasty weather and told him to wait a moment so she could give him a tip. She went into the bedroom for her purse, and when she returned, he tried to grab it. But your mom put up a fight. She screamed and ran for the balcony door. The curtains were open and the door unlocked. He ran after her and was able to get the purse away from her. But she slapped him in the face and made him mad. He managed to pin her against the railing, then pushed her over. He locked the balcony door and drew the curtains. He took the carton of liquor with him when he left."

Marcie cried. "Why didn't she just let him have the purse? I doubt she had much money on hand, and I know she only had one credit card. Why'd she have to put up a fight?"

"I guess it was her first response. After all, she didn't have much time to think."

Marcie couldn't help but visualize her mother's final moments. Those images would stay with her forever.

"He's been charged with second degree murder. He'll be in prison for a long, long time."

Marcie fought to control her emotions. "Thank you, Detective."

"Ms. Freeland, we just go where our investigation takes us."

After the detective left, promising to keep Marcie in the loop, she made herself a cup of tea and went out to the balcony. The hurricane was now a thing of the past, and it was just a question of repairing the damage it had wrought. Very much like her life.

In the morning she'd begin. First would be a call to Seth to tell him about all that'd transpired. After that? Time would tell.

Yolanda Karp Finds Her Inner Sleuth

Martha Rosenthal

Let me start at the beginning:
Tuesday morning the secretary of Lincoln Middle School found a cassette tape affixed to the office doorknob with blue duct tape. It had no note and no name. Betty, the aforementioned secretary, gave it to Mrs. Harkin, the principal, who scrounged up a tape player from the special ed room. In her office she and Betty leaned toward the device as Betty pushed play. After some static a distorted male voice came on delivering an Ogden Nash poem in an exaggerated sing-songy tone, the exact rhythm teachers try to persuade their students *not* to use. They listened intently to the humorous poem about Professor Twist being sent to a jungle, where his bride was eaten by an alligator, or as the professor observed, "a crocodile."

"Is this a threat to someone's wife or a comment on ineffective teaching?" asked the principal. There was a long pause on the tape, and just when she was about to push stop, the same voice said, "Check the third stall in the boys' main hall bathroom."

Mrs. Harkin called to Betty who was already halfway out the door, "Whatever is there, be careful." She looked down at the silent tape player. "Especially if it's an alligator...or a crocodile."

I believe there are two types of people in this world. There's the type who wakes up early on Monday morning, eager to get to work, dying to dive into whatever lies ahead. Then there's the type who drags herself up from the bliss of unconscious sleep only to remember she has made a pact with the devil to appear at a certain time, at a certain place, to kill time until she returns home to prepare herself for the next day's bout of crushing tedium. I'm sad to confess that I am of the latter type. My name is Yolanda Karp, Ms. Karp to the students here at Lincoln. I know I'm in the wrong profession. I just don't have the passion to be a seventh grade teacher, but until I figure out what it is I *do* have a passion for, I'm chilling. Don't worry. I'm not scarring anyone for life. I'm just not inspiring anyone.

As I trudged to my classroom clutching my mocha grande double whammy latté, I almost collided with Betty. "You're smart. Come with me," she said. She grabbed my arm with the hand that wasn't holding a walkie-talkie and pulled me along. En route to wherever, she explained the unusual circumstances of this morning. Now, this was unexpected. I immediately felt an unfamiliar surge of, what? Excitement at work?

We pushed our way inside the boys' bathroom to the third stall. There, in the toilet bowl was a small, confused garter snake. Betty brought the walkie-talkie to her lips. "It's a reptile all right. Over." I think she got some perverse pleasure out of tormenting Harkin. There was no debate about which of us would pick up the snake. Betty shoved a pair of latex gloves at me and nodded.

We tried to exit the boys' bathroom casually, but it didn't take long to attract the attention of a few students who had trickled on to campus. Several of them ran up and offered to adopt the wriggling thing. "Aw, Ms. Karp, it's so cute," cooed a tiny girl wearing striped leggings. I think she was one of the Kates in my sixth period class.

Behind her, I saw David Sandoval, one of my best students. He didn't talk much, but when he did, he was worth listening to. "Are you taking it to a science teacher like Mr. Oliver, or maybe to Ms. Spelling?"

Not a bad idea, given that the snake was crawling down my blouse. I convinced Betty to detour to Ed Oliver's room to get a terrarium. He was hurrying from one lab bench to another setting out lumpy rocks and eyedroppers. At my request, he snapped, "Over there," and pointed to some shelves with his chin. Not even first period yet and he already had circles of sweat under each arm. Talk about tightly wound.

By now the campus was teeming with curious teenagers, but Betty was all business as we strode back to the office. "Clear the way. Nothing happening here."

"Jeesh," said Mrs. Harkin staring at the snake on her desk. It behaved like most middle school students in the principal's office; it coiled into a ball. "Do you think it's poisonous?"

"It's just a harmless ringneck garter snake," I said.

"You're not a science teacher. What do *you* know?" said Harkin.

At the same time I registered my hurt feelings, the words "science teacher" tickled my temporal lobe as if they should connect to something, but I couldn't say what. "Well, there's no crime here. Unless you want to count vandalism or animal cruelty," I said.

"Just a prank," said Betty.

So help me, she looked profoundly disappointed. I felt a letdown, too, but that could be because it was time to psych myself up for my first period class, a group of students whose brain development hadn't yet caught up with their hormones.

Mrs. Harkin announced that now that the "fun" was over, she had to leave for the weekly district administrative meeting. She gathered up her briefcase and headed for the door. "Betty, don't forget to check with UPS about that iPad shipment. They were supposed to be here yesterday, and the pilot program launch is less than a week away."

"The launch" was a photo op with the local newspaper to show what a twenty-first century school we were. Candid shots of students uploading, downloading, researching, and posting all on their very own iPads. That reminded me: I had to come up with some creative project to make it appear that the students were more engaged than ever in their education.

I plodded through the first three periods of the day facilitating a wrap-up seminar on *The Call of the Wild* with each class. Many students engaged in a lively debate about whether a life in the wild trumped a pampered domestic existence, but some had parked their brains in the Klondike along with Buck. By the time my prep period rolled around I had perfected my I'm-really-listening facial expression while my mind reviewed the events of the early morning. Someone had gone to a lot of trouble for a prank. What if that person was trying to send a message? Maybe there was animal exploitation going on right under our noses. Or someone knew that one of the teachers was planning a sabbatical for the purpose of offing his wife. Oh sure, it sounded far-fetched, but how many murderers are described by their neighbors as totally normal? I had to keep reminding myself that this *was* a middle school. Pranking was big. Still, it had gotten my attention. If I were a terrier, my ears would be standing straight up.

At recess I returned to the office and through Harkin's half open door saw the terrarium and cassette tape on top of her desk.

"Hey, Betty," I said to the back of her head. "Do you think Harkin would mind if I took these things?"

She gave a limp wave. "Go ahead. We've got bigger problems than pranks. The iPads were delivered, but no one knows where they are. I've got to break the news to our fearless leader." She picked up her cell and started texting.

Call me crazy, but I had a feeling that the recording and snake meant something, and I wanted the perpetrator to know I was in the loop. I took a circuitous route back to my classroom. On the way I "accidentally" dropped the tape a few times and kept switching the terrarium from hip to hip. The terrarium especially garnered a lot of double takes, and I made a point to stop and make some small talk with a certain clutch of girls. A middle school is like a neighborhood. There are always the know-it-all types, the organizer types, and the people who will spread stories, true or not. The benefit of such people is that they provide free publicity. A conversation with Rachel McNulty, for example, was as productive as making an announcement on the school TV.

"Ms. Karp, I *loooove* your little snake. Is it a class pet? Come see this, Margo." She summoned a girl in a blue T-shirt. She'd been hanging back, but when Rachel called her, she approached with interest, even pressing her fingers to the glass walls of the terrarium.

"He looks happy," she said. Did I detect a note of relief in her tone? As in, relief that he's not in the toilet anymore.

At lunch I took another meandering walk around school. This time I cooled it with the terrarium. I'm not the kind of teacher who likes giggly clumps of students collecting in my classroom, and this wriggly little reptile, was quickly becoming an attraction. Go figure. Instead I idly passed the cassette between my fingers, a leftover skill I'd mastered when I aspired to be a magician. Let me just say that I'm very good at this trick, but to draw attention I had to blow it by letting the tape slip from my grip.

I was near the basketball courts when I dropped the cassette tape for the third time. It bounced across the asphalt narrowly missing the underside of a dribbler's shoe. Before I knew it, the dribbler swept up the tape. "Wow. This is, like, an antique. Cassettes came right after vinyl, right?"

"Correct. After records, before CDs, back in the last century," I said holding out my hand.

His blond hair had the hint of green that swimmers get from a daily dose of chlorine. When he placed it in my palm, I thought I detected a look of meaningfulness in his eyes. You won't find many middle school boys who will look a teacher straight in the face. "Thanks, er..."

"Roger." In a flash, he was sinking a layup.

I returned to my classroom and settled in to see what my efforts would yield, if anything. Was it possible that I was so desperate to feel passion for something that I had let myself drift into La-La Land where a stupid prank took on profound meaning? Maybe I'd seen something in Roger's face that wasn't there. Maybe? Probably. I gave myself a mental face slap, and checked my email, deleting most without reading them. The only one I opened was from Harkin. Subject: iPads. But, when I saw that it was two huge paragraphs I postponed reading it until after school. The woman could use an editor.

My afternoon classes proceeded with my usual mental tug-of-war between allowing students to think freely and smacking them upside the head, metaphorically speaking. At this age abstract thinking begins to bear fruit; *begins* being the operative word. Students vacillate between expressing profound insights and spewing out inane comments. Sometimes I think my main job is to categorize their observations for them. *Good point; take it further. Seriously? Think about that for a minute. Okay. That's obvious; go deeper.* I felt like *I* could use that kind of guidance to help me figure out which train of thought to follow.

After school I forced myself to grade some essays. It was a brutal task. Being a puzzle person I found the reading of the essays to be almost enjoyable, sort of like deciphering a code. However, having to grade them was a different matter. I reached my tolerance level about four o'clock and decided to check my email again. Plowing through Harkin's email was almost as arduous as reading another essay. Long story short: A shipment of forty iPads was missing. The administration suspected theft. Be on the lookout.

It had to be an adult, someone who knew when the order was going to arrive and had the wherewithal to bamboozle the shipper into delivering it to an alternate receiving area, so he or she could sign for it and spirit it away from the school grounds. And it had to be done during school hours, or close enough to school hours that the shipper could reasonably expect someone to be around. Was it possible that two mysteries were unfolding on the same day? I was sure the snake in the toilet and the missing iPads were connected. But how? My brain needed a break.

I decided to go to the office to check my mailbox, which was sure to be crammed with workshop announcements guaranteed to make me a better teacher. I stood in front of the fifty-plus cubed spaces, absent-mindedly scanning the various names. They were arranged by department—no doubt to make the disbursement of those workshop flyers easier. History teachers, English, math. The bottom row belonged to the science department: Jake Goldberg, Roy Hernandez, Ed Oliver, Nan Spelling, and Jeannie Washington.

I scooped up the contents of my box and stood over the recycling container separating out the few envelopes with actual information. Betty was still at her desk. "Any further developments on the iPads?" I asked.

"UPS faxed us a copy of the signed receipt. It's indecipherable."

"Can I see it?" What the heck. I might as well apply my highly developed decoding skills. Betty handed me the paper with a fatalistic shrug. For good reason. The signature was a cavalier circle followed by a no-nonsense straight line. I handed back the paper in defeat.

When I exited the office, David Sandoval fell in next to me. "Why are you still here?" I asked.

"Homework Club."

David fell silent, but I knew he would get to the point soon enough. When we rounded the first turn, putting us out of sight of the office, he spoke. "You still got that snake in your room?"

"Yes. Do you want to visit it?"

"No. I don't like snakes."

"Okay." We walked along the corridor outside the library.

"Do you know what the Latin name is for its species?"

"I haven't a clue," I said.

"Well, 'bye," he said, and with that he was gone, heading back to Homework Club, no doubt.

That was strange even for a middle school student. Was he trying to tell me something?

When I got to my room the first thing I did was Google ringneck garter snake species. It came up as *diadophis punctatus edwardsii.* I guess some guy called Edward got a thrill having a snake named after him, though it would not make me tremble with ecstasy. What *was* making me quiver were those two little *i*'s at the end of the name. It reminded me of the lower case *i* on Apple products, like iPhone, and iPad.

The next thing I did was pull up the Ogden Nash poem that had been on the cassette tape. I read it through three times. There was a clue here, but what was it? It's called *The Purist*. I don't know any teachers here with a reputation for purity. I mean, criminy, this is a middle school, not a monastery. The scientist in the poem is named Professor Twist, but none of our science teachers are named Twist or anything that rhymes with Twist. I went through the teachers' names four more times. Okay, it's Ed Oliver, but I thought the species name was meant to clue me into the iPads, not a person's name. I suppose it could be a double hint, but how does the poem fit in?

Suddenly the clouds parted and the sun shone through. Ed as in Edwardsii. Oliver as in Oliver Twist, like the professor in the poem. Was he the culprit?

I ran out of my room and sprinted to the library where Homework Club was held, but the supervisor was just locking the doors. I remembered seeing David Sandoval on a bicycle one morning. Maybe I could catch him at the bike racks, but there were three sets of racks. The nearest stood between the art and history wing. No dice. Next were the racks between the science wing and the auditorium, halfway across campus. When I arrived, there was still no David. I bent over with my hands on my knees, sucking air into my lungs. Above the sound of my labored panting, I suddenly heard angry shouting.

I followed the noise to a hedgerow of tall oleanders that separated the bike racks from the rear of the science wing. It was definitely an argument. Through the bushes, I saw an almost private parking lot semi-hidden by another row of tall oleanders on a second side.

"I saw you! I saw you load them into your car!"

"You didn't see anything! You hear me?"

Mr. Oliver stood next to the driver's side of his Smart car, parked on the far side of the lot. David, grasping his handlebars, had positioned his bike lengthwise between himself and the teacher. Across the boy's chest, slung like an ammo belt, was a heavy chain with a bike lock. I could see David's chest expand and depress. Mr. Oliver towered over him a good ten inches.

"You're lying!" yelled David.

"Listen, you little worm, I can make your life miserable. It's easy to find a way to flunk you, or accuse you of cheating. Think about it."

David didn't back down, but he quieted his voice a little. "Just bring them back. You can make up some excuse. I won't tell anyone if you just bring them back."

The teacher threw his arms into the air. "I can't bring them back! They're gone. Get it? I can't undo it."

I got out my cell phone and called the office praying that Betty was still there. She was. "Betty, call the cops," I whispered. "Then come to the back of the science wing. Hurry!" After I hung up I set my phone on record, pushed it through the bushes, and hoped that Ed would incriminate himself further.

David, with the idealism of youth, continued to appeal to Ed's better self. "But, why, Mr. O? You're a great teacher."

"Grow up! It's business. It's money. I can't even afford to live in the district where I work." He tapped his chest. "Guess what it feels like to be teaching kids whose parents make five times what I make. And, now the school is set to buy you all your very own iPads? It's crazy!" He dramatized his point by seizing his hair. Or was he dramatizing? His eyes opened wildly.

Suddenly he leaned toward David and said through gritted teeth, "Stay out of my way, mister."

David pushed his bicycle toward Mr. Oliver to keep him at a distance, but the man reached over the bike, placed both of his hands on David's chest, and shoved.

David stumbled backwards and fell to the pavement, the heavy bicycle chain landing on top of him with a sick clank.

I struggled through to the other side of the oleanders, hoping that my mere presence would stop Ed. But, upon seeing my cell phone he put two and two together and charged at me like a wounded bull. I faked right and then ran left in a wide arc until I had put his car between us, but now I was in the corner of the parking lot. Ed hesitated, but only for a second. Then he barreled right at me. I clawed my way over the top of his ridiculously small car, stumbled over David's fallen bike, and turned, holding my cell up. It was still recording.

Ed stopped in his tracks. I heard sirens approaching. Betty rushed in wielding a three-hole punch like it was a machete.

"Damn, Ed," I said. "It's come to this?" In his desperation, I recognized someone even more ill suited to this profession than I.

David got up slowly and wiped at his lip, which had suffered a cut from the bike lock.

He later confessed that he had confronted Mr. Oliver the previous afternoon, but the teacher had threatened him. Hence the cryptic hints. But, then he got a burst of adolescent righteousness and thought he could reason with Mr. Oliver.

I have given notice that I will not return to Lincoln next year. I'm thinking of starting a private investigation agency. I caught a glimpse in Ed's misery of what could happen when one settles for the wrong life. Thanks, Ed. I needed that.

SAUNA

KM ROCKWOOD

" A sauna? You had a sauna built in the family room?" Megan rubbed the side of her face and tried to sit up. Groggy, she fell back onto her pillow.

Jeremy smiled as he laid a soft white robe on the edge of her bed. He was wearing an identical one. "Yes, my dear. You will love it. I promise. It's relaxing. And soundproof. We can meditate there."

"I don't understand how you could have done that without me knowing about it." She thought about adding, "and with my money," since Jeremy had none of his own that she knew about. But that would only upset him.

"I wanted it to be a surprise. For your twenty-first birthday. And our anniversary. Both today! So I had the work done only in the afternoons, when you take your nap."

Yes, today was Megan's twenty-first birthday. The day she was to come into her inheritance instead of getting a monthly allowance.

And the first anniversary of her marriage to Jeremy. Shouldn't she have a clearer mental image of her wedding day? And the courtship that led up to it?

Perhaps her confusion was understandable. Her father had passed away after a long illness. She remembered feeling adrift. What more logical person to turn to than her father's good friend, Jeremy? He was a doctor who had given up his promising private practice to care for Father in his last few years, staying in a spare bedroom of the big old house. That way he was always available.

As Jeremy said, there had been no need to call in a hospice group. Jeremy was there to provide all the medical service needed, and once Megan came home from college to keep her father company, they did quite well with only a few hourly home health care aides.

Father died peacefully in his sleep, Megan and Jeremy by his side. Megan remembered burying her face in Jeremy's starched white jacket, feeling his protective arms around her. And the little orange pill, the first of many, he gave her helped her get some much-needed sleep.

Whose idea had it been to marry so quickly? When she'd asked him about it, Jeremy said he thought they should wait, but that Megan was adamant she wanted to marry immediately. It was what her father would have wanted. And he confessed that he loved her dearly, immensely, even lustfully—and was easily persuaded to accede to her wishes.

Megan did recall wanting to invite some of her college friends to the ceremony, but in deference to her father's recent demise, they had a courthouse wedding with only official witnesses.

Jeremy said, "Later we can have a lovely reception, my dear, with all your friends. And mine. Perhaps on our first anniversary? When a decent time has passed and you're feeling stronger."

But today was their first anniversary. She was not feeling stronger. If anything, she was feeling weaker and more confused.

And did Jeremy *have* any friends? Megan had not met any.

What had happened to her plans to go back to college, to study a year in France, to go on to graduate school?

Jeremy devoted himself to her and her care, just as he had her father's. They still slept in their separate rooms—Megan could not bear to think of moving into the master suite, where Father had drawn his last breath—but on his visits to her childhood bedroom, which was really another suite with its own bathroom and a sitting area, Jeremy proved to be a tender and considerate lover.

He was in constant attendance. Except for a weekly cleaning service, Jeremy saw to all their needs. He was careful about what he prepared for her to eat and prescribed medications that he promised would help her recover from the terrible shock of losing her father—her only family.

Lately Megan had been having doubts about how helpful all this medication was. She'd taken to palming some of the orange pills Jeremy set out for her, flushing them down the toilet when she got a chance. She wasn't sure that made her feel any better physically, but it did make her feel less helpless and more like she could think about the future. Of course, she didn't mention it to him. That would only cause hurt feelings, with Jeremy withdrawn, sulking, claiming she was ungrateful and perhaps no longer loved him.

"Come, my dear." Jeremy's words broke into her thoughts. He held out a hand and helped her sit up. "Put on this robe and come help me try out our new sauna. I'll go make us some yogurt smoothies. With fresh raspberries and bananas. You like those, don't you?" He smiled and headed to the kitchen.

Megan slipped into the robe. She snuggled down into it, letting its softness surround her. It smelled of soothing lavender.

As she slid her feet into the equally soft spa slippers he'd left by her bed, the phone rang.

She used to have an extension in her room. But Jeremy had it taken out, saying she didn't need her sleep disturbed by insurance salesmen and fundraisers. He'd discontinued her cell phone, too. Now the nearest phone was in the hallway.

She picked up the receiver. "Hello?"

"Megan! So glad you answered!"

Confused, Megan looked at the phone. "Yes?"

"It's Julie. Your old college roommate. A few of us were talking, and we remembered it's your twenty-first birthday. Look, kid, we want to take you out for a few legal drinks. And dinner."

"That would be nice." Megan hesitated. "But Jeremy may have plans…"

"Oh, the hell with Jeremy. His plans can wait. He keeps you so tied up it's been ages since we've seen you. Jeremy always answers the phone. And you never call us back! This time, we won't take no for an answer."

They heard Jeremy's voice as he picked up another extension. "I got it, Megan."

"Megan's already answered," Julie said. "And we're going to take her out for her birthday."

"How lovely of you to offer." Jeremy's voice was harsh and didn't sound like he thought it was lovely. "But Megan and I are having a special dinner tonight. Just the two of us. It's such a special day for us."

"Oh, okay. Then we'll just have to swing by there right now and take her out for an hour or so. We can have her back in time for your dinner. We'll be there in twenty minutes."

"That would be too much excitement for Megan, I'm afraid. You know she's not well. She has to conserve her energy."

"Pooh. That's what you always say. But you can't keep Megan entirely to yourself forever."

"Not forever," Jeremy said, his voice slipping back into its usual soothing tone. "Just until she feels a bit better. How about you call back in, say, another two weeks? I've definitely seen an improvement lately, and if it keeps up, she should be able to enjoy an outing then."

"Okay," Julie agreed. "But when we call back, we'll definitely schedule something. So keep a time slot open for a girls' night out."

Megan stood holding the phone as the others hung up. What would be different in two weeks?

And if there was any improvement in her condition, she thought, it was because she had stopped taking so many of those damned orange pills.

Jeremy led her into the family room. With its inviting soft cushions and afternoon sunlight streaming through the windows, it was her favorite room in the house. She'd sit by the fireplace, in front of the weathered red bricks and the black iron fireplace tools. In the cold weather, a fire would radiate welcome heat. A huge television hung on the wall, but she seldom watched it. She would study. Or read. How long had it been since she'd picked up a book? Or even sat in the family room?

Now, a ceiling-high cubicle of blond wood blocked off one corner. Jeremy swung the glass door wide and proudly displayed the slatted wooden floors and seating. Even slatted wooden headrests. Welcome dry warmth spread from a glowing heating unit on one wall. A huge thermometer hung on the back wall. The temperature was just over 100 degrees.

"Lie down," Jeremy said, arranging one of the headrests.

"I'd rather sit for now."

When she was settled on the bench, he brought two tall glasses filled with a creamy liquid and sat down next to her. He left the door to the sauna cracked open. "Here's your smoothie," he said, handing her one glass. "Drink up!"

She sniffed it. Banana and yogurt. She couldn't smell the raspberries, but the drink did have a reddish tone.

"Can I have a straw?" she asked.

A flicker of annoyance crossed Jeremy's face, but it quickly changed to a smile. "Of course, my dear. Let me get you one." He put his glass down on the floor at the far end of the bench and went back to the kitchen.

Megan looked at the glass in her hand and at the one on the floor. Moving more quickly than she had in months, she switched them. If they were both the same, no harm done. But if, as she suspected, he had put some type of medication in hers, she would be skipping yet another dose.

Jeremy came back with the straw. Once again he left the door open a bit. He watched critically as she put the straw into the drink and took a sip. Nodding, he sat down next to her and tipped his glass toward her in a toast. "Now, isn't this better than going out partying with some drunken college girls?" He downed half the contents in one swallow.

No, Megan thought. It's not. Not when she'd just turned twenty-one and hadn't been out with her friends in over a year.

She took another sip and put her glass down. Putting her hand to her forehead, she said, "I feel a little woozy."

"Probably the heat. You have to get used to it. Shall I open the door a bit more?" He upended his glass, finishing his drink.

"No, thank you. I feel a little sick to my stomach."

"Do you feel like you're going to throw up?" Jeremy frowned. "The smoothie should settle your stomach."

Megan clutched her midsection. "More like cramps. Maybe a touch of diarrhea." She stood up. "I have to go to the bathroom."

Jeremy wrinkled his nose and grimaced. "Will you be all right on your own? Do you want me to come with you?"

"I'll be fine by myself." She gathered the robe around her and hurried out, pushing the sauna door shut behind her.

She went toward her bedroom, but stopped by the phone in the hall. Was the sauna really soundproof? She picked up the phone and hit star six. When the mechanized voice gave her the last number that had called and offered to dial it for her, she accepted.

"Julie? It's me. I changed my mind. I want to go out with you girls."

"Atta girl, Megan. I know you're married and all, but you can't spend *all* your time stuck in that stuffy old house!"

Megan's first instinct was to defend Jeremy and the house, but she was afraid she'd lose her nerve. "Can you pick me up in twenty minutes?"

"You bet."

"I'll meet you in front of the house, down by the street."

Jeremy might cause a scene in the house, but he wouldn't outside for all the neighbors to see.

Megan opened her closet and surveyed the contents. When was the last time she'd gotten dressed? Really dressed, underwear and shoes and all, not just put on a clean nightgown?

She pulled on her clothes quickly. If she took too long, Jeremy would come checking up on her. She was tempted to just sneak out, but decided she owed it to Jeremy to tell him what she was doing. He would worry if he found her missing, and leaving a note would be cowardly.

Squaring her shoulders, she went to face him. He would be hurt, but she would deal with that later, when Julie dropped her off at home again. It would just be a few hours.

As Megan grabbed the handle to the sauna door to open it, it came off in her hand. She watched in horror as the other part of the handle, inside the sauna, fell to the slatted wooden floor. She didn't hear it; the sauna must really be soundproof.

Inside, Jeremy sat on the bench. He looked up at her with stupid eyes. A bit of drool gathered in the corner of his lip and dripped down his chin. When he saw her, his mouth fell open and his tongue lolled out. As she watched, he leaned back against the wall and slumped on the bench.

Megan glanced at the thermometer. It registered 150 and climbing. She twisted the control knob beside the door. It spun freely, but didn't seem to be catching.

Frantically, she tried to fit the door handle back on. It wouldn't go. This could be dangerous. She had to do something.

Break the glass in the door. She picked up a poker from near the fireplace and swung it at the glass, turning her head to shield her face. But the poker bounced off. She tried again, with the same result.

Maybe call someone? And in the meantime, go down into the basement and pull the circuit breaker that controlled the sauna heater? Or, if she couldn't figure out which one it was, pull the main breaker for the whole house.

Was Jeremy passed out from the heat? He might die.

Suppose she'd been in there with him? They might both be passing out. Then what would happen? They both might die.

How could Jeremy have let this happen? He was such a careful man. Didn't he try the controls and the door latch before they used the sauna for the first time?

She peered through the glass in the door and tried knocking on it. Jeremy didn't respond. Her eyes took in the wooden slats of the floor, the glowing heater, the glass lying at Jeremy's feet.

He had drunk the smoothie intended for her.

Until she'd closed it, Jeremy had left the door open a crack, not engaging the latch. Had that been deliberate?

Did this have anything to do with what might be different in two weeks?

Megan shook her head, trying to clear it. She straightened the collar of her jacket and stared at Jeremy. His chest heaved as he inhaled, but otherwise he was unmoving.

The conclusion was unwelcome but unavoidable. Megan turned and left the family room. She went to the kitchen and took a house key off the rack by the back door, and some money from the stash always kept in the otherwise empty sugar bowl in the cabinet.

Then she headed out to meet Julie and the girls.

THE DAMN DIVA

KARI WAINWRIGHT

"Oh no, I broke a fingernail," the Diva cried. She dropped the box of flowers she carried onto a table near my hospital bed and studied her jagged crimson nail.

I sighed. I was the one who had just had an appendectomy, but her total attention focused on her hand. To most of the world, she was known as The Divine Diana. But to me, she was The Damn Diva. I'd worked as her personal assistant for over forty years, forty-three to be exact. To be even more exact, forty-three years, four months, six days—I glanced at the clock—two hours and thirty-three minutes. But who's counting?

Finally, she looked at me. "You wouldn't happen to have any topcoat, would you, Jenna?"

"Sorry, I didn't think to grab any manicure supplies before the ambulance came."

"Oh, dear, I'll have to get this fixed before my show tonight. It's on my mic hand."

I rolled my eyes, then worried that she'd seen my silent revolt. But I needn't have felt concerned. Her attention was on herself again.

"Could you be a dear and call Lisa, my manicurist?"

"Her name is Laura, but her number is on my cell phone, which is at home on the floor by my bed."

"Not your usual efficient self today, are you?"

"Guess not," I replied. It didn't even occur to her to ask why my phone would be on the floor, where I dropped it after dialing 9-1-1 while doubled over in pain.

She leaned on the bed with one hand and removed one of her stiletto-style shoes with the other.

I groaned. The mattress shift caused my body to roll to the side, just a bit, but more than enough to trigger pain near my incision. But she didn't seem to notice my problem, just continued taking off her shoes. I pressed the nurse call button. Someone needed to care about me.

Diana glanced around, then pulled a chair closer. "I really must sit down. Those heels are killing me and I have to save my strength for tonight. You know how those concrete arena floors are."

The Damn Diva was kicking off her latest farewell tour tonight at the Parkway Arena in downtown Phoenix. I'd never missed one of her opening performances before, but enduring blood tests and eating hospital food was a welcome respite from weathering her diva-strength backstage storms.

A knock at my door sounded, then Nurse Nancy in her cheerful-print smock and blue pants entered the room. "You rang," she started to say to me before she saw my guest. Suddenly, I was invisible. "Ohmygawd, ohmygawd, ohmygawd," she squealed. "It's you! The Divine! It's really, really you."

The Diva preened, pushing her bleached blonde curls off her high plastic-taut cheekbones. She extended her non-damaged hand to the nurse as if offering the middle-aged woman the keys to the city, the crown jewels, the attention of the singer, The Divine Diana. She smiled her most gracious smile, bestowing upon the woman her whitened pearly teeth.

Nancy clasped the Diva's hand in both her own and gushed, "I just love your singing. Why, I've attended the openings of your last two tours."

Yeah, I thought, her third and fourth "farewell" tours. The woman doesn't know how to say goodbye and mean it.

"Are you coming tonight, dear?" Diana practically cooed the question.

"Oh, I wish I could, I really, really do. But it's my grandmother's ninetieth birthday and the family is celebrating tonight."

"You should have bought a ticket for her as her present."

"She couldn't handle the walking and the crowds and all. The last concert she went to was probably thirty years ago and that's when she swore off events at large venues."

"Why was that, dear?"

"As I recall, she thought the opening act was way too loud and the main attraction appeared on stage two-and-a-half hours late."

Diana tsked, tsked, tsked. "Why, that is simply downright rude. Who was this person?"

Nancy mentioned the name of The Divine Diana's most hated rival, Scarlet Gleeson. Scarlet, a good ten years older than Diana, had once stolen the attention of the Diva's latest boy toy. Plus, had the effrontery to marry him. Scarlet also had only one farewell tour, maybe because she had a husband to go home to when the audience quit applauding.

I watched for steam to spew out of Diana's ears when she heard the other woman's name. But she merely lifted her chin as if to show the other entertainer was beneath her. "It's too bad your grandmother didn't come to one of my concerts instead of *hers*. I'd never have put her through all that."

Right. You've never had a loud opening act that pounded people's eardrums into the base of their skulls. And of course, you've never thrown a petty tantrum moments before the concert that kept audiences twiddling their collective thumbs while you threw things at assistants, made angry phone calls to managers, or ripped costumes to shreds.

Diana continued speaking as she lightly hugged Nancy. "If I'd known your lovely grandmamma, I would have warned her about that Scarlet Diva."

I couldn't stop the coughing spell that spasmed through me, causing pain to reach new levels at my incision site. As I doubled over, I seemed to finally garner Nurse Nancy's attention.

"My poor, dear Miss Harper," she said as she handed me a cup of water, then fluffed my pillows. As my coughs dissipated, she glanced at her watch. "It's time for your pain meds. I'll go get them now."

She tittered a nervous goodbye to Diana, then backed out the door as if in the presence of royalty.

The Diva took a wet wipe from the container on my tray and wiped off her hands. In the process, she rediscovered her broken nail. "I should have asked Nurse Sally if she had some topcoat." She tilted her head to the side, obviously in deep thought. "No, her nails needed a manicure, so she probably wouldn't have any."

I didn't bother correcting her regarding the nurse's name. She never remembered people's names unless she deemed them important. It was my job to recall them along with any pertinent information.

And I'd done my job well. Until two days ago, when I had to be rushed to the hospital with an inflamed appendix. The irony is that if anyone else in the Diva's life needed flowers for a hospital visit, it would have been my job to order them, find a suitable card, and make sure the appropriate photographers were there to document The Divine Diana's altruism. Maybe I should be grateful she managed to make her way to the hospital without my help, even if the flowers were still in a white box instead of a vase and there was no evidence of a get-well card.

Too bad The Damn Diva wasn't in bed instead of me. I'd show her where to stick the flowers.

Three weeks later, I arranged yellow roses in a Waterford crystal vase in Diana's hotel suite living room. It was my first day back on the job, the day after the Diva's latest tour appearance in San Francisco. I opened the envelope that came with the bouquet to find a surprising name as the donor—Antonio de Molis, the one-time boy toy who had left one diva for another. Looked like Diana had yanked him back like an errant yo-yo. I couldn't wait to hear all the glorious details.

As I steeped green tea in a rose-patterned bone china teapot, I heard rustling movements coming from The Diva's bedroom. I could picture her stretching her elegant long limbs as she prepared to face another day. To her, it didn't matter that it was mid-afternoon and most people had been up for hours.

Half an hour later, she appeared in the doorway between the two rooms, languishing against the doorjamb in a long, white, terry-velour hotel robe. "Darling Jenna, you're back. It's about time. Did you manage to get a decent berry parfait with my tea? Yesterday's order simply wasn't fresh enough."

"Yes, Diana." I sighed. Welcome back to me. "I made sure the fruit was fresh. And the sliced pineapple on the side is divine."

"Just like me," she simpered.

Well, a whole lot fresher than that. Of course, I couldn't say that out loud. Oh hell, there were lots of thoughts I hadn't been able to say out loud for years. Not if I wanted to keep my job.

Some people might have envied my position so near the blazing talent of The Divine Diana. Others who knew her better might have wondered why I'd stayed so long. Neither side knew the whole story. Diana and I had both moved into the same neighborhood in Scottsdale, Arizona, when we were sophomores in high school. Neither of us fit in—she was the gawky one, I the shy, pimply one.

We bonded one day at the "outcast" lunch table when she saw the brownie I pulled out of my lunch sack.

"That looks good," she'd said.

"It is," I'd answered.

"Homemade?"

"Kind of. I baked it in Home Ec."

"Are there nuts in it?"

"No. Why?"

"I'm allergic. So many people put nuts in brownies, and then I can't eat them."

Feeling sorry for someone who couldn't enjoy chocolate when they wanted, I handed her my dessert.

Thus began our friendship, a relationship that deepened our senior year when her mother was diagnosed with cancer. I spent almost as much time at Diana's house as she did, both of us taking care of her sick mother. It had been just the two of them for most of Diana's life, and it was apparent how much her mother doted on Diana. Both my parents had busy careers and didn't seem to mind where I spent my time.

By now I'd discovered my friend's singing talent and loved nothing more than to sit at the foot of her bed as she belted out the latest pop song. Her mother loved it, too. A month before the woman died, she called me closer to her bed while Diana warmed up some broth in the kitchen.

"Jenna, sweetie," she whispered. "Please watch out for my daughter after I'm gone. I worry so about her."

"We're friends, Mrs. M. Of course, I'll be there for her."

"She has such a talent," her mom had continued. "There will always be people trying to take advantage of her. But I know you would never be one of those. Promise me, you'll be there for her."

I closed my eyes and swore an oath of fealty to Diana. More than anything, I wanted Mrs. M to be at peace. I later learned from Diana that she had promised her mom to look after me, as well. Mrs. M had sealed our fates.

Less than two weeks after her mother died, Diana entered a local singing contest and won a trip to L.A. for the next round. She won that, too, and soon the legendary Divine Diana was born. Wearing flamboyant costumes and outrageous hair, she delivered her throaty renditions with passion and style.

When she got her first recording contract, she called and asked me to join her. We'd be a team. With her singing gigs, my temp office work, and our waitress jobs, we managed to pay our bills.

The Damn Diva didn't develop until several contracts and concerts later. Little by little fame chipped my friend away and left in her place a self-centered, spoiled-rotten shell of her former self. By the time the shift finalized, I felt ensnared in the web of our lives.

Diana lured me from my thoughts of the past as she nestled into the couch cushions. "I see you arranged my latest arrival of flowers." She waved an indolent hand. "Did you happen to notice who they were from?"

She knew I did because she knew my work habits. "So, Antonio is part of your life again?" I asked.

Her eyelashes batted a response. "I guess he discovered his mistake after he left me for *her*. He came backstage after my performance last night and then we went out for a talk and drinks and…"

"I see."

She licked the last of the parfait's whipped cream off the spoon like a fastidious cat, one that not only got the canary, but a whole covey of them. I guessed canaries didn't come in groups called coveys, but I had no idea what a bunch of canaries was called. All I knew was that my Diva finally felt revenged upon the Scarlet one.

That evening Antonio arrived. He didn't even acknowledge me as I opened the hotel suite's door for him—he only had eyes for Diana's glittering silver top draped over the black slacks that lingered on her long legs. I noted a few gray strands in his once-totally ebony hair, some crinkles at the corners of his eyes. He'd better watch out, I thought. Diana likes sparkling new toys, not recycled used ones. The exception this time might last awhile, but I doubted it would be permanent.

Even so, I felt envious. I'd never had a man look at me like that. Once in a while, one of Diana's admirers would notice me, approach me, and sidle close to my side. But that was only to ask my advice on how to get closer to *her*.

Tired after my first day back at work, I left them gazing at each other like hormone-driven teenagers.

A few weeks later, we returned to the Scottsdale mansion, Diana and Antonio arm in arm. Me, toting a bucket of mail to sort through before I could settle into my guesthouse quarters behind the main house.

At my workstation tucked in a small study in Diana's residence, I kicked off my shoes and sipped a cold diet soda. As I studied the huge bucket, I felt like tipping it over into a dumpster. Ever since my appendix scare, I'd been depressed, depressed and tired. I hated my life.

Surely, the warranty on my promise to Diana's mother was up by now. The Diva had someone else in her life. If she didn't keep him, that shouldn't be my problem.

I'd given enough. I deserved to have a life of my own. To put myself first for a change. To consider my needs, my wants, my desires. I decided to give Diana two weeks' notice. It would come at a cost. As long as I remained with her, I would receive a lovely sum of money when she died. If I left, that bequest would most likely leave the will.

Still, I could take no more. I would have to come up with a plan that my current savings could handle. I'd concoct one as I did the mindless task of going through her mail, envelope after envelope. Then I saw a package addressed to me. The postmark was from San Francisco, but there was no return address. I tore off the brown paper to find a beautiful tin container full of brownies from a famous wharf-side bakery. An enclosed note said: Hope you can find a use for these delicious brownies. It was signed: S.G.

The only S.G. I'd ever met was Scarlet Gleeson. What was she doing sending me brownies? And what did that note mean, find a use for the brownies?

A brief knock rapped on my door and Diana entered. Without thinking about it, I crumpled the note in my hand and dropped it on the floor next to my shoes under the desk.

"Anything of importance in the mail?" she asked.

"I haven't finished sorting it."

"Brownies," she exclaimed. "They look so good. Are they for me?"

"Guess they are now." I held the tin out to her and she took one with her delicately manicured fingers.

"Hmmm." She licked her lips before turning and leaving the room.

After she left, I spied a paper in the tin that listed the information about the enclosed food—calorie count, fat grams, ingredients. I considered going after her when I discovered chopped walnuts in the list. For a second, I thought about calling out a warning to Diana. But only for a second. It looked like I'd found a use for the brownies after all—at least one of them.

A few minutes later, I heard a thud, then Antonio's yell for help. I licked the chocolate from my half-eaten brownie off my fingers, pushed my chair away from my desk, and put on my shoes. I strolled out of my tiny study toward the sounds emanating from the top of the stairs near Diana's bedroom.

Dressed in a paisley robe, Antonio knelt over her body. One of his knees crushed the remains of the brownie next to her. He stroked her cheek. "Diana, darling, speak to me. Speak to me."

I knelt on the other side. "Is she breathing?"

He brought her head closer to his. A sob seemed to catch in his throat. "I don't think so. What should we do?"

He certainly wasn't the brightest bulb. "Allow me," I said. I put my fingers on her throat. No pulse resonated.

His eyes watched me with dark brown hope.

I shook my head. "You stay with her," I ordered gently. "I'll call 9-1-1." While in his sight, I hastened down the marble stairs, then ambled back to my study. I finished my brownie, especially enjoying the tiny bits of walnut.

Then I picked up my cell phone and placed the call. I had to work to keep the smile from my voice.

The Damn Diva was dead.

TRIAL RUN

MARY ELLEN MARTIN

"Huh, there you go, first one of the shift. Aren't you glad you started on Friday?"

Jeanine looked at Matt, her supervisor for all of five minutes. She recognized him from some classes they had shared, so he was a familiar face on her first night. Jeanine looked at the bank of security cameras, each showing a different viewpoint of the store.

"What am I looking at?" Jeanine asked. "I was only hired this afternoon."

"Yeah, Rick told me. See this one here?" Matt pointed to one screen, which showed a thin young woman with long hair and a red sweatshirt emblazoned with the local team logo, furtively looking around as she stole makeup items and shoved them into her purse.

"That's bold." Jeanine said, shaking her head. "Is it always like that?"

"On Friday? It's makeup to look good at the party, booze for the party, or condoms and pregnancy tests after the party. And your shift just started. It's going to be a long night."

"So what now?" Jeanine asked.

"Now, we wait for her to buy a couple of things, while hiding the other stuff, and then nab her outside the store. We bring her here, call the cops, and they slap her wrist and send her on her way. If she's juvie, we call her folks, too."

"Sounds easy enough," Jeanine said. "Why wait until she's left the store?"

"That's how we prove intent to steal. We get her outside, find what she stole, match that to her receipt, easy-peasy." Matt shrugged and drank from a liter bottle of soda. "She's small, so if she fights, she'll be easy to hold down."

"They fight?" Jeanine asked, trying to imagine wrestling some teenager to the ground over ten dollars in mascara.

"This may surprise you, but many people don't want to get caught. She's heading to the registers now. And she never went to the bathroom, so she didn't try to lose anything there. Let's go." Jeanine didn't have a uniform, but followed Matt out of the security office, trying to look official.

They caught up with the girl just as she stepped into the road in front of the store. "Excuse me, miss, but we need you to come back inside," Matt said. She turned and looked at him, a questioning look on her face.

"Why?"

"Miss, we believe you have stolen property, and we need you to come back into the store."

"But I didn't steal anything."

"Come with us, now." Matt's voice had become firm, and he had shifted his posture in a manner that made Jeanine think he was getting ready for trouble. The girl shrugged.

"Yeah, whatever. You wanna search, fine. You won't find anything." They walked back into the store, with Matt in front and Jeanine in the rear, and the girl between them. They filed into the small office, and Matt asked the girl to sit in a chair next to the row of monitors. He took the shopping bag from the girl and dumped its contents onto the desk. A pair of socks, some hand lotion, and a package of pencils. Jeanine grabbed the receipt and checked; it matched what came out of the bag.

"Miss, please empty your purse," Matt said. The girl rolled her eyes and began taking items out of the purse. Movie ticket stubs, some lint, and her cell phone. Jeanine raised her eyebrows. She and Matt had clearly seen this girl stuffing things into her purse.

"See?" the girl said. "I told you I didn't take nothin'. Can I go now? And who's your boss, by the way? You're gonna lose your job, fat ass." She smiled smugly. "This is the last time you see me. At least until you ask me if I want fries with my meal."

After that, the night went quickly, contrary to Matt's prediction. Jeanine didn't get much training, except for when Matt sent her to the ladies' room to look in the garbage for packaging. Another person had boosted some jewelry, tossed the packaging in the garbage, and tried to walk out of the store wearing it. That, and several other shoplifters, made the night go by faster than expected. It made staying awake easy.

Jeanine finally felt it as she pulled into the lot of her apartment complex. She turned off the car, looking at the stairs. Three floors was suddenly a hell of a climb. The blinding sunlight made blinking difficult. She wanted to close her eyes for a minute, but knew she'd fall asleep in the car. Not good for the neck. She sighed, grabbed her bag, and trudged up the stairs. She opened her apartment door, frowning. Dusty had left it unlocked again. Damn.

Dusty was a nice enough roommate, Jeanine supposed. He was quiet, didn't have any parties until after she left, and stayed out of her room, which she kept locked, anyway.

Jeanine looked around. It seemed she had the place to herself. Dusty's bedroom door was open, showing piles of clothes on the floor and an unmade bed. The TV and stereo system were still in the living room, so it looked like they got lucky again. She rolled her head, trying to relieve the stiffness in her neck, and decided bed would be a good idea. She'd yell at Dusty later.

Her phone rang. She looked at the caller ID and groaned.

"Hi, Mom."

"Hey, honey. How was the first night?"

Jeanine made sure the Bluetooth was snug in her ear, and began undressing. "Okay, actually. I'm going to try to sleep early, so I can have a little 'chat' with Dusty when he gets back from class."

"Oh, is he giving you trouble?" Jeanine heard some muffled sounds, while her mother presumably talked to the cat. Or the vodka. Even odds.

"He keeps leaving the door unlocked. We're going to get burglarized if he isn't more careful. But he only has six months left on his scholarship. So either I'll be moving or looking for a new roommate."

"Why would you move? That's a nice apartment."

"Mom, it's essentially student housing. I'm not a student any more, and when the neighbors find out I'm basically a rent-a-cop, my tires will be slashed in a New York minute."

Her mother chuckled. "You are not a rent-a-cop."

"No, I'm a Loss Prevention Officer. Except I don't actually arrest anyone. I spy on people with store cameras and wait for them to be stupid. I can't be a real cop until the local department lifts their hiring freeze. They said they would keep my application on file. Hope it's not the circular kind."

"You could always come home. Dad could find you something." Jeanine rolled her eyes.

"Mom, I can't get a job in law enforcement with Daddy holding my hand. And with him on the city council? Please. Conflict of interest would be the tip of the iceberg. Besides, I'm doing okay, so far. I probably will be calling you soon, though. My first paycheck won't come for another two weeks. And that will be the last time I ask for money, promise."

"Humph, never say never. Isn't there something else you could use your degree on?" Her mother asked. "I just hate the idea of you taking down bad guys, or whatever the term is."

Jeanine laughed. "You didn't care when I did ride-alongs with cops. This is okay, really. I'll work nights, so I won't be kept up by the parties in my building, and nobody I know shops at my store, so I doubt I'll be harassing anyone I know. This is good, honest."

Jeanine managed to get into a sleeping shirt and shorts, and crawled under the sheets. "Okay, Mom, listen, I really need to sleep. Say hi to everyone."

Jeanine plugged her phone and Bluetooth into their chargers and tried to rest. But sleep wouldn't come. Sunlight shone around her window blinds, and the apartment was quiet in a way she never noticed before. Usually, the TV was on, or Dusty was playing the Xbox or Wii, and something was always happening. Is this what the place is like when we're gone? Jeanine thought to herself. It occurred to her that perhaps night shift wasn't going to be as kind as she thought. She threw the pillow over her face and tried to relax. Two hours later, sleep finally claimed her.

Over the next week, Jeanine encountered, and learned to watch for, several shoplifters. She joined in on teasing another co-worker who let a suspect with an entire shopping cart full of beer get away from him. She finally got her uniform. She also got a mask and a white noise machine, considering herself lucky she got both on the employee discount. The shoplifting happened often enough that she began to learn the names of the police who came to deal with them.

And twice, looking over the logs, she found similar reports of employees confronting a thin woman with long, dark hair who appeared to be stealing, but no hidden items were found. No explanation had been given as to why they hadn't been able to pin anything on her, but an employee meeting had been scheduled. Mandatory.

"Mandatory? Crap, like we don't have enough to do. You know how much stuff goes missing when Rick has one of his meetings?" Jeanine shrugged, figuring Matt's question was rhetorical. She had also learned that Rick, while nice to her, did lean rather hard on some of the other employees. Whoever this girl was, she was popping up on Twitter and Instagram, bragging about her exploits in the store. #Stickyfingerproho was her handle. It made everyone look bad, and Rick was getting cranky about it. She knew the days of him being nice to the new girl were numbered.

Frustrated, Matt went downstairs to get more soda, leaving Jeanine alone in the security room. She looked over the monitors, not really seeing anything, until a policewoman came through the checkout. Frozen dinner and a Coke. Jeanine thought about it, and made a decision, knowing Matt would hate her for it. This particular move was going to be risky on many levels.

"Huh, sneaky little bee-yatch, isn't she?" Officer Heather Bascomb watched the tapes, chewing on her dinner, which had been nuked in the employee break room. The smell of bogus cheese and tomato sauce filled the small room. "Any cameras out front?"

Jeanine shook her head. "No, they only go as far as the front doors. After that, we're blind. And before you ask, the cameras in the parking lot are broken. They went up after that one case several years ago, when that baby-snatching thing happened. But store managers after that never bothered to fix them when they broke down."

Officer Bascomb nodded. "Well, based on what I'm seeing here, we could file a report with the prosecutor's office, since you can clearly see her take merchandise. You have her information?"

Jeanine grabbed a clipboard. "Dawn Larson, born in 1995. White female, brown hair, a hundred pounds even, five feet two inches tall. This is from her driver's license."

Heather reached for the clipboard, and Jeanine passed it to her. The officer contacted Dispatch on her radio, reading off the information on the board, and asking for any warrants. She had an earpiece attached to her radio, so whatever Dispatch said, Jeanine wasn't able to hear it. But Officer Bascomb frowned again.

"What do you mean, correction, Dispatch? Please repeat." Another pause while Dispatch talked, and Jeanine saw the policewoman smile. "Copy." She put her radio back in its holster and started dialing on her cell phone. "Hey, Shane? Yeah, I need you to get the IR goggles and meet me this time tomorrow night. Yeah, yeah, I know, but you're on SWAT, and you can get the goggles signed out. Oh, okay, fine, just at least get the binoculars." The conversation lasted a few more seconds, and she disconnected, smiling.

"What is going on?" Jeanine asked. "I'm so totally lost."

"Why file a report, when we can catch both girls in the act?"

Jeanine hardly slept after her shift, partly because Dusty was home, singing in the shower. Badly. Partly, too, because of the plan Officer Bascomb hatched to catch their serial shoplifter. It seemed a bit contrived, but it was a small college town, and Jeanine figured that perhaps the cops were making things more difficult than necessary out of sheer boredom.

The whole plan depended on Dawn Larson showing up to steal more merchandise tonight. Otherwise, the stakeout would be a waste. But what they were looking for, or what they thought they would see, was something that Heather wouldn't tell Jeanine or Matt. He'd come into the office while the officer was explaining things, and afterwards he lit into Jeanine for calling the cops. Apparently, he wanted to be the one to figure it out and get the credit.

"Stop pacing, you're driving me crazy." Matt glanced away from the monitors to look at Jeanine. "If you keep distracting me, we won't catch Dawn, and Rick will can you." She knew he was right, but she couldn't sit still. She was sweating, and kept sitting down, only to get up and pace a few minutes later. It didn't help that she kept jumping at every dark haired girl that entered the store.

"Okay, there she is," Matt said, zooming in a camera on Dawn as she entered the store.

"God, finally," Jeanine muttered.

"You need to realize there is nothing we're going to do except our jobs, right? No big takedown or anything. We do what we always do. Confront her outside. The cops do the rest." Matt swigged from his soda bottle. "You'll probably have to testify against her if she pleads not guilty and this thing goes to trial, but that could be months down the road."

Jeanine nodded, watching the monitors. Matt stopped talking once they saw Dawn get to the Health and Beauty section, and begin stealing more makeup.

"Jeez, how much makeup does a girl need?" Matt asked. "We've seen her take, what, at least three lipsticks now?"

"Do you think she could be stealing it for other people? That may be why she keeps doing it. Look, she's heading to the registers," Jeanine noted.

"Already? That was quick."

"Whatever," Jeanine said. "We should go." She reached for the door.

"Not yet. There's a bit of a line, we have time. Cool your jets." They watched Dawn as she got closer to the attendant. "Okay, now we go. And be cool, for Christ's sake."

Jeanine and Matt walked up to Dawn as she stood on the sidewalk, stepping into the road to get to the parking lot.

"Can I do it?" Jeanine mouthed to Matt. He rolled his eyes and shrugged.

"Excuse me, miss, but you need to come back into the store with us." Dawn turned around and smiled.

"Well, well, if it isn't Dudley Do-Right and Nell. Tell me again, which of you is which? I always get confused." Dawn smirked.

"Do others have the same trouble with you?" Another voice asked. The three of them turned to see Officer Bascomb leading a young woman towards them. The woman was thin, with long brown hair, and wearing the exact same clothing as Dawn.

Dawn's face fell. "Damn it."

"Loss Prevention team, allow me to introduce you to Danielle Larson." Officer Bascomb walked her charge past them and into the store. Matt grabbed Dawn's arm before she started running, and turned her around towards the store.

"Twins?" Jeanine asked. "How did they do it?"

The officer looked at the twins. "Do you want to tell them, or shall we just play the tape?"

"What? Bullshit, you don't have tape on us," one of the sisters said.

"Let the newbie take a crack," Matt suggested. Jeanine froze, and looked at Officer Bascomb, who shrugged. Give it a shot, her motion said.

"Uh, um. Okay." Jeanine looked at the twins and thought furiously. "Okay, I think I got it. Danielle, here—" she pointed to the girl sitting on the left. "—would steal some stuff, buy some other stuff, and leave. Then she would hand the bag to Dawn outside, where there are no cameras. Danielle would take off running with the stolen loot, and Dawn here, holding the legal purchases and nothing else, would look like she had bought the stuff. Wearing matching clothing was supposed to throw everybody off. The girls would get away clean."

"Not bad, Jeanine. And they were sort of smart about it. Always small items, no electronics, nothing that would bring them to the felony level. But an officer with binoculars watched the exchange from afar, and caught them both." Officer Bascomb said.

"Have you had crimes like this before? With twins, I mean." Jeanine asked.

Officer Bascomb shook her head. "Not exactly. Usually one sibling gets in trouble, and they give us their sibling's name. Then, when they don't show up for court, or pay the fines, we end up contacting the wrong sibling and sending them to jail for something they didn't do. It usually takes both siblings being fingerprinted to sort everything out. That is how we first met Dawn and Danielle, about a year ago. Dawn gave us Danielle's name when she was arrested for Minor in Possession. So they were in our system."

Jeanine helped Matt and Officer Bascomb search the girls and get their identities sorted. The cops then took them away. Jeanine smiled, never imagining she would deal with something quite so creative her first week on the job.

Matt touched her shoulder. "C'mon, shift's not over. Let's get back to it."

Jeanine walked through her front door, locked it behind her, and leaned against it. She felt like she'd earned her exhaustion.

"Hello?" Dusty's voice called from the kitchen nook. Jeanine walked farther into the apartment to see him cooking breakfast.

"Hey, you think you could make me a margarita? I feel like celebrating."

Dusty's eyes opened wide with feigned shock. "What? It's seven-thirty in the morning. Shame on you. That's the first sign of a problem, you know."

Jeanine smirked. "Baloney. It's five o'clock somewhere, right? And I don't have to work tonight. And you make the best margaritas of anyone in the whole building. And—"

"Okay, I get it." Dusty laughed. "But you share, and take the blame when I get kicked out of class for being drunk."

Jeanine rolled her eyes. "Like that'll happen. Everyone in your classes is stoned or hung over anyway." Dusty handed her the glass. The drink was cold and good, and strong. Soon, her lips were tingling.

"By the way, there's a package on your bed. From your friends at Double D Enterprises."

"Yeah, I think they'll be shut down after tonight. Thanks for the drink. 'Night." Jeanine went into her room and shut the door, looking at the bag on her bed. Taking one more sip of her drink, she put it down and dumped out the bag.

Packages of lip gloss, foundation, mascara, perfume, and other sundries poured out of the bag. Damn, despite getting busted, Dawn and Danielle, otherwise known as Double D Enterprises, were fabulous at distracting the staff from the other girls in the store, and their activities.

She'd made one stupid mistake, reviewing things in her head. She'd picked Danielle apart from Dawn in the security office. On a first meeting, no one could tell them apart. Sloppy, but amazingly, no one caught it.

All in all, it was a good test run. Now it was time to be careful. She'd tell the others to chill, lay low a bit, before coming up with another scheme. Dragging the cops into it sucked, but it kept them off of her.

Jeanine reached for her drink when she heard a knock on the front door, and Dusty talking to someone. Then a knock on her door.

"Uh, Jeanine, you better come out here," Dusty said in a quiet voice. Dusty was never quiet. Jeanine opened the door and found Officer Bascomb in the entryway, holding up a business card. A Double D Enterprises business card. She flipped it over, showing Jeanine's name and phone number on the back.

"I think we should talk," Officer Bascomb said.

Cups

Mitch Hale

"I Gotta Feeling," the rhythm of the song made famous by the Black Eyed Peas vibrated through the four, beautiful women dancing on the bar. As promised by the lyrics, it would be a good night.

The music stopped. The rowdy Saturday night crowd at the, now famous bar, Cups went quiet.

Hobe Wilson looked at his watch, and yelled, "Go!"

The race was on. Four, drop-dead gorgeous women's hands rummaged inside their blouses like gunslingers from the Old West at high noon. They withdrew at the same instant, each holding an unsnapped bra above their heads.

Hobe pointed. "Mindy," he yelled.

Mindy whirled a pink forty-two D cup bra over her head like a lasso.

Hobe whistled. "Tara."

Tara Evans gave a sexy smile, peering over the top of a black, lacy, forty-four C cup bra.

Tremendous applause rang out.

Hobe pounded on the bar. "Jasmine!"

Holding up a flesh-colored thirty-eight D cup bra, she gave a pronounced hip thrust, which gained her scattered hoots.

Hobe held his hands high. "How about the owner of Cups, Jen Martinez?"

Jen held a thirty-eight C sexy, striped, pink and lavender bra in her beautiful, white teeth. She gyrated, wiggled, squirmed, and went to her knees. In one fluid motion, she pulled a pair of matching panties from the leg of her designer capris.

Three hundred people at the grand opening of the third Cups bar franchise went crazy.

Jen threw the twisted lingerie into the crowd. She inserted two fingers in her mouth and whistled a shrill, blood-curdling shriek. Pulling two skewers of olives from a gigantic forty-four D bra-signature-glass-cup-of-martini, she grinned. "Two olives were sitting on the bar. One fell to the floor."

The crowd groaned.

"Oh! No! Poor olive!" Tara Evans exclaimed.

Jen continued. "The olive on the bar yelled to the one on the floor. 'Are you okay?'"

"Slightly bruised from the fall, the other olive answered," she drawled the punch line, "'Olive!'" so that it sounded like "I'll live."

The crowd groaned louder.

Jen took an olive between her teeth and gestured to Hobe, who was now standing beside her on the bar.

Hobe started, "I was walking on the beach, and I found a bottle. I popped the cork and a genie appeared. The genie explained, 'I've been in that glass prison for a thousand years. I will grant you any wish except for increasing the size of any appendages.'"

Hobe smiled, and continued, "Well, I hate boats and I have a deathly fear of flying, I told that genie. 'Would you build me a bridge to London?' The genie shook her head and stated, 'Along with increasing sizes of sensitive body parts, a bridge of that enormity would also be difficult. Do you have a different wish?'"

Hobe grinned and squeezed Jen, "I replied, I've loved a lot of women."

Jen punched him playfully. "Not me."

Hobe shrugged. "I've been lucky in lust but unlucky in love."

The crowd exhaled. "Ahhh!"

A tipsy blonde crooned, "I can help with that."

The crowd laughed.

Hobe held up his hands. "So, I told that genie, 'For my wish, I would like to be able to understand women.'"

Hobe shook his head. "The genie looked dismayed and sighed, 'Would you like the bridge to London two lane or four lane?'"

The crowd exploded in laughter.

Bry Bently pointed. "The winner, Jen Martinez?" Applause resounded. Bry continued, "Or, Hobe Wilson?" Twice the applause followed.

Jen yelled "No *mas!*" She handed the olive skewers from both drinks to Hobe as the prize. "Now, everyone drink up and help pay for this place."

Bry Bently clicked a spoon against a glass. "One more thing." Bry vaulted onto the bar in one smooth jump. "I have two questions for this beautiful woman. Number one—when did olives learn to talk?" Bry knelt to one knee. "And, will you marry me?" He flashed a full carat diamond ring, and smiled.

Jen threw her hands up high. "Yes! Yes! Yes!"

Bry chuckled. "I'm the only man that has already been to second base and third base and his fiancée still has clothes on, but no underwear."

Hobe helped Jen down. "Congratulations. Big mistake— It should have been me."

Jen kissed him. "You're my best friend. I wouldn't want to ruin that."

Jen ran to Ray Wicks.

Ray hugged her. "Jen, your dad would be proud. Bry treats you so good. Are you happy?"

Jen exclaimed, "On top of the world. I'm getting married! Our Cups nightclubs are wildly successful. *The New York Times* labeled Cups as 'a saucy mixture of Coyote Ugly and Hooters, and Jen Martinez is the swizzle that stirs the drink.'"

Ray whispered, "We need to talk when you get a chance."

Jen nodded. "I'll meet you in my office."

Ray confided, "I have six hidden cameras that only you and I know about. You can access them from your phone. Jen, we still have a big shrinkage problem and I'm not talking about Hobe swimming in March."

Jen laughed. "Ray, did you ever think when dad died, and I became your partner in Cups it would be this successful?

Ray shook his head. "No way! Your dad just thought it was a great way to get a woman's bra off." Ray gestured to the security camera showing the main room where a thousand bras hung from the ceiling and were displayed on the walls. "Frank just thought that was one less piece of clothing to remove."

Jen stared at the bar room where bras of every style imaginable hung proudly. Many had autographs from stars like Dolly Parton and Madonna. "Not bad for a couple of undercover DEA cops. You two made it happen, Ray." Jen wiped a tear away.

"*We* made it happen." Ray hugged Jen.

Bry strode into the office. He gave a mock grimace. "Ray, are you putting the moves on my girl?" Putting a playful headlock on Ray, he smiled an infectious smile. Stepping away, he pulled Jen with him.

Ray smiled at the two of them. Bry wasn't a hometown boy, but you had to like him, all six foot three inches of him. From the time he'd walked into their lives two years ago, he'd made the ladies take notice when he walked into a room, athletic build, and muscles rippling. It hadn't taken Bry and Jen long to find they were a matched set.

Bry ran a hand through his wavy, black hair. "It was an incredible grand opening. You know you've made it when everyone from Jennifer Aniston to Miley Cyrus wants their autographed bras hanging from your ceiling." Bry shadowboxed at Ray. "Have you decided to sell me your shares of Cups? I figure Jen and I should be full partners in business and pleasure!"

Ray said, "I'm thinking on it. Frank and I started Cups thirty years ago. A lot of blood, sweat, and alcohol went into this place. Bry, you've done a great job, from head of security, bouncer, and future husband of my best friend's daughter. Jen is the only family I've had the last ten years. What's mine is hers. Congratulations, I'll let you know."

Head waitress, Tara Evans, knocked on the door and walked in. "Everyone is asking for you all." She hooked arms with Ray and Bry and escorted them towards the door. She looked over her shoulder at Jen and winked. "Are my bosses drinking or talking?"

Jen nodded towards the private bath. "I'll be out in a minute."

Bry said. "Bring me and Ray two forty-four double D's stirred, not shaken, Tara."

The drinks Bry ordered were Jen's invention, a forty-four double D bra with the two cups overlapped with a plastic liner to prevent spillage. It had a heavy underwire to give support to the drink. The straps were wound into a handle. Ray had argued with Jen about the expense of the cup but Jen flew to China and with mass production and colors sold the idea. With a thirty-five dollar price tag, you had a unique tasting martini that would last an hour "just add ice." You gained a collector's item, too. A wooden swizzle skewer, long enough to hold five olives completed the drink.

That evening, Bry and Jen made the rounds. Congratulations on all sides resounded.

Hobe Wilson squeezed Ray's shoulder. "Are you really selling out to Mr. Adonis? Hell, I'd buy your half if I had any money." Hobe ate the last olive off his skewer. Then, he picked his teeth with the sharp end of the four-inch toothpick styled swizzle stick.

Ray chuckled. "I want Jen to be happy. If she thinks it's the right move, I'll step down."

Bry slapped Hobe on the back. "Hey, Hobe, thanks for watching after Jen all these years. I know she thinks of you as a brother. I want you and Ray to be groomsmen in the wedding."

Hobe nodded. "Of course, we'll be pall bearers at your wedding."

Ray chuckled.

Bry, oblivious to Hobe's joke, jerked around. "Damn! Derek Jeter just walked in."

Ray asked. "Hobe, you okay? You're bleeding."

Hobe studied the bloody skewer. "Yeah, I poked myself when Bry pounded my back."

Cups Grand Opening wound down with the clock showing 3:00 a.m.

Tara Evans checked the waitresses turn ins. "What a great night. Cha-ching, count those tips. Awesome job, girls!" She glanced at Hobe and Ray still nursing their martinis.

Hobe smiled, wiping down the bar. "We survived another grand opening. Whew! What a night."

Ray ate another olive and coughed.

Tara asked, "Ray, are you okay? Why don't you and Hobe go home? I'll help finish up here."

Hobe announced, "I'm waiting on Jen and Bry. With the cash, we probably need an armored car."

Ray chuckled.

Jen and Bry came out of the office.

Bry said, "Ray, will you and Hobe take Jen home? She's sick and needs some rest. I can finish up. Jen has the money. There's fifty thousand in cash and ninety thousand in credit cards. I think that is a record."

Ray and Hobe helped Jen to Ray's Cadillac.

Ray handed the keys to Hobe. "I'm not feeling so good either. You drive, hot shot."

Jen leaned out the window and vomited.

Ray groaned and did the same.

Hobe said, "I'm headed to the Emergency Room."

Ray moaned. "Jen, only fifty thousand cash? Ninety in credit cards? We usually run fifty-fifty."

Jen countered, "It was a huge night, a lot of celebrities."

Hobe interrupted. "Most of those pro-players and Broadway egos love to throw the cash around though."

"Ohh!" Ray hurled again. "I'm dying here. Hurry up."

Jen punched a sequence on her cell phone and six hidden camera screens appeared. Ray and Jen leaned in close to hear the conversation.

Tara Evans giggled. "What a night, sexy man." Stacks of bills lined the bar top at Cups.

Bry approached, looking cautiously at the surveillance camera angles he'd had installed. Satisfied they were in a blind spot, he smiled. "Cups is a gold mine. Sex and fame definitely sell."

Tara smirked. "There's sixty thousand in cash, here. Do you want to celebrate with a drink?"

Bry grinned. "I'll have a double D."

Tara turned to mix a drink.

Bry unsnapped her spare bra and let it fall to the floor. "I wasn't talking about the drink." He kissed her.

Jen launched a barrage of curses, tears, and puked out the window.

Hobe pulled into the hospital. He asked, "What's going on? What are you looking at?"

Ray groaned. "Get help, quick!"

Hobe yelled at the paramedics.

As the paramedics moved Jen and Ray into the emergency room, Ray said to Hobe, "I have a glass with Bry's fingerprints on it in a Ziplock bag under your seat. Take it along with Jen's phone to Tom Kaplan. He is an NYPD detective, an old friend of Jen's dad. Tom will know what to do. Jen's phone code is 4438."

Eleven a.m. Joshua Barnes M.D. shook Hobe Wilson awake. "Hobe, you met Tom Kaplan last night."

After shaking hands with Tom, Hobe asked the doctor, "How is Jen and Ray?"

"We pumped Ray and Jen's stomachs and found some unexplainable derivatives of cyanide. We don't know if they will make it. Ray's body weight gives him a better chance than Jen. It was fortunate they both vomited some of the poison out of their systems on the way here."

Hobe wailed, "No! This can't be. No!"

Joshua said, "They are in good hands."

Tom confided, "Hobe, Joshua, the information Ray provided last night was crucial to an investigation we've been doing on Bry. We did a forensic check on Bry's fingerprints. He's a dangerous man and a suspect in multiple murder investigations. But the FBI doesn't have enough evidence to prove anything. With the hidden camera recording on Jen's phone, we are closing in."

Joshua muttered curses.

"Joshua, you grew up with Jen. Your families are close. Hobe, I know you are Jen's best friend. I am going to need your help to put this murderer behind bars for good."

Joshua nodded. "I'll do whatever it takes."

"Jen is the most important person in my life," Hobe said. "Ray is like family. Of course, I'll help."

Tom's mouth tightened, his face showing concern. "I've talked to the police chief and the mayor. Extreme measures may be needed to catch Bry. Let's all work together to be sure Bry and Tara have mixed their last drinks."

Two days later, the visitation of Jen Martinez and Ray Wicks was an event. Celebrities, family, and the Cups clientele were shocked to learn that Ray and Jen, who had been so full of life, were now nothing but ashes.

Flowers arrived from around the world. At the services, pictures of Jen were displayed from a baby to a young girl: Jen, riding in a police car with her dad and Ray with lights flashing on their police cruisers. Jen was smiling over a grill in culinary school. A picture of Jen, holding Halle Berry's autographed bra, with Jimmy Fallon, in front of Cups.

Beautiful urns of ashes protected Jen and Ray's images from the public eye. Discoloration and bloating of their faces were rumored to be the reason for the cremations.

A small group of family and close friends gathered at Cups after the funeral.

Bry Bently jumped up on the bar, "Thank you all for being here. I assure you that Cups will continue to move forward as Jen would have wanted. Jen and I were to be married as a formality. We had slipped away and were married in Vegas at the Little White Chapel three months ago." Bry, tears streaming down his face, jumped to the floor.

Tara moved to his side to console him.

Bry reached for Jen's urn, which was displayed on the bar where she'd stood so often. He held it high. "Beautiful, vivacious, sexy, the love of my life, here's to you, Jen."

Everyone sipped a martini in Jen's honor.

Hobe Wilson wiped down the bar after the crowd dispersed.

Bry and Tara came out of Jen's office. Tara was sucking on a skewer of olives. Bry came to the bar and reached for Jen's urn.

Hobe turned on him. "I know you killed Jen and Ray. I have proof."

"You're fired, Hobe. Get out of my club."

Hobe held up the remote and clicked it at the giant television. It came to life. Bry and Tara's images appeared.

"I'll have a Double D," Bry said, on screen as Tara's bra fell to the floor.

Tara answered, "I love you, Bry. Poisoning the olives worked perfect."

Bry set Jen's urn on a table. In one quick move, he had Hobe in a headlock. "You couldn't leave it alone."

Hobe pushed off the bar for leverage, arms flailing. The two men tumbled into tables and slammed into Tara. Her screams turned into a gurgling sound as she fell to the floor.

Bry snarled, "I took care of Ray and Jen. Now, I'm going to kill you, Hobe. You planted hidden cameras. Always with your jokes, you played Jen's best friend. Hell, Jen got a double dose of death when you gave her olives that night. Cups is mine and I'm keeping it."

Hobe choked. "You're a fraud!" He punched Bry in the groin. The two men crashed to the floor along with Jen's urn. Glass shattered and ashes scattered.

Hobe aimed a flurry of punches to Bry's stomach.

Bry's breath went out with a shoosh. He gasped for air. When he inhaled, his lungs were filled with ashes. He loosened his grip on Hobe, trying to recover.

The doors to Cups burst open. Tom Kaplan and an army of NYPD detectives, guns drawn, entered the room.

Ray Wicks stepped forward. "Bry Bently, you are under arrest for conspiracy to commit murder."

Bry, gagging, looked on in disbelief. "You, Ray Wicks, you are dead."

"No, I'm not a ghost and those weren't my ashes. We didn't really know much about you. I was investigating you before I sold my shares of Cups. I learned you and Jen were already married. So, I started digging deeper, Bry. Or, is it Brian or Bill? I uncovered scheme after scheme. You're a murderer and an embezzler. Crime is your business. Then, the hidden cameras told it all. The cyanide olives in our drinks were deadly!"

"Oh, my God! What about Tara?" Ray turned Tara Evans over. The four-inch skewer of olives she'd been sucking on had been driven through the upper pallet of her mouth and into her brain. She was a casualty of Bry and Hobe's fight.

Bry collapsed.

Ray yelled, "Call an ambulance."

Ray explained, "Bry and Tara were a con-artist team. They were wanted in several states. We had to fake my death to catch them."

"I was in love with Jen. I could never break out of the friend zone. I should have helped her see Bry was a phony." Hobe buried his head in his hands. "Jen will never know how much I cared for her."

A familiar voice asked. "Do you think you'll ever understand women?"

Hobe looked up. There stood Jen Martinez.

Bry groaned, handcuffs biting into his wrists. "Jen!" he gasped, in stunned disbelief. "I thought you were dead. I went to your funeral."

Jen placed papers in Bry's pocket. "Bry Bently, or, I guess your real name is William Hardaway from Munster, Indiana. You are served."

"Divorce papers? Jen, you're unbelievable." Bry shook his head. "You're alive?" Bry's words echoed as he was led away.

Hobe gave Jen a hug. "I love you, Jen."

Jen gave him a long kiss. "I love you, too." She held up a pitcher of margaritas. "I think we are ready for a different signature drink." Jen winked as she ate a cherry off the skewer.

"You're alive?" Hobe grinned as he mimicked Bry.

Jen chuckled. "Olive. I'll live!"

REARVIEW MIRROR

SHARON WOODS HOPKINS

Dusty Shaunessy, erstwhile tomboy and horse trainer, now grandmother to four screaming boy children, tucked her gray ponytail under her ball cap, sucked in a deep breath and pushed open the door of the Best Mechanic Garage on Sepulveda. She was prepared for bad news about her 1965 Mustang.

Not that the news should've been bad. She believed the problem was in the carburetor. Most of the mechanics in Los Angeles these days tried to baffle her with bullshit about her car. She figured they assumed her gray hair meant she'd be discouraged enough or dumb enough to sell it to them. Whenever that happened, she'd never gone back. She'd never sell her car.

She hoped that handsome Hector Fernandez would be different.

She loved and understood every nut, bolt, and valve on the 289 V-8 beauty. After all, she'd owned it since she was eighteen. She'd bought it new off the showroom floor for cash with the money she'd saved for an intended trip to Europe following her high school graduation.

That special day had started out like any other August afternoon in 1965. Her uniform was stained with sweat, spilled soda, and ketchup as she sauntered home from her job at Smiley's Drive-in. When she strolled by the window of the Ford Dealer on La Cienega Boulevard, the crimson pony car whinnied to her and she veered in. Within minutes, she'd plopped down a fifty-dollar bill from her pay envelope as a deposit. Then she ran ten blocks home to get the rest of the cash. Nineteen hundred ninety-five dollars. She didn't want to go to Europe anyway. That was her parents' dream, not hers. *I'm going to get that car, Father be damned.*

She'd been an obedient daughter, working since she was sixteen, giving her folks some of her money, saving the rest. What she wanted was that new, incredible machine. She hadn't discussed it with her parents, just bolted out the door with the cigar box full of cash, heart pounding with excitement. She'd first fallen in love with the Mustang while watching a news report when it had rolled out the previous year.

The car had fully captured her soul as she cruised away from the dealership, windows down, wind in her hair, and joy in her heart. She had caressed the red fenders as tenderly as a lover stroking his beloved's cheeks. The first song that had blasted out of the little AM radio and dash speakers was "Fun, Fun, Fun" by the Beach Boys. That song still made her smile. Except, when she sang along, she substituted "Mustang" for "T-Bird." By the time she'd reached the little bungalow she shared with her parents, her face hurt from smiling.

Michael Shaunessy, stern and intolerant, met her at the door. He glanced from the car, gleaming at the curb, to her. "And whose car would that be?" Her father's brogue picked up a little, a sure sign that his temper had, too.

"Mine," she answered, happy and breathless. "Isn't it beautiful?"

Wordlessly he'd turned his back on her and pointed to her room. He met her there with his belt, and when he was through, he'd muttered that she'd better have enough sense to get it insured.

The next day, not only did she get insurance, she got an apartment. She never saw her parents again.

"*Buenos dias, Señora* Shaunessy," Hector said, interrupting her mental return to hell. Although he had a little trouble pronouncing the Shaunessy part. Her late husband, a heathen Louisiana Frenchman, himself with the unpronounceable name of Thibidoux, had wanted her to change her name to his. She adamantly refused to take a name wherein all the letters weren't sounded out. Besides, her family roots went all the way back to the tenth century, to the last pagan king of all of Ireland, King Daithi. Even if her paternal unit was a demon in man's skin, all of her life she felt the magical Irish connection clear through to her bones. Her black hair may have turned silver and her bones ached from time to time, but her spitfire dark eyes could still shoot sparks. Too many green horses.

At sixty-seven, she was divorced, retired and living alone in her Craftsman-style house, raising veggies and flowers on her acre tract out in the valley. Her car was still the love of her life. Her son, Michael, father of the screaming grandchildren, had died for his country in Afghanistan. Her daughter-in-law had remarried within eighteen months. Dusty didn't blame her. The girl was young and life does go on. Dusty hated that the kids' mother said that being around Dusty made her feel uncomfortable. As a result, Dusty never saw much of the screamers. It was as though they didn't exist.

"So what's the verdict, Hector?" She leaned over the motor as Hector pointed to the offending part.

"Nothing too serious, *Señora*. The carburetor, she needed cleaning. That's it." He wiped his hands on a shop rag, then set the hood down gently.

Dusty grinned. She liked Hector. He obviously respected her baby. His thick gray hair flopped down over one eye. If she were younger, she could go for him. If she were younger…

"How much?" She pulled herself back to reality. She fished in her jeans pocket for her wallet.

He waved her off. "Nothing, *Señora*. All I did was clean the carburetor. This car…" He patted the hood. "I love these cars. It is my pleasure to fix them. I know them well." He waved his hand around the spotless work area. "I work on them right here since 1965."

His smile lit up the garage. Her stomach fluttered. A kindred spirit.

"You can't make a living giving your work away." She tugged a fifty-dollar bill out of the recesses of her wallet and folded it into his stained hand. "Keep this off the books, if you like. I don't need a receipt. Take your wife out for dinner, okay?"

Hector smiled. "I have no *señora* at home. I never found the right lady. It is just me and my little dog, Pancho." At the mention of his name, a little Chihuahua wagged a spindly tail.

Hector pointed to an old rearview mirror that lay on top of a pile of boxes. "I notice when you come in, that your mirror, there, she was broken."

Here it comes, she thought, anger bubbling. *There was nothing wrong with my rearview mirror. Wonder what he thinks he's going to charge me for that? And just when I was beginning to like him.*

"I don't recall that it was broken," she answered, trying to keep her voice calm and her tone as sweet as saccharine. "Maybe you should take this new one out and put my old one back in." She knew her old mirror wasn't broken. She had checked her hair in it just before pulling in to the shop. That's when she'd seen the fourteen new wrinkles that had popped up along her upper lip along with new laugh lines that framed her mouth in parentheses. And the drooping eyelids that curtained her still-dazzling black eyes. She knew the mirror wasn't damaged. It was both unbroken and truthful. She'd have preferred the mirror to fib to her at least a little.

Hector leaned in through the passenger door window and caressed the new mirror. "There is no charge, *Señora*. I do this for you. You are a special lady with a special car. The mirror, I already have. Look at it. It is beautiful, no?"

It was indeed, a fine, new mirror, same size as the old one. In fact, it looked identical. No, wait. Not identical. There were buttons along the bottom. "Yes, Hector, it is beautiful."

"Like you, *señora*." His dark eyes flashed.

"You are too kind, Hector, too kind." She felt herself blush. When had she last blushed? She couldn't remember. Was it because Hector was so good looking? Or that he was so caring? Or both?

She slid into the driver's seat and inserted the key into the ignition. Hector moved away from the car, and smiled, the kindest smile she'd ever felt. She reached up and adjusted the new mirror. She started the car, and shifted into reverse. "Oh, Hector, I almost forgot to ask. What do those buttons do?" She pointed to the three buttons lined up along the bottom.

"One is for the direction, you know, like north or south. The middle one, it is for day or night. It just flips the mirror. But the third one? That one is very special. You'll see." He returned to the car, leaned in through the passenger door window again, and gestured toward the buttons. He smelled of Irish Spring mixed with a little motor oil. Not an unpleasant combination. "Once you touch it, it will ask you 'are you sure?' If you are not sure, it will not change anything, but if you say you are sure, and touch it again, you can never go back."

Although she didn't smell any alcohol on his breath, she wondered if Hector had been drinking. *What did he mean?* She felt a quiver tickle her spine. She blinked at him wordlessly. He stepped away from her door, humming a tune she couldn't place. She backed out of the garage, her heart fluttering more than a little.

The Mustang roared down the alley and onto the street. She braked at a red light. Glancing at the new mirror, she reached up and skimmed her fingers along the bottom, barely grazing the third button. She didn't press it. Bolder by the next stoplight, she gave in to her curiosity and firmly pressed the third button. The daylight brightened around her and the mirror glowed. She stared at the radiance spilling out of it. *What kind of mirror is this?* She peered at her reflection. Her eighteen-year-old face looked back. She shook her head. Had to be her imagination. The light changed, a '62 Chevy Nova honked at her. She spun around for another look. *A '62 Nova?*

She gazed out at the street she knew so well. Hundreds of old cars zipped everywhere. Confused and shaking, she pulled to the curb, parking in front of a '63 Coupe de Ville. Was she hallucinating?

A small light at the bottom of her mirror blinked. She squeezed up close to it and squinted at a message scrolling across the bottom. "Do you want to continue? If No, This light will go out in ten seconds. If Yes, Press the button again. WARNING: If you press it, there is no going back." She watched the LED display count back, 10, 9, 8…until it reached zero, and lights flashed once more. Dusty blinked in confusion. The day returned to its lackluster smoggy self, and she found herself parked in front of a white Camry or Taurus, or maybe it was an Impala. They all looked alike to her.

She pounded the steering wheel. "What the hell just happened? It has to be a trick mirror." *That was it. A trick mirror, not a hallucination.*

She had trained horses, and men, too, for that matter, so she wasn't about to let that trick mirror get the better of her. She took a deep breath and pressed the button again. The silvery light reappeared, the timer ticked down. This time, she didn't give the mirror a chance to ask her. She hit the button again and held it.

The afternoon sky brightened and she did too. Her face was eighteen again. The streets were jammed with fifties and sixties collectible cars of every type. She turned on the radio. "Fun, fun, fun…" blared out of the speakers.

She spun a U-turn. Then she grinned and gunned the Mustang. There was no going back.

She knew Hector would be waiting.

IF NOT FOR THE DOG

ROSEMARY SHOMAKER

Irene's transition to retirement wouldn't be as smooth as her husband's. Three years ago Joe transformed from engineering firm vice president to neighborhood go-to gardening guy overnight. In the past week, she'd recovered from her own accolade-laden retirement receptions. Sleeping late for two days accomplished that. She read four books. She reorganized the linen closet. At a loss for what to do next, she followed Joe around the yard. His loving attention converted to irritation, and he suggested she structure her retirement time. She stepped up to his challenge and joined a walking club.

She drove their Ford Ranger to the meeting place and left her Audi A4 at home. "Get used to being a regular person," Joe said. "Don't advertise your pre-retirement status." Irene parked and, looping her sling water bottle across her chest, strode toward people gathering near the trailhead. A sluggish breeze moved the humid air. One man took a lawn chair from his car's trunk and positioned it in the grass. A woman vacated the car, sat down, and began knitting.

According to the county's recreation bulletin, the Walking Club used a Rails-to-Trails section. Using old rail corridors as "greenways" for recreation appealed to Irene as did the Rails-to-Trails Conservancy slogan "healthier places for healthier people."

Wellness Coordinator Melanie Watson greeted the group, "Welcome, everyone. This is the Tuesday/Thursday morning Walking Club. Some of you are new. Some of you have walked here before. It's a 'come as you can' commitment, but I hope to see you often. Now, let's introduce ourselves and begin with some warm-ups." She demonstrated simple leg stretches and said, "Let's start over here," nodding at two women who'd been gabbing since they exited their respective cars.

"I'm Bea and this is my friend Renata," the shorter of the two women said.

Introductions continued as Irene sat in a hurdler's stretch. An involuntary "Ow!" escaped her mouth; her leg didn't splay sideways like it had in college. She switched quickly to easy toe touches.

Irene registered that the gray-haired compact man was Gino, the tall shorthaired woman was Jan, the two chatty women were Bea and Renata, and the trim Helen Mirren look-alike was Louise. The large man was Larry, and the woman in the lawn chair was Laura.

Absently she pegged them as a mechanic, gym teacher, retail cashier, dry cleaning clerk, doctor's wife, furniture salesman, and housewife. She mentally kicked herself for hastily judging these people. For all she knew, the group's make up included a biomedical researcher, quantum physicist, plastic surgeon, and, she smiled, a judge.

When her turn came for introductions she said, "Hi. I'm Reenie," and startled herself at the childhood name she used. Maybe she was opening up to her husband's "start again" retirement mentality.

Melanie explained that the route was one and one-half miles out and back with a targeted three miles per hour pace. The procedures were: leave electronics in the car, stretch to warm up, carry water and keep hydrated, stop at benches to rest, monitor one another for injury or illness, regroup regularly along the trail, and not disband until everyone returned to the starting point. A three-mile distance struck Irene as ambitious for a first jaunt, but she expected the gentle, level surface and cleared easement of the Rails-to-Trails allowed for easy walking.

A car rolled into the parking lot, and a woman waving a cane emerged. Her featureless sunglasses and a gray headscarf reminded Irene of an aging incognito movie star. Melanie moved to meet the woman and after a few words, they both approached the group.

"This is Faye," Melanie said, indicating the newcomer. Then she gestured toward the knitting woman and continued, "Laura cannot walk with us, but she's here to support her husband, Larry. I've taught aerobics and led one walking club already this morning, so I'll stay here and keep her company. I deputize Bea as substitute leader. She's in several walking clubs and knows the route. Bea, please take the emergency phone and call if any problems arise."

Bea patted the front of her plus-sized stretch shorts and shrugged as Melanie led them up the gravel path to the asphalted Rails-to-Trails.

"She's got nowhere to carry the phone," Faye said as she plucked the phone from Melanie's hand. "I'll put it in my pocket."

As they began, Louise in her tennis whites strode forth like the gleaming sail of a regatta's leading yacht. The other walkers followed, shifting positions and walking a bit with different members. The tall woman fell in beside Irene.

"Good morning," she said keeping pace but looking sideways at Irene.

"Hi. You're Jan, right?" Irene responded.

Faye shuffled next to them. A telescoping metal walking stick, not a cane, propelled Faye's irregular gait. She wore a lightweight elastic hemmed jacket that filled with the breeze like a beach ball. Whenever Irene glanced at the woman, she found Faye already looking at her. Irene's brows unknitted when Faye settled to walk with the two non-stop talkers next in line.

Irene looked back. Faye gazed at Bea and Renata with examining intensity.

Jan said, "Dodged that bullet, right?"

"What?" Irene asked.

"The new lady. She's walking with Bea and Renata now and *not with us*."

Irene raised one eyebrow at Jan.

"Yeah. Funny thing. I bet they take that creepy stare of hers as attentiveness to their every word," Jan quipped.

Irene choked on a laugh. While warming up Bea and Renata had commented on television shows, manicure shops, and new recipes.

"Funny, yes," Irene agreed, "and odd, too," she added, comforted that Jan validated her own impressions of the women.

"Bike up!" Jan yelled—the signal for trail users to move right and let a bicycle pass. Bea dodged in front of Renata and Faye as the bicycle whizzed past. Irene, unable to stymie her habit of enforcing order, walked with Bea to disperse the walking trio and keep them from stretching across the eleven-foot wide trail.

Bea was plump, eager to please, and accommodating. She asked about Irene's health and her recent movie viewing. Talking to Bea was soothing, and Irene felt genuine care. When Bea slowed to walk again with Renata and Faye, Irene happily walked alone, leaving the reformed trio to its chattering.

She noticed that Jan had dropped back to walk with Gino and Larry. Large Larry ambled in a drenching sweat. Even with his long strides, he trailed the pack. Gino stayed with him, perhaps to enjoy man-talk or, Irene thought, to avoid the prattling women.

A snarling shape darted from a side path and bounded at Louise. Jan pushed Irene towards the trail's edge and then turned to help Louise. Faye leaped past her, walking stick upraised, yelling, "Get! Get! Gee-Yaw! Gee-Yaw!"

She lunged at the dog, swatting it with the stick. The German Shepherd whined and ran back into the neighborhood, a shower of rocks loosed by Gino hastening its departure. Larry stood ready with more rocks at Gino's side. Bea and Renata cowered on the nearest trail bench ten yards away.

They all looked at Faye, astonished at her fearless, aggressive response.

"What?" Faye asked. "Let's go. That dog won't come back."

Irene stepped forward and to lighten the mood said, "If you screamed at me that way, I know *I* wouldn't. Now, are we all okay? Shall we turn back or go to the one and one-half mile mark?"

They decided to go on. Jan and Irene led. Bea, Renata, and Louise grouped around a now-popular Faye, and hailed her as the savior of the group, the great dog battler. Irene wondered at this mysterious woman who resumed her meek shuffling way. Her forceful outburst was surprising.

After reversing course at one and one-half miles, they heard the faint chopping sound of helicopter rotors.

"Wrong time for the traffic 'copter, isn't it?" Gino observed and jokingly added, "Maybe it's a news 'copter tracking the vicious dog."

"West Side General isn't too far away. It could be a med flight helicopter," Bea offered.

While others gazed aloft at the approaching helicopter, Faye's motions attracted Irene's attention. Faye collapsed her walking stick and clipped it to her cargo shorts. She then extracted a handgun from her waistband.

Instantly Gino was in motion. He dropped low to charge her. Her shot grazed his leading shoulder and knocked him off balance. Faye then shot a stunned Larry three times before she roundhouse kicked the unsteady Gino, knocking him to the pavement.

Irene next saw Jan reach beneath her over-shirt and draw a sidearm. For the second time in twenty minutes, Jan pushed Irene hard, heaving her towards the weedy trailside. Irene's face brushed something dangling from above. As she toppled into straggly vegetation, she saw Louise collapse and heard Bea and Renata screaming.

From her sprawled position, Irene saw Faye strip off her balloon jacket revealing a tank top with harness strapping. Faye hooked onto the dangling line and tossed her gun and the phone into trees beyond the trail's edge. As the line retracted and she rose skyward, something fell from Faye's body. She reached for it, but it eluded her grasp. Faye turned back to the group on the ground and hurled items at Jan who'd been firing upward. A four-inch throwing knife caught Jan in the arm.

"Stay down!" Jan commanded, and she retreated into the brush.

Once Faye climbed on board, the helicopter withdrew to the east.

Irene and Bea were the first on their feet, and they ran to Larry who lay crumpled on the pavement, Gino leaning over him.

"I'm a nurse," Bea said.

"That doesn't matter now," Gino said. "He's gone." Gino clutched his arm to his chest, immobilizing his shoulder and strode to Jan. Her arm bled from a knife gash, but her pistol was up as she eyed the perimeter. Renata helped Louise stand and confirmed she was not shot; she had fainted. Shaking, Louise said, "W-W-What happened?"

Bea looked for a pulse and checked Larry's head and chest wounds. She confirmed Gino's conclusion: Larry was dead. She covered Larry's face and body with a rain poncho from Renata's daypack.

As Irene vomited into the grass, Jan came to her side. "Judge Cahill? Are you all right?"

"What? Yes," Irene said wiping her mouth with a tissue. "Wait. What did you call me? Who are you?"

"Janice Bell, ma'am. I'm a retired Federal Marshal on part-time protective detail. As a retired Federal judge, you're on our 'monitor for safety' list."

"What happened here, Marshal Bell?"

"Off the record, Judge, Witness Protection gone awry according to Gino. He's also on a protective assignment."

"So who was Larry?"

"You know I can't say. Right now, can you help us calm these women?"

Irene agreed. She directed Renata and Louise to sit on nearby benches and put an arm around the sobbing Renata. The first police cars arrived along with the rescue squad. They'd bypassed the trail's "no motorized vehicles" barrier at the parking lot, more than a mile away.

All were checked by the rescue squad and identified to police.

A police sergeant said, "We're taking some of you to the hospital and some to Police Headquarters. We'll call your families to pick you up, but first we need your statements about what occurred here. We'll have you on your way as soon as possible."

A large van arrived. Crime Scene Investigation Unit, thought Irene. She, Bea, and Renata were herded towards police cars. Gino, Jan, and Louise entered rescue squad vehicles.

Irene rode with Bea. At the trailhead, they passed a police car transporting Melanie and Larry's wife Laura toward the shooting scene.

"Oh, God. They've not removed Larry's body. I guess that's where they're taking his wife—to see him." Bea reached over and took Irene's hand.

At Police Headquarters, officers led Bea and Irene in separate directions. Irene told the officers what happened, but her recollections were fuzzy. The events were improbable for a county Walking Club.

Before Irene was released to go home, Jan appeared, bandaged but well. "I'll give my arm a rest for two weeks. A few sessions of physical therapy, and I'll be fine," Jan said handing Irene a cup of coffee. "Let me walk you out. I met your husband on my way in. He's waiting for you in the lobby."

Irene embraced her husband, relieved to be going home. In parting, she hugged Jan also. "Call me in a few days, okay?" Jan said. Irene nodded, and they exchanged phone numbers, but she reserved her first calls for the Federal Court Personnel Office and for the United States Marshals Service.

Jan did not wait for Irene's call. She called Irene the next day.

"The Walking Club will wait a month before resuming the Rails-to-Trails walks," Jan told Irene.

"Good. Next week I'll go to the gym instead."

"Great," Jan said. "Hey, I'd like to thank you for not decrying me to the Marshals Service."

"Ha. I didn't eviscerate you, but I did have choice words for the judicial administration. I don't think the Marshals Service will run shadow protection on retired judges anymore. Jan, are you investigating the case?"

"No, but I did spend hours with investigators. The FBI directed news outlets not to release Larry's true identity. The Bureau is stressing the 'no terrorism connection' and falsely portraying the case as a homicide by a grudge-holding veteran from Larry's service days."

"Good luck with that. The helicopter involvement plus the witnesses make it hard to downplay the murder. Surely the tiny detail that a woman killed Larry can't be hidden?"

"The FBI is allowing the question 'Was it a woman?' to circulate. Supposedly, we witnesses are so shaken up that we're unsure if Faye was female."

"It's a wonder anything reported by the media is true. I answered a lot of questions yesterday, too, but I feel so helpless."

"So do I. Yet, I have an idea."

"What?"

"Judge, can you meet me at ten tomorrow morning at the trail? Let's get out there and literally walk through what happened."

Thursday morning Jan and Irene walked side by side on the Rail-to-Trails. By ten o'clock, a lemon-yellow sun shone in a cloudless sky. Irene noted how Tuesday's humidity had receded. "No clouds today, and the air feels light instead of cloying. We definitely sweated more on Tuesday. Will that help with DNA retrieval?"

"Agents found Faye's jacket and Melanie's emergency phone. If the technicians get a good DNA sample, the best hope is for a database match," Jan said.

"Unbelievable that the helicopter just disappeared. It headed east, so it could be in the foothills or even the mountains."

"Gino pegged it when he said it was a news helicopter. It was an Airbus AS350 B2, the kind used by news stations. It's only as long as a city bus, so you could hide it in a barn or a warehouse, or cover it with camouflage tarps under some trees."

"We've just got to find Faye! How could I be so wrong? When Faye joined us yesterday, I dismissed her as frumpy and inconsequential."

"Yeah. Her tiny-stepped gait and rounded shoulders had all the hallmarks of docility. She became straight-backed and agile when she fought off that dog and when she attacked us, though. You know, she wore those beige sunglasses and gray scarf through it all."

"What about her walking stick? Did the police find that?"

"No."

"Well, let's see if we find anything," Irene suggested.

They walked about thirty yards examining the area until urgent barking upset the quiet.

"Hey! Isn't this where Faye challenged the dog?" Irene asked.

"Yes. There's a neighborhood path. Maybe that's the same dog," Jan replied.

"We're not getting anywhere here. Let's check it out," Irene suggested.

As they followed the packed dirt leading toward the subdivision, a fenced brick rambler materialized on their right and a blue split-level with an open yard on their left.

A barking, tail-wagging black shape dashed at the fence. "Jan, that German Shepherd—"

"Yes! It looks like our attacker!"

Irene spoke kindly to the dog. It responded with more barks and tail wags, and then it took off running around the yard. On one pass it tossed a tennis ball towards them inviting a game of fetch.

"I can't resist, Jan," Irene said, and she threw the ball. After four fetches, the dog stopped to drink from a bowl near its doghouse. Irene noticed an old lady turning from the street to come up the path. "Look, Jan. We can ask her who lives here."

She looked back at the dog. It held in its mouth not a tennis ball, but something short, tubular, and gray. Plus now the dog was growling.

A knife nicked Irene's hand. Another hit the dog. It cried out but didn't back away. Instead, it barked ferociously and leaped at the fence.

"Damn it! It's Faye!" Irene yelled.

Irene ducked to the right, reached under her shirt, and drew her Colt Defender semiautomatic. She checked Jan's position, pulled back and released the slide, sighted, and clicked off the safety. As Faye released another knife, Irene squeezed the trigger, heard the shot, felt the recoil, sensed pain near her neck, and heard a knife thud on the compacted earth.

Irene staggered. Touching her neck she felt blood, but her fingers found only a wound to her jaw. Faye lay on the ground under Jan. Irene expected Jan had tackled Faye and was handcuffing her or that Jan was checking Faye's gunshot injury.

Irene lowered her gun, slipped her cell phone from her pocket, hurriedly punched 9-1-1, and reported their location to an emergency dispatcher. Jan lifted Faye to her feet. She appeared unharmed and was *still holding a knife!*

"Thanks, Jan," Faye said. "I'd have been ripped by that bullet if you hadn't knocked me down."

"Sorry. I didn't realize the judge was packing," Jan apologized. They both moved closer to Irene.

Irene gaped, too stunned to aim her gun. Jan and Faye each held knives, but they weren't poised to injure each other, those knives threatened *her*.

"Don't even think about it," boomed a voice behind Irene. Two warning shots preceded the next command, "Drop the knives *now*." Jan and Faye lay down their weapons and raised their arms over their heads.

A shaking Irene looked behind her to see an armed Gino emerge from behind a tree.

"Three weeks in a neck cone, and Griff will be okay," Gino said. "His haunch will heal. He's famous now as the dog that solved the Carini case."

"How about your injuries, Gino?" Irene asked. She and Gino sat in the police chief's office. The morning's Rails-to-Trails drama necessitated that she spend yet another afternoon at Police Headquarters.

"Yeah. Tuesday's shot to my shoulder handicapped me but left my shooting arm unaffected. Luckily, today neither Jan nor Faye had a sidearm, but Faye's knife arsenal was intimidating."

"No kidding. She and Jan both looked ready to carve me up at the end. What made you suspect Jan?"

"Her enthusiasm. After separate questioning, agents interrogated Jan and me together. She was zealous about details, asking repeatedly what investigators found at the site. Her name also spurred my suspicion. I checked, and sure enough. Ellis Island officials Americanized her Bellincioni grandparents' name to Bell when they arrived from Italy in 1908.

"Lorenzo Carini, a.k.a. 'Larry,' testified against the Gambino Syndicate back in the 1990's. That's what put him in the Witness Protection Program. Any connection to Italian families drew my suspicion."

"Jan and Faye were stunned to see you, Gino."

"Not as surprised as they were to see your semiautomatic, Judge."

"I pocketed my Concealed Carry Permit and cleaned my Colt last night because I was impressed with Jan's shooting against Faye's attack. Too bad her heroics yesterday were a ploy. She must have been firing blanks."

"Yeah. I didn't realize it until today, but I saw an exchange between Faye and Jan when Faye ascended to the 'copter. I saw something drop—her walking stick. She reached for it and missed, and then hesitated and motioned to Jan before she loosed those last knives. Jan asked in our interview if evidence technicians found the phone *or anything else*. She wanted the walking stick.

"I followed Jan this morning and was surprised to see you meet her. Knowing you were above suspicion, I almost joined your walk," Gino finished.

"If not for the dog! Griff knew something we didn't—he retrieved the walking stick. What's so important about that stick?" Irene asked. "DNA? Some identification or emblem? A compartment or chip?"

"Maybe we'll learn at the trial. The importance for us today was that Faye and Jan came looking for it. Because of that, we captured Faye and uncovered Jan's complicity. Now we can get justice for Larry."

Trompe L'Oeil

Steven Clark

"So Nadia is working at the Smithsonian?" I said with studied caution. "That's so unlike her."

Polly gave me a meaningful glance as she guided Ben and Crissy onto the Metro. "Her work is her therapy. That's the way Nate and I see it. She's still intense. And a great actress. You should have seen her at the one-acts we did at the SOURCE."

"It's the performance off-stage that always disturbed me. That's why I got out of the roar of the greasepaint and smell of the crowd. Journalism lets you observe. Study. Get a steady paycheck."

The train jerked as I gripped the rail. "And she can get us in? Wants to get me in?"

Polly shrugged. "Look, Stephanie, you said you wanted to see the American Realism exhibit. There's going to be a line for tickets a mile long, and since you were in town..." She placed a rambling Ben in her lap. "I'm not trying to be peacemaker for you two, but you know she still takes it hard. Working around art relaxes her. Steffi?"

"I should see her," I said absently, "and yes, I want tickets. Okay, and to make sure Nadia's better. I'll be polite."

Emerging from the Metro station, I was blinded until I put on my sunglasses and made the world an aquatic green. After we watered the kids, we weaved past flocks of tourists to the Smithsonian, or rather by the side of the red-brick castle to a newer addition sticking out of the ground like a twelve foot tall chrome soda can. We entered it, submerged again and waited at the guard's desk flanked by a herd of well-scrubbed, Midwestern adolescents all wearing Future Farmers of America T-shirts and baseball caps. The elevator chimed, its silver doors swished open, and there was Nadia.

As always, she was in costume. A rainbow sash was deftly tied around her black muslin dress. The jewelry was subtly Egyptian. Nadia's limbs were tanned and firm, her hair tied into a low ponytail. In profile, she looked more like a frieze then a friend…or rival. Always that remote beauty, always on stage. Also the scent of lemon and rosewater, her perfume. A twinge went through my veins, but I suppressed it.

"Polly," her soft voice purred. "And Steffi."

I waited, expecting something catty, if not leonine. I'd stolen her boyfriend and a major part. Nothing.

Her eyes turned from me as she scooped up Ben and Crissy.

On the ride down, the elevator hummed as Polly and Nadia conversed. How's Nate? Did Raoul get the part? Read Trevor's latest screenplay? Like that. I knew Nadia was ignoring me because what she had to say would come later. She only gestured at me as she held Crissy…a shrug of her head that reminded me the visit was, after all, for my benefit. Talk of the exhibit only so much carrot leading into the box.

We entered a marbled lined underground corridor that had a distinct odor of fresh paint and new carpeting. Construction scaffolding and plastic covering flanked the doorways. Despite the usual gabbling about a tight budget, it was a good year for arts funding.

As we entered a lobby, I heard water gurgling and saw a fountain in the center surrounded by palms and ferns. Children eagerly charged it and splashed their hands in the water. They begged Polly for coins. Before she could fumble into her purse, Nadia handed the kids two bright pennies. They giggled as they plinked into the water. Nadia's eyes centered on me.

"That's the first wish of the fountain," she said.

"A wish for what?" I asked. "Or should I say, whom?"

She ignored this. "We just moved in last week. It's going to be officially dedicated next month."

Polly nodded. "Why the delay?"

"The director is on vacation in the south of France. His yearly retreat. When he returns, we become official."

Nadia observed me and almost winked. "You like it, don't you?"

I did.

A trompe l'oeil painting covered the entire wall; the perspective attempting three dimensional. It seemed to begin at the brick floor. Steps in front of it merged into the wall, and I had to concentrate to make out where the base of the work started. The brick changed into a path with verdure on either side of it leading to a classical ruin whose Doric columns had thick twists of ivy and laurel around them. The top of the path changed into stone whose chips and edges could almost be felt. In the distance, past a wood, one could almost glimpse the Smithsonian. Here, underground, the painting didn't seem incongruous at all. With the dim light, tropical plants and fountain and breath of air conditioning, it appeared as a grotto leading to an Arcadia. The only contradiction to this illusion was the smell of paint, whose pungent oils almost invited inhalation.

Nadia studied my gaze. "You really like it, Steffi?"

"Interesting."

"You always find everything 'interesting,'" she gently rebuked.

Ben and Crissy went up to the work, baffled by the reality of the bricks. Polly explained to them how the painting was done. Despite this, they kept wanting to go up the steps. Nadia smiled at this then spoke to me.

"It was a popular style in the Renaissance, and also in the classical world. It was said Zeuxis was the master of the style. He painted such realistic grapes that birds flew up and tried to pick them."

"You like it very much," I observed.

Nadia was meditative. "Art is so complete. It's permanency is reassuring. Unlike people."

I detected an attack, but before she could say more, an overjoyed Ben ran up to her to point out bugs he'd seen on the ferns nearest the path. I found their miniature realism disturbing. As Nadia stroked his hair, I tried to ignore the slash on her wrist. After two years, its puckered scar was still an accusation. Perhaps it was my fault. After taking the part, and then when Tad left her, I refused to answer her pounding on my door at two a.m. "You have to come out and face me." Her cry couldn't be ministered by me. Emotions...

I came out of this somber flash as Ben was taken by Polly, Nadia pointing to the painting for my benefit.

"The painting confronts reality and absorbs it. Don't you find that reassuring?"

"You do."

"It reassures me," Nadia said with a pleasant gaze, "of the serenity of art. It makes things last."

"Do you know the artist?"

"His name is Zaubermann. I watched him work." She narrowed her eyes. "He saw me watching. He became interested in me."

"Do any modeling?"

"He sketched me. It was…like being in a trance. Better than yoga."

So, I inwardly sighed, she was under the charms of another director's ministrations. "He sketched you but didn't put you in the painting?"

"He said," she frowned, "and this is important…that the oils must dry properly before it is completed. Zaubermann has a really unique perspective. His vision of art and life so encompassing…" Her voice dropped. "He helped. Helped me forget."

I instinctively touched her arm. "Nadia, I'm sorry about us. About how it ended…"

She pulled her arm back and nodded. "It's okay," she whispered. "Really. It's okay." She brightened. "Hey. Let's see my office."

She led us into the honeycomb of cubicles to hers. Then a tour of the conference room, its dark wood paneling reminded me of the ones you see in movies where the president and his court flee while we citizens are left to duck and cover.

Nadia paused as her fingers drummed on the table.

"I've gotten better since I took this job."

Polly nodded. "Have you, Nadia? I'm so glad to hear that. So does Nate. We've told you things would pick up. Do you still go to the counseling?"

"I don't need to," she said with mysterious satisfaction. "Not anymore. Used to, I always blamed myself."

She stopped, then continued, her eyes again pleading, as they so often did. "I'm not like you, Steffi. I can't walk out."

"Nadia…"

"From performing," she added quickly. "This is my life. The one-acts were good, but it was only a couple of weeks. I didn't have the long-playing part. Like you did." I was bracing myself for the blowup, but she only inhaled and smiled again. "Zaubermann…has the most wonderful techniques." She lit up. "He's shown me things. He studied in Mongolia and Tibet…art and theatre a synthesis…"

I frowned. "I didn't realize Mongolia was a hot spot for theater."

"There are a lot of things you don't know. But Zaubermann does." Her pride was deep as her pain—conspiratorial. "Just watch."

She had to get back to work.

"Something more than a part." I said to Polly as we left the building.

"I was hoping to see the exhibit," shrugged Polly as she led the children. "Nadia's being evasive again, and that worries me."

"She's always been like that."

"Nadia is a good actress, but what kind of long-running part could she keep? I really couldn't see her on the Soaps."

"I shouldn't have taken that part."

"Hey, hey," Polly said. "You were the best one. Everyone agreed. You were Celimene."

I agreed, still troubled by Nadia's smile and confidence.

"I shouldn't have slept with Tad."

Polly sighed and passed that one over.

If Nadia was involved in a conspiracy, then it was a damned good one.

The next day I told Polly I had to visit a friend at the *Post* before I left town.

Of course, I went back to the Smithsonian. When I got to Nadia's office, I was told she hadn't come in. I left, then checked the next day. Same answer. They were as surprised as I was, and then I hit the panic button. I called Polly and got Nadia's number. No answer. A hurried visit to her apartment brought me to a street off George Washington University, one of those brick houses whose plain bleakness called to mind frock coats and republican simplicity.

In the hall of rented rooms, I found her door and pounded. Nothing. Old, bad memories tingled. Her crying and shaken fists while we were on tour, that long night at the ER. All of her calm a ruse. Had she run off with this Zaubermann?

Had she OD'd again? I kept telling myself I was only a concerned friend, not the chick who'd taken her guy away from her, a Samsonette who pushed down the pillars of her emotional security. It was wrong, but Tad and I...I was better for him, and that was the version I kept, and my trying to comfort Nadia when Tad broke up with her was like a razor on the skin. To say I was the woman who took away her man and destroyed her happiness...that was so fifties, but after I'd distanced myself, after Tad went onward and upward, after I tried to mend fences and failing...wanting to get in touch with Nadia, rebuild and reconstruct. She spurned this. Until the trip to the painting.

I didn't have anything else on my platter, so I went into the lobby. It was crowded with a flock of Chinese businessmen. After twisting trade concessions out of our elected solons, they were here to enjoy art and partake of the newly opened exhibit of American Realism. When they filed past the entrance, I was alone with the gurgling fountain and the two pennies of the kids. Head lowered, I smelled a familiar scent of lemon and rosewater. Through the heavy smell of paint, it came through, like a petal floating in the smog. I looked up and saw her.

Nadia was in the painting, on the path to the forest. Her back was turned to me, but there was no mistaking the dress, sash, and ponytail. Her sandaled foot was in mid-step above a stone.

I looked at the back of her wrist and swallowed hard. The scar. It couldn't have been painted. Daring to move closer, I touched it, pulling back my fingers in cold shock; the wrist was warm. It pulsed.

A guard called out and ordered me back to the velvet rope draped across the front. Gasping for breath, my fingertips felt her warm shoulder blade until he pulled me away. I tried to stammer a reason as he called a code whatever, and two more guards escorted me away. I begged forgiveness and was finally allowed to stay on the bench by the fountain, closely watched until closing time.

Reentering the ground, my eyes painfully contracted at the blazing afternoon sun, reminding me of deep-sea fish who burst if brought to the surface.

I can't describe the fear, anxiety, the sheer awful terror I felt. I called Polly, but she wouldn't believe me. Even a trip back failed to convince her it was Nadia. My appeals to the bureaucracy went unheeded. I had to get closer to the painting, but after a third day of approaching, was finally escorted out. When I left Washington, it was in a torment I'd never anticipated.

I've measured her progress, and judge it to be one quarter of an inch per week. It is steady. Nadia is in no hurry to rush this, her longest playing role. I've given up hopes of greater employment in coming back to Washington, barely able to report on its doings as I spend every moment here that I can.

Summer has passed. Orange, red, and gold trees serenely flank and shield the white marble and avenues of the capital. My attempts to contact Zaubermann have failed. He is an elusive artist, much in demand throughout the world. At last count he's done commissions in Abu Dhabei, India, and after a gig with the Vienna opera, has disappeared in China creating murals for the country's new, out-of-sight bureaucrats. My letters and emails demanding he lift his spell go unanswered.

I'm prepared to hunt down the mystical snipe, find him, wrap my fingers around his neck and keep choking until he gives Nadia back. But for now, I can only watch. With every visit, I sit on the edge of the bench, guards sternly watching me, as I see her shoulder inch closer to the pillar. The outline of her face is beginning, like the dawn on the horizon's crack.

Exact calculations are hard, but Christ, I've done the math a hundred times over. In three months, I think her ascension to the top of the stairs will be complete. What will Nadia do then?

Will she turn and begin her descent, content I've returned? Can she? Or will Nadia continue into the parallel world of her longest performance, forever onstage in an eternity of color and surface, tempera and oil?

I don't know. But I'm here, Nadia. I'm here for you.

ALL DRESSED UP

CAROLINE DOHACK & JODIE JACKSON JR.

Nothing in her police academy training prepared Laurel Goodman for this.

When she arrived at the scene, Laurel saw a road-killed deer posed and propped up against the Route M signpost with its legs crossed, a pipe drooping from its mouth, and a jaunty monocle on one eye. Scrawled into the dirt: "*Aujourd'hui, maman est morte.*"

As she examined the scene, Laurel wondered if she had stumbled onto a lead on the latest rustling case. That's what had brought her to Jewel Box, the "crown jewel" of Diamond County, as the chamber of commerce liked to say. Sheriff Claude Norton had requested help from the Columbia Police Department, and they had sent Laurel, much to her chagrin. As soon as this case was settled, she would head back north to civilization. But now the cattle rustling investigation had turned strange. Laurel was sure this bizarre deer setup had something to do with it. The latest rustling site, where someone clipped four strands of barbed-wire fence to escort about forty black Angus off the property, was on Route M, no more than two hundred feet from the rakish ruminant.

Her radio squawked to life as Sheriff Norton reminded her of the errand he'd asked her to run.

"I got that, Sheriff. Get Mrs. Norton to her hair appointment by ten. And Sheriff, I might have something here," she added.

Laurel sighed as she drove her cruiser up to the local Casey's. She had just dropped off Norma Jean Norton at the Mane Attraction, and Sheriff Norton had asked her to pick up his favorite chocolate-filled pastries before she returned to the station.

As she made her way to the register, what passed in Jewel Box for a sharp-dressed man—dark-wash jeans, perfectly pressed shirt, and boots that had yet to be broken in—cut in front of her. It was Barry Newman, an attorney-turned-rancher who'd relocated to Jewel Box about a year earlier.

"Oh, excuse me," Laurel snapped. "Was I in your way?"

"Wha...?"

Barry stood blinking. Despite his cluelessness, he was kind of cute, Laurel hated to admit. But even so, she had no time for this podunk prince. If all went well, the Sheriff's Department would finish the rustling case and she could return to Columbia. She had a long and growing list of things to catch up on: sushi, concerts, cappuccinos that didn't come out of an automated vending machine...

The cashier, Crystal Beth Mayberry, interrupted her reverie.

"I guess you've both heard: The animals have voices," she said.

Crystal Beth, who claimed to be clairvoyant, spent much of her time writing letters to the editor of *The Jewel Box Jewel* predicting the next big earthquake. The publisher, Douglas Garrison, sometimes ran her ramblings if her vision coincided with the anniversary of another seismic activity. As Jewel Box was on the New Madrid fault line, Crystal Beth practically had a regular column.

"I've not," Barry said, staring into his gas-station latté. On a good day, he found Crystal Beth amusing and indulged her penchant for oddity. She was in his book club and always had strange but thoughtful comments about the readings. But lately she'd been a little cloying, particularly at their weekly meeting, where Crystal Beth had taken to reprimanding anyone whose literary interpretations differed from Barry's. And today was not a good day. His neighbor's cattle had vanished in the night. Though his own herd was accounted for, he hated to see someone else lose his livelihood. And now the beautiful cop, whom he had hoped to get to know, was upset with him. If he hadn't been so distracted, he might not have made such a fool of himself.

"Something's happening," Crystal Beth said. "Something big. I've seen it, and soon all will hear it."

"Hear what?" Barry said. Once the wannabe-seer got going, there was no way to stop her.

"The animals! They walk amongst us, and soon they will talk amongst us."

"I guess we'd better hire a translator," Barry said.

Laurel perked up. A translator? Of course.

"I've really got to be going now," Barry said. "I'm having security cameras installed today. Can't be too careful. Officer, can I make it up to you? I'll buy your coffee and, um, whatever those chocolate things are."

That's okay," Laurel said, plunking a tenner down onto the counter. "You already have."

Laurel sneezed as she followed Jacqueline Sneed through the stacks at Southeast Missouri State University's Kent Library. After hearing the story of the deer, Jacqueline, an associate professor of French literature, moved swiftly through the stacks until she reached her Dewey destination and pulled a tattered paperback from the shelf.

"*Voila!*" she said. "I think you'll find your answer here."

Laurel squinted at the book cover. "'*L'Etranger?*' Professor, I can't even pronounce that, much less read it."

"The line—'*Aujourd'hui, maman est morte.*'—translates into 'Mother died today,'" Jacqueline said. "It's Camus, and it's one of the most famous openers in modern literature."

"I was a poli-sci girl," Laurel said sheepishly. "So what's going on here?"

"What indeed!" Jacqueline crowed. "That's the central question in all Existentialist literature. I can tell you one thing, though: This is only the beginning. Whoever did this put some considerable effort into crafting this message. I imagine there will be more until its intended recipient takes the hint."

"So what am I supposed to do? Wait until I see an opossum wearing a beret?"

Jacqueline smiled as she handed Laurel a book. "*Non!* But you should read up. This has the English translation right next to the French."

As soon as Laurel got to her cruiser, she could hear a voice coming over the radio. It was Sheriff Norton.

"*Merde,*" she muttered, pleased with her burgeoning French-language skills.

"Officer, I need you to report to the square. Some pervert is dressin' up them critters again," Sheriff Norton said.

A small crowd had gathered by the time Laurel reached the town square. "Police! Step aside!" she ordered.

There, just outside the Mane Attraction, was a small boat. A bloated raccoon wearing a chambray shirt sat with its paws resting on two oars. A flattened cat wearing a blue Swiss dot dress was propped up facing the rower. A banner along the side of the boat read, "It still isn't over."

Laurel frowned and started flipping through the book Jacqueline had given her.

"Whatcha lookin' for?" came a voice.

It was Cicada "Cissy" Jones, owner of the Mane Attraction.

"I cannot reveal details on an open police investigation, ma'am," Laurel intoned.

Cissy rolled her eyes. "A police investigation? Sure don't look like any policing going on."

It was Laurel's turn to roll her eyes. "And what would you even know about that?"

"Well, nothing I guess. But I do know that the Hinkles' cattle turned up missing this afternoon. Broad daylight, can you imagine that? Anyway, sixty-some head gone, and you're standing here looking at some dead animals acting out that scene in *The Notebook*."

"*The Notebook?*"

"You know, Rachel McAdams and Ryan Gosling. Gosh, it's been forever since I've seen that movie."

"This is a scene from a movie?"

"Sure is! The book isn't half-bad either."

"It's based on a book?"

"Yep!"

"Do you happen to have a copy? I think this is important."

Cissy smirked. "I don't have the book, but I can lend you the DVD."

Laurel walked up to Crystal Beth's counter, this time with her own snacks. Twizzlers, cashews, and coffee—it was going to be a long night if she was going to get through a contemporary classic and a chick flick.

"Can I interest you in a lottery ticket?" Crystal Beth asked as she rang up Laurel's items.

"No, thanks," Laurel said.

Crystal Beth shrugged. "Your loss. Who knows? Today could be your lucky day."

"Aren't *you* supposed to know?" Laurel snapped. "Some psychic."

Crystal Beth bristled. "I'm not a *psychic*," she said. "The universe speaks to me and I *listen*."

"I'm sure she didn't mean it that way," came a voice behind Laurel. It was Barry. "We've all been a little tense today."

Crystal Beth softened. "I had a feeling you'd be back. Can I interest *you* in a lottery ticket? Today could be your lucky day."

"Oh, sure," Barry said. "And ring me up for whatever Officer Goodman is buying. I owe her after being so inconsiderate this morning."

"So what're your numbers, Barry?" Crystal Beth asked cheerfully.

"Why don't you pick for me?"

"It would be my pleasure."

Laurel stalked out of Casey's, Barry in hot pursuit.

"Officer! Officer!"

Laurel whirled around. "What?"

Barry stopped. "You, um, forgot this," he said, proffering the paper bag with Laurel's snacks.

Laurel snatched the sack from him. "Thanks."

"You know, you don't have to be so rude," Barry said.

Laurel sighed. "I'm sorry. It's been a strange day. A hundred cattle went missing just today, but Sheriff Norton only wants me looking into these stupid animal scenes. I might be able to figure it out, but first I have to get through all of *this*," she said, opening her purse to reveal the novel and the DVD.

"You might be in luck," Barry said.

"Luck, huh? Don't *you* go Crystal Beth on me."

Barry laughed. "I don't have visions, but I did minor in French when I was an undergrad. And as it just so happened, I spent a whole semester on Camus. I could fill you in on the story. Maybe over dinner?"

"Well, you'd save me a considerable amount of time, and I haven't eaten all day. Any chance you can give me a synopsis on *The Notebook*, too?"

Barry grimaced. "Funny you should mention that. It's my book club's current pick. I pushed for Atwood's *MaddAddam* trilogy, but got outvoted. Anyway, I've been putting it off, but I do own a DVD player."

Laurel frowned. "Look, I'm not really looking for a relationship, so…"

"Oh, gosh! I didn't mean to come off that way. I just thought, you know, I could help."

Laurel hated to admit it, but Barry was cute, especially when he was flustered.

"Well, so long as it's work-related," Laurel said.

Dinner had been surprisingly enjoyable. Over Budweiser and burgers, Laurel learned not only the tale of Meursault, but of how Barry had come to Jewel Box.

After graduating from the University of Missouri School of Law, Barry worked as a public defender in St. Louis County. State budget cuts eventually cost him his job, so he went into tax law in Chesterfield. He turned out to be good at it, but he didn't enjoy it. Seeking a simpler life, he bought a farm in Jewel Box and thirty head of Charolais.

"Starting small, you know?" Barry said.

The townsfolk had regarded him with suspicion, just as they did all newcomers, but they warmed to him when he traded in his Bimmer for an old Chevy Silverado and became a regular at the livestock auctions. And come tax season he could be relied on to dispense solid advice openly and—perhaps more importantly for some of the cash-strapped farmers—freely.

"And so how about you?" he asked Laurel. "How did you come to settle in our fine hamlet?"

"Oh, I haven't," Laurel said. "As soon as this rustling thing is dunzo I am gonzo. But that's a story for another day. If you don't mind, I'm ready to get this movie over with."

"You really are all business," Barry said. "Shall we at least drive over together? Save the county some gas money?"

"I'll tail you."

"Fair enough."

As they approached Barry's ranch, Laurel smiled to herself. The fences were whitewashed and immaculate. The pasture was neatly trimmed and the round bales of hay were arranged in perfectly spaced rows. Laurel didn't know anything about agriculture, but she could appreciate Barry's sense of tidiness.

Ahead of her, Barry's truck stopped suddenly. Laurel slammed on the brakes, put the cruiser in park, and jumped out. Illuminated in Barry's headlights was a grisly scene: A dead armadillo with its short, fat neck locked in the frame of a guillotine. Scratched in the dirt: "Since we're all going to die, it's obvious that when and how don't matter."

"Camus," Barry said, coming up behind Laurel. "But why here?"

"You've got bigger problems," Laurel said.

In the field just beyond the scene, several dozen cattle mooed and milled about.

For Sheriff Norton, Laurel's discovery was a tremendous coup.

"Well done, Officer Goodman. Soon we'll be able to return the cattle to their rightful homes, and then Newman can go on to his rightful home—probably Potosi," he said.

"Sheriff, something's off. I don't think Barry stole those cattle."

"The cattle were on his property. We tried to check the footage from his fancy new surveillance system, but it'd been erased. What else do you need?"

"But what about the road kill?"

"What *about* the road kill? There haven't been any more of those…'displays' since we nabbed Newman last week."

"Why would Barry have invited me to his house if he was rustling cattle?"

"Do you see a white coat?"

"No."

"That's because I'm not a psychiatrist. But I've got some good news for you: You're cleared to go back to Columbia. You'll still have to come back to testify at the trial, but your work here is done."

Laurel stood in front of Crystal Beth's register for the final time.

"Headed home, Officer?" Crystal Beth asked.

"You're as good as they say you are," Laurel said.

Crystal Beth laughed. "Oh, it wasn't a vision. Just what I heard from the other folks. Can I interest you in a lottery ticket? Last chance. I'll even pick the numbers for you."

"Oh, sure," Laurel said.

"It's a lucky day, I can just feel it," Crystal Beth said. "*Bon chance.*"

"I didn't know you spoke French, Crystal Beth," Laurel said, eyeing the woman closely.

"I love to expand my horizons," she replied. "It's too bad about Barry. We were on the same page, so to speak. Everyone else in our book club wanted to read Jennifer Weiner. One of the first books Barry suggested was *Candide*. That got voted down pretty quickly. Personally, I thought it was nice to have such a sophisticated person in our book club, and I was surprised when he kept coming back—especially since he and I were the only ones who ever wanted to read anything worth discussing."

Well, thought Laurel, *book buddies. How interesting.*

"I don't think Barry stole those cattle," Laurel said.

"Officer, he erased the surveillance tapes. You know that as well as I do. Why would he do that if he didn't take them cattle?"

"How do you know that, Crystal Beth?"

"Everyone knows that!"

"Do they? He'd only had the system installed a few hours before he was arrested. Why would he have bothered setting it up just to dismantle it?"

"To throw everyone off? I don't know!"

"Actually, it sounds like you do. Barry had only decided that day to have the system installed. We have phone records to prove that. And he didn't tell many people he was getting the system. In fact, the only time he left his home between the time he called the security company and the time it was installed was when he came in to get coffee, and you and I were the only ones in here at that time."

Crystal Beth started to fidget.

"Are you psychic, Crystal Beth? Or is there something else going on?"

"I'm not psychic!"

"Yeah, the universe speaks to you. I know. So what did the universe tell you about these cattle?"

Crystal Beth's eyes grew wide and round as she grabbed Laurel by the forearms.

"We have to get out! Something's coming! I can feel it!"

"Cut the crap, Crystal Beth."

Crystal Beth started to convulse, shaking Laurel vigorously.

"It's the big one!"

"Knock it off!" Laurel shouted, grabbing the Dolly Parton's Imagination Library donation box from the counter and clocking Crystal Beth over the head.

Crystal Beth confessed everything. She'd been smitten with Barry since he first joined the book club. It wasn't often she came in contact with such an intellectual. And the way he interacted with her at the convenience store? It was as if he understood her, whereas the rest of the town laughed behind her back. Even when Douglas Garrison had the good sense to run her predictions in the paper—*especially* when Douglas Garrison ran her predictions in the paper—Crystal Beth was the butt of everybody's joke.

And so when she saw so many gaining from Barry's largesse—all those other farmers who made fun of him after asking for his legal advice—she had to act.

She'd hired her brother to haul the cattle down to Arkansas to sell, but then this other woman—this cop—had come onto the scene and led Barry astray. To be so summarily dumped was more than Crystal Beth could bear. Barry was going to pay.

Then Crystal Beth had second thoughts. What if she was wrong? What if she was misconstruing the interactions she saw between Barry and this interloper? The only way to know for sure was to send a message; a message only Barry could decipher.

But it hadn't worked. Laurel had traced it all back to her before Barry could.

Crystal Beth pled guilty to cattle theft, fraud and assaulting a police officer.

The case closed—for good this time—Laurel had packed her belongings and was prepared to head back to Columbia. She stood by her cruiser, taking one last look at the quaint downtown near the sheriff's office when Barry pulled up.

"Do you really have to go?" Barry asked her.

"I really do," she said.

"You know, we never did get to watch that movie. My book club says it's actually pretty good. Better than the book, even."

"That does not surprise me."

"Well, my offer stands."

"Barry?"

"Yes?"

"Do you still have your lottery ticket?"

"I think so."

"Maybe today is your lucky day."

DECEPTION AT MALLARD COVE

LINDA FISHER

Callie leaned back in the Adirondack chair and pushed on a pair of sunglasses to cover the fear in her eyes. She attempted to steady her coffee cup by holding it between her trembling hands.

Callie had just completed her morning laps in her indoor pool when her daily routine was interrupted by a call from Deputy Dexter Lower.

"I have news about Mr. Gaines." To most people, Dexter's drawl would have sounded casual and unimportant. Callie knew better. She had reported Alastair missing three weeks, two days ago. What could they have discovered? A tremor went through Callie's body as she pondered the possibilities.

"Wh...at?" Her voice cracked.

"I'd like to talk to you in person. I'm on my way now."

"I'm in the pool house. Come on around when you get here." She had known Dexter since he was a chubby teenager in her finance class at Mallard Cove High.

She sat down her cup as Dexter rounded the corner of the country mansion her second husband, Barry, had left her.

"Good morning, Mrs. G." Dexter was still chubby, but he wore a serious expression rather than his usual happy smile.

"Sit down, dear," Callie waved him toward a second chair with fluttering hands.

He sat on the edge of the chair facing her. "I guess there's no easy way to tell you this." He cleared his throat and repeated the sentence. "We've been investigating your husband, and we've discovered he has a criminal background."

"You must be mistaken!"

Dexter ducked his head and speeded up his delivery. The drawl disappeared. "He romances wealthy women and drains their bank accounts. Then, he disappears, steals someone's identity, and does it all over again."

Callie gasped. "That isn't possible. He is my husband and loves me. He would never do that. Something has happened to him."

"Mrs. G., since you taught finance at Mallard High, he may have had more trouble stealing from you than his average target."

Callie buried her head in her hands. "Uh, he handled all our finances after we were married. He wanted to, and since I've retired, I thought it would give me a break from managing the money Barry left me."

"Have you checked your bank statements?"

"Everything is online now. I don't get statements, they're all sent to our email account. Alastair monitors the account so I never bother." She jumped up from the chair and crossed the flagstone steps to the patio door. Dexter pushed himself up from his chair, and removed a handkerchief from his back pocket to discretely wipe the sweat from his face. He hesitated, to see whether she meant for him to follow or if she was dismissing him. When she left the door open, he followed her inside to the sunroom.

She plopped onto a desk chair and after punching a few buttons, pulled up a list of bank statements, clicking on the links one by one. "Oh, no. Most of the money is gone. Thank goodness he couldn't touch the Trust so I should be able to live comfortably."

Callie had met Alastair at a three-day retirement seminar in Las Vegas. During the cocktail mixer, he introduced himself. "You look really young to be at a retirement seminar," he commented, stirring his drink without taking his eyes off hers.

Callie knew she looked good. Sure, she'd had a little work done to smooth out the lines around her eyes and a few nips and tucks, a little enhancement. It didn't hurt that her ruby-red dress draped her body showing off her curves.

She smiled, "Oh, I'm old enough to want to enjoy life." She had turned fifty, but with her inheritance, she had decided to quit her teaching job. "You, on the other hand, cannot possibly be old enough to consider retirement." She was good at judging age and figured he couldn't be more than forty.

He laughed, and his blue eyes snapped with humor. "I'm getting ready to sell my construction company in California and move to a quieter place. My doctor tells me to get away from the stress before it kills me." He looked pretty darn fit to Cassie. He was muscular and trim, no sign of middle-aged spread.

"You should move to Mallard Cove. There's nothing there but fresh air, sunshine, and a peaceful lake complete with, you guessed it, Mallard ducks." She felt a connection with this ruggedly handsome guy wearing his jeans and plain black T-shirt. He was a few inches shorter than her, but at five foot eleven, she was used to shorter men.

"Sounds like what the doctor ordered," he said. He snapped a picture of her with his phone and punched in her phone number. "I'll call you."

And he did call, several times. Their titillating conversations led to an intimacy beyond any Callie had previously known. Before long, they ended each conversation with "love you."

Two months later, he called with exciting news. "I'm flying in to Kansas City and want to look over your Mallard Cove. Would you be willing to show me around?"

"Of course!" Callie was giddy with the prospect of spending time with him.

At the airport, she stood on tiptoes and waved frantically as he walked through the glassed-in secure area. He carried a small bag in one hand and a single rose in the other. After a bear hug, he handed her the rose. "A single rose means love," he said. His lips touched hers lightly, sweetly.

"Did you reserve a room for me at a local hotel?" he asked after he loaded his suitcase in the trunk of her Blazer.

She laughed. "There are no hotels at Mallard Cove. You can stay in my guest suite while you look for a place."

Well, there was never a need for him to find his own place. They were married at the courthouse within a month. "I want to spend every minute with you," he said. He had placed his belongings in storage in California, and told Callie there was no need for his immediate return.

Since they had met at a retirement seminar, it only seemed natural that he wanted to help her with her investments. "Callie, your money should work for you. Having all your money so conservatively invested is costing you a fortune."

"I never trusted investors with my money. I just left it where Barry had it."

He massaged her shoulders and said, "You have someone you can trust now, sweetie. I would love to help my beautiful wife be financially secure for the rest of her life. You are spending down instead of growing your investments."

When had she become suspicious of him? She wasn't sure she could pinpoint the exact moment, but she did know when she confirmed her suspicions. He said he had to fly to California to tie up some loose ends with the business. She wanted to go with him, but he assured her, she would be bored to tears while he spent his days in meetings.

After he left, the house felt so empty that Callie was happy to see the cleaning lady, Claranita, when she came on Monday. Alastair would never let Claranita clean his office, so after she left, Callie thought she would tidy it up a bit. She turned the knob to find the door locked. *That's strange*, she thought. *Maybe he accidentally locked it, or thought Claranita might decide to clean it while he was away.*

Callie checked the key box in the utility room and discovered the office key was missing. She shrugged, and rifled through a pile of keys in the cabinet drawer until she found the spare key.

As she straightened papers on Alastair's desk, she noticed a list of accounts and passwords. She smiled at his weakness to remember. He had told her a head injury had affected his memory.

Seeing a list of banks, she decided to check and see how much Alastair's investments had grown her accounts. She turned on his computer using the password listed on the sheet and then began to check the account balances.

Before long, she realized the accounts listed were in the Cayman Islands. She shook her head at the amount of wealth he had accumulated. She noticed his recent deposits were transfers from her portfolio to his. After a few hours of browsing, she came to the conclusion he was siphoning off her accounts and the only evidence of investment growth was to his accounts.

She checked his email, using the password list, and discovered a receipt for a plane ticket to the Caymans, not California. Fear washed over her in a powerful wave of nausea. He didn't have all her money yet, so perhaps he really would come back to finish what he had started. As she sat at his desk pondering the situation, the phone rang. Alastair said, "I'm coming through town. Do you need anything from the store?"

She took a deep breath to steady her voice. "Could you pick up some eggs and milk?"

"Sure thing!" his voice sounded upbeat. Why wouldn't he be cheerful? He certainly had added to his wealth since their marriage.

Callie mussed the papers as close to their original position as she could. She used the printer to copy the passwords, just in case, and put the original back in the pile. She locked the office door.

She lay awake beside him that night trying to decide what to do. How long would it take him to clean out her accounts? Did he really have feelings for her? Is that the reason he was taking his time?

The next morning, Callie suggested they go for a boat ride in Mallard Cove. "Let's take a picnic lunch. I'll fix all your favorites."

His boyish grin lit up his face. He loved riding in her cabin cruiser. It was late in the season, and the tourists had gone home so they would have the cove to themselves on this crisp September morning.

Callie cut the motor and stopped in the middle of the cove. "It's quiet this morning," he said.

"Yes it is," she replied. After lunch, she reached beneath a cloth in the bottom of the picnic basket and pulled out a pistol. She pointed it at him. "You've been stealing from me."

"I have not!" He sounded indignant, but his expression was a mixture of guilt and fear.

"I know about the accounts, and I know where you went. Before I married Barry, I had nothing. I know what it's like to be poor and you, you son of a bitch, are not taking my security away from me."

"I love you, Callie. I only moved your money to those accounts to invest it. You know, grow your money." His voice shook. "Don't do this, sweetie. I'll put it back if that'll make you feel better."

"You know what would make me feel better?" Callie asked. "To have my money back and you out of my life forever."

"I'm so sorry," Dexter said. "Are you going to be all right, Mrs. G.?"

Callie nodded. She didn't need Dexter to tell her that the construction company in California was fictional. Alastair, or whatever his real name was, had become wealthy by marrying widows and stealing their life savings.

After Dexter left, she pulled up her new accounts to reassure herself that her money and Alastair's millions were safely in her new Cayman accounts. "It's a nice day for a boat ride," she said aloud.

Callie steered the boat to the middle of Mallard Cove where she and Alastair had their heart-to-heart. She remembered their talk about his past and his thievery, culminating in his pitiful attempt to convince her that he, and he alone, could return her money to her accounts.

Tears misted her vision as she leaned over the side of the cruiser to stare into the murky waters of Mallard Cove. The deck still smelled faintly of bleach and its clean scent blended well with the dank scent of the lake water.

"I really did love you, Alastair." She inhaled the fragrance of the single red rose before she dropped it over the side of the boat. "Rest well, my love."

Author Bios

David K. Aycock and his wife, Mary, moved to Missouri from Austin, Texas, in 2002. He earned a B.S. in Elementary Education from Drury University. *David and Dad Catch the Rainbow*, his first children's story, was published by Windstorm Creative of Port Orchard, Washington, in 2007. David currently works as an assembler for Quaker Window Products of Freeburg, Missouri.

He and his wife are active members of Phelps County Animal Welfare League. They both enjoy gardening and reading, and are dedicated vegans. They share their home with two dogs, an undisclosed number of cats, and a rat named Templeton.

David maintains a website at davidkaycock.info.

A legislative attorney and former law librarian, **Paula Gail Benson**'s short stories have been published in the *Bethlehem Writers Roundtable*, *Kings River Life*, *Mystery Times Ten 2013* (Buddhapuss Ink), and *A Tall Ship, a Star, and Plunder* (Dark Oak Press and Media 2014). She regularly blogs with others about writing mysteries on *Writers Who Kill*. Her personal blog is *Little Sources of Joy*, and her website is http://paulagailbenson.com. She is a member of the Mystery Writers of America, Romance Writers of America, and Sisters in Crime. She serves as a Member-at-Large representative to the SinC Guppy Chapter's Steering Committee.

Steven Clark's novel, *The Green Path*, was published in 2012. The *St. Louisans*, his next novel, will be published in 2015 by Walrus Press. His stories have been published in *Black Oak Presents*, Mozark Press, and *UMSL Litmag*. His play *The Love Season* won a national award in 1985.

Lisa Ricard Claro is an award-winning short story author and Pushcart Prize nominee with published articles and stories spanning multiple media. She is a mother of three and resides in Georgia with her husband, two dogs and three cats, and dreams of living at the beach. Lisa is an active member of Romance Writers of America and Georgia Romance Writers, and her novel *Love Built to Last* (the first in the "Fireflies" series), will debut in 2015 with Black Opal Books.

Please email Lisa at lisa@lisaricardclaro.com and visit her website and blog at http://www.LisaRicardClaro.com.

KAREN MOCKER DABSON has authored two novels, *Tarentum* and *The Muralist's Ghost*, and several of her poems and short stories have been published. In 2013, she received one of the Judge's Picks for fiction from the Columbia Chapter of the Missouri Writers Guild and placed second in the Life-Writing contest of the national Story Circle Network. She is a member of the Columbia Chapter as well as the Missouri Writers Guild, the Story Circle Network, and a local writing group. Originally from Pittsburgh, Pennsylvania, Karen resides in Columbia, Missouri, with her husband, Brian, and Jack the Dog. Her blog, Writings from Covered Bridge can be followed on www.mockerdabson.com.

E. B. DAVIS writes crime fiction. "Compromised Circumstances" appeared in the anthology, *Chesapeake Crimes: Homicidal Holidays.* "The Ice Cream Allure" a romantic mystery spoof was published in *Carolina Crimes: 19 Tales of Lust, Love, and Longing.* A young thug proves no match for chemo patient/mother in "No Hair Day," contained in *A Shaker of Margaritas: Bad Hair Day.* Look for more of her stories in previous volumes of the *A Shaker of Margaritas* anthologies. Her current novel manuscript, *Toasting Fear*, is a supernatural mystery set in the Outer Banks, North Carolina.

She blogs at http://writerswhokill.blogspot.com, and is a member of SinC, the SinC Guppy Chapter, and The Short Mystery Fiction Society.

CAROLINE DOHACK grew up on a goat farm in the Ozark foothills. She misspent her youth traveling and playing punk rock shows before becoming the lifestyle editor at the *Columbia Daily Tribune.* She lives in Columbia with her husband, her stepson, and their half-wild dog.

EILEEN DUNBAUGH's short stories have been published in the Mystery Writers of America anthology *The Prosecution Rests,* edited by Linda Fairstein, in the Central Coast Mystery Writers historical anthology *Somewhere in Crime,* edited by Sue McGinty and Margaret Searles, and in two Sisters in Crime anthologies from the New York/Tri-State chapter: *Murder New York Style: Fresh Slices,* edited by Terrie Farley Moran, and *Murder New York Style: Family Matters,* edited by Anita Page (September 2014).

LINDA FISHER, Mozark Press, is the project leader and editor of the *Shaker of Margarita* series. She has published five books of essays from her award-winning Early Onset Alzheimer's health blog. She has been published in *A Cup of Comfort, Chicken Soup for the Soul,* other anthologies, and online publications. Linda has won awards and prizes for her stories and essays. She is a member of the Missouri Writers' Guild, Ozarks Writers League, and the Columbia Chapter of the Missouri Writers' Guild. She blogs at http://earlyonset.blogspot.com and her websites are www.lsfisher.com and www.MozarkPress.com.

J.D. FROST's short fiction has appeared in *Nuvein Magazine* and *Christmas is a Season!,* an anthology edited by Linda Busby Parker. His thriller, *Dollface,* from The Ardent Writer Press is available in ebook or print. He lives with his wife near Huntsville, Alabama. They enjoy keeping up with Lizzie, Nicole, and David.

ROBERT MITCHELL "MITCH" HALE lives in Buffalo, Missouri. He graduated from the University of Missouri in Columbia in 1980 with a bachelor's degree in Animal Science. Mitch is an owner of Hale Fireworks, L.L.C., a wholesale business of over eight hundred customers and four hundred family operated retail locations and other businesses. He has three children, Nick, Chayla, and A. J.

Mitch's hobby of writing was inspired by his mother, Jane, showing him a different world of imagination and intrigue. They enjoy friendly competition when writing for contests. Mitch's first published work was "The Business of being a Father" in *Every Day Is Father's Day,* 2006. His short stories "Checkmate" and "GPS" are published in *Mysteries of the Ozarks, Vol. III* and *Vol. IV,* 2011. "Double Dare Ya" was published in 2012. "The White Wolf" will be published in *The Best of Frontier Tales* in 2015.

CATHY C. HALL is a (mostly humor) writer living in the metro Atlanta area, published in fiction and nonfiction, for both children and adults. She blogs about the writing life at Women-on-Writing.com and shares writing tips and adventures at c-c-hall.com. She likes the beneficent Mr. Hall, her grown-and-out-of-the-house kids, reading in a lounge chair at the beach, and her five (soon-to-be-six) cows. Not necessarily in that order.

SHARON WOODS HOPKINS is a branch manager for a mortgage office of a Missouri bank. She is a member of the Mystery Writers of

America, Sisters in Crime, the Southeast Missouri Writers' Guild, and the Missouri Writers' Guild. Her first book, *Killerwatt*, was nominated for a 2011 Lovey award for Best First Novel, and was a finalist in the 2012 Indie Excellence Awards in the Mystery category. Her second book, *Killerfind*, was a finalist in the 2013 Indie Excellence Awards in the Mystery category, and won first place in the Missouri Writers Guild "Show Me" Best Book Awards for 2013. The third book in the series, *Killertrust* was released in August 2013.

Sharon lives on the family compound near Marble Hill, Missouri, with her author husband, Bill (*Courting Murder* and *River Mourn*). Sharon's hobbies include painting, fishing, photography, flower gardening, and restoring muscle cars.

JODIE JACKSON JR. married a farm girl who once asked him, "Are you sure you want to stand behind the manure spreader?" Jodie survived that lapse of common sense and has managed to make a living as a professional journalist for thirty-two years, covering county government and health care for the *Columbia Daily Tribune* since 2008. He hopes to be a fiction writer someday, although many allege that's what he's been doing the last thirty-two years.

JENNIFER JANK is a mystery lover writing and reading in Reston, Virginia. She also enjoys hiking, swimming, and volunteering at the local Humane Society.

SUZANNE LILLY writes stories with a splash of suspense, a flash of the unexplained, a dash of romance, and always a happy ending. Her short stories have appeared in numerous places online and in print. She is the author of the historical fiction series, *The California Argonauts* of which *Gold Rush Girl* is the first book, as well as the following novels: *Shades of the Future*, *Untellable*, and *A Thousand Little Secrets*. She lives in Northern California where she reads, writes, cooks, swims, and teaches elementary students. Sign up for her newsletter to read about new releases. Every issue a subscriber wins a prize. http://suzannelilly.com/subscribe-to-my-newsletter/.

Suzanne's website is www.suzannelilly.com and her blog is found at www.teacherwriter.net. Her Goodreads author page is at www.goodreads.com/author/show/5258804.

MARY ELLEN MARTIN has enjoyed writing her entire life. She has published stories for Mozark Press, Hadley Rille Books, *Idaho*

Magazine, and *Have Heart Magazine.* She lives with her incredible family, calling north Idaho home, where she is buried under unfinished manuscripts and children's toys.

EDITH MAXWELL writes the Local Foods Mysteries (Kensington Publishing). The latest, *'Til Dirt Do Us Part* (2014) chronicles the murder of a CSA member after geek-turned-organic-farmer Cam Flaherty's Farm-to-Table dinner. She also writes the Lauren Rousseau Mysteries (Barking Rain Press) as Tace Baker, and the Country Store Mysteries (Kensington Publishing) under the pen name Maddie Day. The first in her historical Carriagetown Mysteries is in development.

A fourth-generation Californian, Maxwell has also published award-winning short stories of murderous revenge. She holds a doctorate in linguistics, is a long-time member of Amesbury Friends Meeting, and previously was an organic farmer, a doula, and a childbirth educator, among other careers.

Edith lives in an antique house north of Boston with her beau and three cats. She blogs every weekday with the rest of the Wicked Cozy Authors (wickedcozyauthors.com).

CAROLYN MULFORD writes the award-winning *Show Me* mystery series featuring an ex-spy who applies her tradecraft honed in Eastern Europe to solving homicides in rural Missouri. The first book, *Show Me the Murder* (Five Star/Gale, Cengage Learning, 2013), received the Missouri Writers' Guild's Walter Williams Major Work Award. MWG awarded the second book, *Show Me the Deadly Deer,* honorable mention in the Best Book category, and DearReader.com named the book a Mystery of the Week. Carolyn served in the Peace Corps before working as a magazine editor in Vienna and Washington, D.C. She survived for decades as a freelance writer/editor, producing everything from calendars to conference reports, travel articles to how-to books. After returning to Missouri in 2007, she changed her focus from nonfiction to fiction. Her first novel, *The Feedsack Dress,* was Missouri's Great Read at the 2009 National Book Festival. To read excerpts from her books, visit http://carolynmulford.com.

KM ROCKWOOD draws on a varied background for stories, among them working as a laborer in a steel fabrication plant, operating glass melters and related equipment in a fiberglass manufacturing facility, and supervising an inmate work crew in a large medium security state prison. These jobs, as well as work as a special education teacher in an alternative high school and a GED teacher in county detention facilities, provide most of the background for novels and short stories.

MARTHA ROSENTHAL taught public school for twenty years. Since retiring she has had stories published in *Talking Writing* magazine and *Shark Reef* magazine. Beyond writing, her interests include swimming, yoga, upholstery, and tutoring young writers. She lives in Los Gatos, California, with her husband and two dogs.

GEORGIA RUTH lives in the foothills of North Carolina. Now retired, she managed a family restaurant for ten years and worked in sales for fifteen years. Both experiences produced rich soil for her fertile imagination. Georgia is a member of Sisters in Crime and Short Mystery Fiction Society. She has stories published online for *Stupefying Stories* and *Bethlehem Writers Roundtable*, and in *Mystery Times Ten 2013* by Buddhapuss Ink. Her story "The Mountain Top" will be published in a Sisters in Crime anthology in 2015. Follow her historical whimsies at http://georgiaruthwrites.us/

HARRIETTE SACKLER is a longtime member of the Malice Domestic Board of Directors. Her short stories have been published in numerous anthologies, including "Thanksgiving with a Turkey," which appeared in *A Shaker of Margaritas: A Bad Hair Day*, from Mozark Press. She is a past Agatha Award nominee for "Mother Love," published in *Chesapeake Crimes II.*

Harriette is a member of Mystery Writers of America, Sisters-in-Crime National, Chesapeake, and Guppies, as well as the Rockville Writers Group. An avid pet lover, she is vice president of House with a Heart Senior Pet Sanctuary. She lives in the D.C. suburbs with her husband and their three pups.

Visit Harriette at www.HarrietteSackler.com.

ROSEMARY SHOMAKER writes about the layers beneath seemingly ordinary happenings. She's an urban planner by degree, a government policy analyst by practice, and a fiction writer at heart. She lives in Virginia with her fine husband and exceptional children.

MARTHA ROSENTHAL taught public school for twenty years. Since retiring she has had stories published in *Talking Writing* magazine and *Shark Reef* magazine. Beyond writing, her interests include swimming, yoga, upholstery, and tutoring young writers. She lives in Los Gatos, California, with her husband and two dogs.

SUSAN THOMAS' work has been previously published by *Focus on the Family*, *CBH Ministries*, Judson Press, and Mozark Press. She won first place in a short-story contest with Mozark Press in 2010 and Grand Prize in the Women's Memoirs First Paragraph Contest in 2014. She has her B.S.E. in English Education and a master's in philosophy. She owns The Dramatic Pen Press, a small publishing company for drama and party games. She works and lives in Lolo, Montana, with her husband and three children.

From an early age, DONNA VOLKENANNT has loved to read and write. Her favorite books growing up were the Nancy Drew and Hardy Boys series, and she still loves curling up with a good mystery yarn. Among the awards she's won are first place in the 2012 Erma Bombeck Global Humor Contest and top-ten finalist in the 2014 Erma Bombeck Human Interest Competition. Essayist, short story writer, editor, blogger, and workshop presenter, she's also an adjunct creative writing teacher at the University of Missouri St. Louis. She has presented seminars and workshops at numerous venues, including the Missouri State Teachers' Association annual retreat. Donna lives in Missouri with her husband, their two grandchildren, and one lovable black Lab. Visit her at http://donnasbookpub.blogspot.com.

KARI WAINWRIGHT divides her time between her Colorado mountain home and an Arizona desert residence near her sister, Ronda, and her dog, Willow. Kari tries to spend the seasons in the place with the best weather, but doesn't always succeed. Wherever she lives, she shares her life with husband Tom, son Travis, and Shih-Tzu lapdog, Oscar Wilde. She belongs to the Desert Sleuths chapter of Sisters in Crime and has a story published in their 2013 anthology, *SoWest: Crime Time*. She is currently working on a traditional mystery.

FRANK WATSON has spent most of his adult life involved in some type of writing—primarily journalism, technical writing, and business writing—but never lost his love for fiction.

Frank published *A Cold, Dark Trail* and *The Homecoming of Billy Buchanan* with Fawcett/Random House under his own name and other historical novels for Zebra, which he wrote under a pseudonym.

He has not limited his work to westerns. For example, a literary short story, *Where the Yellow Flowers Grow*, won the Graduate Fiction Prize from the University of Missouri—St. Louis and was subsequently published in *Mysteries of the Ozarks, Volume 1* from Skyward Publications. Another literary short story, *When Bonnie and Clyde Came to Town,* won recognition from the Ozark Writers League and was published in *Echoes of the Ozarks, Volume VI*, published by High Hill Press.

Visit his website at www.FrankWatsonWriter.com.

22985416R00133

Made in the USA
San Bernardino, CA
30 July 2015